MURDER IN LOVERS' LANE

An absolutely gripping crime mystery with a massive twist

DANIEL SELLERS

DCI Lola Harris Series Book 2

Joffe Books, London
www.joffebooks.com

First published in Great Britain in 2023

Cover art by Nebojša Zorić

ISBN: 978-1-80405-931-9

For Gordon

AUTHOR'S NOTE

A number of the places referred to in this novel are real, as are some institutions. The characters and the events are fictional.

Please follow me on Twitter (@djsellersauthor) and on Instagram (@danielsellersauthor), or by following the hashtag:

#WhatWouldLolaHarrisDo?

CHAPTER ONE

Sunday 23 October
6.49 a.m.

The alarm went off for a second time and Lola Harris groaned with something approaching despair.

She reached through the dark for her phone and stopped the bleeping, then lay on her side, eyes screwed tight, curled up like a foetus, as a fist of dread closed round her heart.

How had she — a practical, confident, grown woman — come to this? *And it's my own fault*, she told herself. *I chose this. What was I thinking?*

For God's sake, get a GRIP!

She hauled herself into a sitting position and turned on her bedside lamp, then took a deep breath and heaved out a sob.

She was exhausted. She felt it in every muscle, in her bones, in her spirit.

Work had been intense. She'd only just wrapped up the investigation into a series of murders linked to Glasgow's newest art gallery, when she found herself heading an enquiry into the death of a mother and her young son in a flat owned by a gangland boss. The case had come to its grim conclusion within a month, but it had left Lola feeling drained and depressed. Add to that the usual stresses of office politics, and she generally ended every working week feeling like she needed a holiday. Or to retire.

Then there was Joe, the married man she'd been seeing on and off for the best part of twenty years — an affair that was now over, romantically, at least. They were still "friends" — whatever that might mean — and in regular contact.

Which is why she'd made the decision she had. The one that now prompted this sense of horror mixed with an urge to crawl into a hole, one that caused palpitations in her chest and brought her out in a clammy, cold sweat.

6.53 a.m. Seven minutes to go.

Adrenaline sparked like electricity in her chest. This must be how it felt on death row. To sit in your cell, in the dark hours before dawn, knowing that the guards would arrive, the executioner with them, ready to escort you to the noose or the chair. She'd seen the films — the Stephen King one, and the one with the nun. She'd seen the looks on those men's faces.

6.54.

Lola, you're not dying!

Out of bed and into the bathroom, where she gargled mouthwash and eyed herself miserably in the mirror. There were bags under her eyes and her hair was like a burst couch.

Then back into the bedroom, where she tugged on leggings and scrabbled in a drawer for a long-sleeved top.

6.58.

Two minutes and her executioner would be here. He was never late.

You'll be fine, she told the reflection in the mirrored door of her wardrobe. *There's nothing to fear.*

Except humiliation. Pain. And a deep-down reminder of why she was doing this . . . Not the reason she'd given herself. Not the one she'd given her sister, or Kirstie at work.

The real reason . . . The same old reason. The only one.

The doorbell chimed. She closed her eyes and swallowed hard.

It was time.

* * *

7.07 a.m.

'We'll do intervals, but first you're gonna run a mile,' Johnny said, grinning widely and bouncing from foot to foot. 'I'll time you, and I'm looking to see an improvement on session one, 'kay?'

'Just . . . give me a minute . . .' Lola was still getting her breath back after the warm-up, or "pulse raiser" as Johnny called it: a jog from her front door, across an empty Dumbreck Road and into neighbouring Pollok Park, then the dreaded "dynamic" stretches on the grass beside the allotments.

The language of personal training was as new and objectionable to her as the training itself.

Johnny, to his credit, was less objectionable, being tall, strappingly handsome, tanned and charming.

While Lola puffed mist into the chilly morning air, Johnny jogged on the spot, beaming to reveal whiter-than-white teeth. His blond curls, held back from his forehead by a kind of Alice band, bounced too, giving him the look of a giddy kid. She'd found him on the online noticeboard of the Glasgow Police Fitness Club, advertising a special deal for "more reluctant" clients. His six-week, twelve-session programme was branded "Feel the Fear with Johnny Blake", and there was a fifteen percent discount for serving or retired officers. She'd emailed him and asked for an introductory call before she had time to think about it and, within minutes, she had her debit card in her hand, ready to read out the long number, because — *sod it* — something had to change. He'd sounded nice. Kind. Funny. When she'd said, 'Can I tell you to bugger off if you're doing my heid in?', he'd laughed uproariously, and replied, 'You can call me all the names under the sun. It'll be great.'

'Right,' he said now, his stopwatch in his hand. 'Deep breaths!'

'Okay.'

A mile . . . She gazed miserably at the road stretching away into the misty wooded park.

'We'll follow the road from here, along the side of the golf course towards Pollok House, then round towards the museum. I'll tell you when to stop. Nice steady pace. You set it, I'll keep up with you. But *no stopping*, got it? Now, three, two, one — *GO!*'

She stumped cheerlessly along, the impact of each step reverberating up into her hips. Her calves and thighs soon hurt like hell, as did her chest, but she kept going, performing the prescribed method of breathing: four shallow intakes of breath, timed per step, then four out.

Despite the cold, she began to sweat.

'You're doing great, Lola. You're gonna smash this.'

"Smash" was a very Johnny word.

'Am I?' she panted, wiping her brow.

Breathe, breathe, breathe, breathe.

'You'll smash your own time and I'll be mega proud of you.'

She endeavoured to distract herself from the pain by focusing on her surroundings. Mist swathed the trees to her left. The pre-dawn light made their brown and yellow leaves glow dully. On her right were the playing fields of Lochinch, a former police gym, now home to a football club; then the golf course, undulating away into the mist. A group of deer stood in the distance, their heads turned her way, no doubt wondering what on earth the large woman in leggings thought she was doing.

She'd announced it to her sister a month ago. 'I've booked a personal trainer.'

'Have you? Wow . . .' Frankie, ever the cynic, had barely been able to contain her amusement.

4

'I need to do something, sis. Look at me. If I'm going to move on from Joe and meet someone else, I'm going to need to look after myself a bit better.'

'You're not fat, Lola.'

'I'm bigger than I want to be,' she'd said, sitting in her sister's new kitchen, while Frankie's two brown Labs rested their chins on her thighs so she could fondle their ears. 'Besides, I want to eat healthier too. Mum died of a heart attack. I don't want to go the same way. Not yet, anyway. This Johnny — he's going to do me a nutritional plan as well. I'll be a new woman, Frankie. A different one, at least. Thinner. Healthier. Happier, maybe.'

'How far?' she wheezed to Johnny now.

'Just over a third of the way,' he said.

They'd descended into a shadowy dip where the air was colder and unpleasantly damp.

'The road climbs as it goes round the house,' Johnny said. 'I want you to slow it down a bit and keep breathing. Just like a car going into a lower gear.'

'A lower gear,' she said, nodding, liking the analogy.

Frankie had asked her if she was planning to start shopping around.

'For men? Aye, maybe.'

'I think you should. I think it'll do you good. But aim low. Go on a few dates. Have some fun.'

'Aye, well . . .'

'You're a good-looking woman, Lola. You're in your prime. Any bloke'd be lucky to have you.'

'That's you past halfway,' Johnny said. 'You're ahead of where you were in week one. I'm proud of you.'

'Thanks.' A croak, because her chest was tight now. The muscles of her ribcage were screaming with pain.

On she stumped, as the blood filled her muscles and made her face burn. The road was still climbing and her legs felt like jelly. Her breath went before her in steamy gusts.

'How far?'

'See the junction? We'll carry on beyond it another hundred metres or so, as far as the holly tree, and that'll be us. You're so gonna smash this.'

They reached the junction, where the road split off in the direction of the Burrell Collection, the newly reopened museum that lay at the heart of the park.

The holly tree was only metres ahead — then something caught her attention. She stopped, staring into the trees.

'Keep going!' Johnny yelled, then followed her line of sight to what was half hidden under the trees. 'Oh!' He stopped and stared too.

It was a car, a BMW — expensive, top of the range, she thought. Both the driver's and passenger's doors were open. It looked abandoned, and yet . . .

'Do you think it was nicked?' Johnny asked, only slightly out of breath. For once, he wasn't jogging on the spot.

'Let me check it out,' she said, her own breathing still coming in painful gasps. 'You stay here.'

He nodded, looking anxious.

She left the road to cross the soggy, leaf-strewn grass under the trees, keeping clear of the twin muddy tracks gouged from the earth where the car had been reversed off the tarmac.

'Is anyone there?' she called.

'Should we call someone?' Johnny shouted over to her from the road.

She raised a hand to quiet him and shook her head.

'Hello?' she said, peering into the car's dark interior.

As far as she could see, there was no one there.

She stepped away from the car and circled to its rear — then stopped dead when she saw the people lying there, as still as the trees around them.

CHAPTER TWO

7.21 a.m.

Even in the gloom, Lola could see the two people were fully clothed and tied together, face to face in an embrace, lashed with ropes round their shoulders, waists, thighs and ankles. One, a dark, stocky-looking man, was clearly dead. There was a bullet wound above one open, staring eye. It had bled, and the blood had dried to a crust. Strapped to him, her face angled away, was a woman, blonde and thin. Lola could see no sign of injury, though she lay as still as the man.

She steeled herself and crouched, stretching over the man's body to reach the woman's throat. It was faintly warm, and there was a pulse.

She stood and turned to face Johnny, momentarily at a loss.

'What is it?' Johnny called. He stepped onto the grass.

'Stay where you are,' she shouted, hand up.

He stopped.

She eased her iPhone out of the strap on her upper arm and peered at its screen in dismay.

'I've no signal. Have you?' she shouted to Johnny.

He checked his own phone. 'No. The park's crap. I . . . I can usually get a couple of bars back down towards the big house. Do you want me to go and call for help?'

'Yes. Ring 999. Ask for an ambulance and police.'

'Right . . . What do I say?'

'Say that there are two people in the park,' she went on. 'Tell them one of them is dead — that he's been shot.' Johnny's eyes widened. He was no longer the bouncy macho lad, but a scared young boy. 'Tell them the other one is alive but unconscious, and in need of urgent assistance. Give them the exact location and do not contact anyone else. When you've called them, come straight back here, but stay on the road. I'll need you to flag them down when they get here. Oh, and take a photo of the car's registration number. Give it to the 999 operator.'

'Will you be all right? You could go make the call and I—'

'I'll be fine. Just go.'

She watched as he took a snap of the car's registration then, with one last nervous glance, sprinted off. Then she turned her attention back to the prone couple. If they were indeed a couple . . . But such details could wait. Right now she had to make a choice. And fast.

She didn't know whether the woman was injured or not — or, if she was, how badly. She could leave her where she was, perhaps finding a way to keep her warm until the paramedics arrived, then risk them destroying forensic evidence in their efforts to free her. Or she could try to free the woman herself now, and move her away from the corpse and to the roadside, ready for the ambulance, thus preserving at least some forensic evidence for the investigation that would follow — an option that risked causing injury.

She played the scenarios over in her head, realising a sickening possibility: that the woman might, at any time, wake up and realise she was strapped to a corpse. If they were a couple, she'd be looking into the dead eyes of her lover.

8

Would see that crusted bullet wound, like a third eye in his forehead — and then what?

Such an experience could scar a person for life. No, she had to act, and now.

Focus. Stay practical. One thing at a time.

Steadying her breathing, she looked quickly about her, committing details to memory, trying to notice anything that might be significant, anything that might explain what had happened here. She opened her phone's camera and took photos of the couple lying at her feet, from several angles. This was not normal practice, but she wanted to capture the scene before she disturbed it.

Phone back in the strap on her arm, she steeled her nerves and turned her attention to the young woman. Gingerly, she stepped around the couple's heads and into the space between the woman's back and the car's rear bumper. She crouched, her knee sinking into cold, wet mulch.

'Okay,' she whispered, more for her own benefit than that of the woman, who seemed completely out of it. 'It's going to be okay.'

She lay her hands on the woman's left shoulder then waited, in case the pressure of her hands should wake her. The woman didn't move. That was good. The longer she took to come round, the better. She studied the rope binding the couple's shoulders, focusing on the bunch of knots to the left of the woman's spine. They looked tight and complex. Not the kind to submit to a fingernail.

She needed something sharp but didn't even have her house keys on her, having stashed them in the wee safe beside her front door.

A minute later she was leaning into the BMW's interior. Tugging the sleeve of her Lycra top over her hand to create a makeshift glove, she began a search, but found nothing of use: a service book, a manual, a wheel lock, small packets of tissues and a roll of mints.

Next the boot, hunting for tools. But again, nothing.

She let the boot lid drop, then reached for her phone again and checked the time. 7.28. How long had Johnny been gone? Four minutes? Five? He should be at the house by now. Might already be on the phone to the emergency services.

A sound from the woman at her feet: the softest moan.

Lola stared, stricken. The ambulance could be another ten minutes. Fifteen. Longer, even.

To think how much she'd been dreading the training session. She'd swap this situation for gruelling intervals any day.

She bent down and shone her torch on the cluster of knots again, noting just how tightly they were pulled, how compressed the fibres were. No way could she attack them on her own. She'd break her nails, make her fingers bleed and compromise the scene all the more. Aware of rising panic in her chest, she looked about for a stone — anything that she could use to cut the ropes.

Then, the sound of running feet. Johnny.

'I spoke to them,' he called from the road. 'I asked for police and an ambulance. They'll be here within fifteen minutes.'

'Good,' she called back. 'Do you have a knife, by any chance? Or keys, or—'

'Um . . . Yeah, I do!' He unhooked his backpack from his shoulder and rummaged for a Swiss army knife. He twisted out a sizeable blade.

'Stay where you are. I'll come to you.'

He gave her the knife, handle first, eyes like saucers.

'What about gloves?' she said.

'Gloves? I've got my cycling ones.' A moment later he was handing her a pair of luminous yellow, lightweight stretchy things. 'They might be a bit big for you.'

'They'll be fine,' she muttered. 'Stay right where you are. Shout when you see a vehicle arriving.'

Back behind the car, the woman was groaning, writhing a little as she tried to move against the constraints of the ropes. Lola still hadn't seen her face. She bent and plucked at the rope to the left of the knot, and began to saw with the knife. The blade was sharp and it parted fibres with ease. After ten or so strokes, the rope snapped.

The woman's shoulder twisted and heaved. Consciousness was returning. She groaned some more, muttering sounds that could have been the beginnings of words.

'You're okay there,' Lola said softly, one hand on the woman's shoulder. 'I'm a police officer.' She kept her voice deliberately low and soothing, though every muscle in her body was painfully tense. 'You just stay still and everything'll be okay. That's right.'

She moved her attention to the rope at the couple's waists.

Seconds later, it gave too.

'That's lovely,' Lola murmured. 'Just a little longer and that'll be us.'

Next she cut away the rope tying their thighs and moved to the ankles.

'Wha . . . where am I?' The words were clear, but the voice thick with sleep.

Eyes locked on the back of the woman's head, which was lifting and turning, Lola cut faster.

'You're hurting me . . .' Rearing back, pushing herself back. '*Oww* . . .'

'Where does it hurt, love?' Lola asked.

'It aches . . .'

'Okay. Just keep calm.'

'Who are you?' Lifting herself now, turning her head. Her face was young, bleary with sleep. She frowned at Lola, perplexed, then swooned, blinking fast, as if unconsciousness was pulling her under once more.

The final rope gave.

Sweating from the exertion, Lola sat up straight. 'My name's Lola Harris, and I'm a police detective,' she said gently, hands on the young woman's shoulders, pulling her firmly back. 'Something's happened here and I need to see you're all right. Have you got any pain anywhere?'

'What . . . ?' The word was thick with confusion. 'My head hurts. Sean? What's going on?'

'I'm going to try to help you stand up. Okay? Take my hand, and I'll help you get to your feet.'

Dumbly, clumsily, like a malfunctioning automaton, the woman staggered to her feet. She took Lola's hand. Lola gripped it, then stood to get her balance.

'That's right. That's good.' She helped the woman to her feet. 'There we go.'

But the woman was focused on the man on the ground. 'What's wrong with Sean?' She peered at Lola blearily, and Lola saw she was shivering.

'You come with me.' A steadying arm round her waist, Lola pulled the woman firmly away from the man's body. 'What's your name?'

'It's Fiona. Where are we?' A note of a panic now, and her teeth were chattering.

'We're in Pollok Park, Fiona. You're safe.'

Moving away from the car, she looked for Johnny, but couldn't see him. Then she spotted him, a few hundred metres away, waving to an approaching ambulance.

'The ambulance is for you,' Lola said. 'To make sure you're all right.'

'Don't understand . . .' Her voice rising.

The ambulance stopped and two paramedics jumped out, one, a man, ready with a blanket for Fiona's frozen shoulders. He pulled it round her and led her gently towards the back of the vehicle.

Lola introduced herself to the second paramedic, an older woman with iron-grey hair. Then she led the way over the grass and under the trees, to the place where a man lay dead.

CHAPTER THREE

8.06 a.m.

The sun was up, and the copper of the autumn trees was more vivid now. The fields across the road from the woods were dark emerald and glittering with dew.

A beautiful day for murder.

The place that had been so quiet, that had seemed so unsettlingly remote, now crawled with people and hummed with low voices.

Inspector Michelle Brown, the senior uniformed officer on duty at the time of the 999 call, had arrived a few minutes after the ambulance, accompanied by a pair of constables, who'd quickly begun marking out a cordon. If she was surprised that a colleague had discovered the murder scene, she didn't show it. Michelle Brown was known for her level-headed approach to work and her dry, laconic manner with people. Lola found her tricky.

'You didn't call it in, though, did you?' the inspector said, frowning.

'That was Mr Blake.' Lola pointed along the road to where Johnny lingered, head down, hands in the pockets of his shorts, kicking the grass, unaware he was being talked about. 'He's . . . He was with me. He went to find a signal while I stayed here.'

Michelle Brown nodded, eyes lingering on the man in the distance. She looked back at Lola with a quizzical, mildly amused light in her eyes.

Lola smiled pleasantly, refusing to rise.

Two more cars of uniforms arrived. Michelle Brown gave orders, and Lola watched as the officers went smartly about their tasks. It was this team's task to lay the ground-work for an effective and efficient investigation: to secure the scene, put in place an entry and exit path, and open a scene log to record comings and goings. It was also their job to assess whether the crime warranted the attentions of CID — a no-brainer on this occasion.

'Your colleagues will be here within the next twenty minutes,' Michelle Brown told Lola now. 'DCI Izatt and DS Pierce.'

'Oh, right . . .'

Her reply was met with a satirical raised eyebrow. The tension between Lola and Pierce was well known in G Division, and no doubt beyond.

'DCI Izatt asks if you'd stay around.'

'Of course.'

She waited until the inspector was away to talk to members of her team before slipping across to the ambulance.

Fiona lay on a bed under a red blanket. The male para-medic was fitting a strap over her waist.

'How's she doing?' she asked.

'She's confused,' the female paramedic said quietly. 'She doesn't know where she is. There are some signs of hypothermia, so we're taking her in to the Queen Elizabeth now. One of the constables is going to come with us.'

'Sean?' The woman on the bed tried to raise her head. 'Where's Sean?'

'Lie still,' the male paramedic said. 'Everything's going to be just fine.' He sent Lola a guilty glance. If Sean was the chap with the hole in his head, then things might not be fine at all.

A female constable appeared at her side, Michelle Brown behind her, eyebrows raised at Lola.

'Just saying my goodbyes,' Lola said nicely to the inspector, and stepped away.

Johnny was pacing in the distance. She half-jogged the hundred metres or so to join him.

'How are you doing?'

'I'm okay.' He looked sheepish. 'Well, you know . . . I've never . . . I've never been involved in anything like this. Feeling a wee bit shaken up, if I'm honest.'

'Aye, well, finding a body is a first for me too. When I'm going about my personal business, I mean. It's bound to be a shock.'

He looked as if he might tear up.

She gave his arm a pat, her eyes falling on a bunch of dead flowers someone had tied to the fence that edged the field. An accident some time ago, perhaps. The drooping, blackened flowers seemed grimly appropriate.

'Will she be okay, d'you think?' Johnny asked her.

'Hopefully.'

'Do you know what happened?'

'Not yet.'

'Do I need to stay?' he asked, and she saw the pleading written on his face.

''Fraid so,' she said. 'There'll be a statement. We'll need to record what you saw, what you did. Anything you might have noticed.'

'Okay.' He nodded, then hitched his backpack a little higher on his shoulder. 'What about my knife? Only, it was my dad's, and he's . . .'

'You'll get it back. Your gloves too. I'll buy you a new pair if you prefer.'

He managed a little smile. 'You did great, by the way.' He pulled out his stopwatch and showed her the display. 'Knocked a minute off your time.'

'Did I?' She gave a dark laugh. 'Well, well. Who'd've thought it?'

CHAPTER FOUR

Lola found a tree stump to lean against while she sipped the coffee one of the constables had produced. From here she watched as DCI Graeme Izatt took over the crime scene from Inspector Brown, negotiating how many of her uniformed officers he could retain to secure the site.

Izatt loved to be in charge. He was a big, grumpy man, with messy grey hair and angry, swivelling eyes. He always gave the impression he'd got dressed several days before and then slept in his clothes, so that his suits were crumpled and his ties ratty. He looked like a man who had lost all ambition, but that was not the case: in fact, his ambition was legendary. He'd made it public that his firm intention was to get out of CID and gain a superintendent's role with the regional Major Investigation Team — or MIT — where he could oversee big and complex cases. Right now, though, his chances of a move and a promotion seemed slim. He'd spent the past six months temporarily promoted to superintendent with G Division CID, during which time he'd repeatedly made poor decisions and wound people up — those under him, and those above — then complained, loudly and publicly,

16

that his seniors failed to see his worth. He'd returned to his substantive rank two weeks ago, and been like a bear with a sore head ever since.

She watched as he marched from his officers to the photographer, then to the police surgeon, frowning as he asked unheard questions and glaring at answers he didn't like, fists on hips like a school teacher in charge of an unruly bunch of kids.

DS Aidan Pierce and DC Marcus McVittie had finished taking details from Johnny Blake and had let him go. Now they were talking to a tall, very thin man in a green wax jacket and flat cap, who'd arrived in a kind of Jeep and now stood, slightly stooped, with his arms crossed and a disgusted look on his pinched face. He was barking out complaints she couldn't quite make out and Marcus was doing his best to soothe him, with open gestures and empathetic nods. Pierce, meanwhile, smirked shamelessly, and spoke the odd word in that snarky way of his.

Marcus effected an escape and headed her way, scene log in hand.

'Who's the chap?' Lola said, nodding over at Green Jacket.

'Park manager, boss. Not happy because DCI Izatt wanted to close the park.'

'The *whole* place?' She had to make an effort not to laugh. Pollok Park was one of the biggest country parks in Europe, made up of hundreds of acres of woodland and incorporating a golf club, a cricket club, a stately home and a museum, all of which could be accessed via multiple routes, by car and on foot.

'They've settled on a triangle from the junction back there down to the post along that way, then through to the field at the back of the copse.'

Lola nodded. That would be a large area to scour, but it was necessary in the early stages. Key evidence might lie hidden in the trees — a gun, for instance. In due course, the area would be reduced to something more manageable.

'I need to know about the gloves,' Marcus said now.

Johnny's gloves were already bagged and labelled. Marcus wrote notes while Lola explained how she'd worn them to free the young woman, and gave details of what she'd touched.

'How long you hanging around for, boss?' Marcus asked when she was done.

'Till DCI Izatt says I can go,' she said, smiling.

It was a lie. Izatt had told her she was free to go, meaning he *wanted* her to go — or so she strongly suspected. But she meant to stay, and for a very good reason: she wanted the case, and she meant to tell Izatt that, this morning, to his face.

Marcus went to talk to the photographer, and she was beginning to relax when a man's voice barked out behind her.

'Who are you, please?'

She pushed herself up from her stump and turned to face the park manager.

'I'm Lola Harris, DCI with Police Scotland,' she said, as the man gave her the once over, screwing up his face as if in disgust at her attire. 'We haven't met, have we?' She put out a hand and turned an ear theatrically to receive his name.

'Jeremy Warren,' he said. 'Park manager.' He was English and sounded upper class. 'I don't suppose you're going to tell me what's going on here either, are you?'

'Afraid not, sir.'

'Is it true a man has been *shot dead*?' he said, nodding towards the newly erected white tent half covering the BMW.

'Can't say,' she said. 'Sorry.'

'Someone moved my rocks,' he said peevishly.

'Your rocks?'

'I specifically had them put there to *stop* people driving into the trees. They do, you know? They pull off the road and into the bushes and . . . *make love!*' He gave her a look of sheer disgust. '*Young* people.'

'Rocks, Mr Warren?'

'Along here,' he said, pointing along the edge of the road. 'Size of footballs, painted white.' Now that she looked she could make out flattened patches of grass, the green faded to a sickly yellow, making a dotted line along the verge. 'Anywhere there's grass where someone could pull off the road. Only put them down a month ago, and they've been moved.'

'Moved where?' she said, frowning.

'Found them piled up under a rhododendron, back there,' he said, nodding. 'Six of the things. Done deliberately, I'd say.'

She thought about what it might mean. 'Did you mention this to my colleagues?' she asked.

'I told *him*.' He waved an irritable hand in Pierce's direction. From over by the trees, Pierce was watching them, head tilted, a look of sly interest on his face.

'I'll see it's recorded, Mr Warren,' she said.

'Very well.' He went muttering on his way.

'Everything in order, Graeme?' she said, when Izatt arrived at her side.

'Car belongs to a Sean Rennie. Sound familiar?'

'Vaguely.' She'd very nearly said, 'Vaguely, *boss*,' and was pleased she'd managed not to. He wasn't her boss for now, but he'd enjoy the slip of the tongue, and she wasn't about to give him that pleasure. 'Who is he?'

'Gangster,' Izatt said. 'His dad was Mickey Rennie — of King's Park. Likely shot dead by Tony Malone in 2005 for cheating on a major heroin deal.'

'I remember.'

'Sean's thirty. *Was* thirty. Flat in the posh bit of Pollokshields. Fotheringay Road. Nice old tenements, those. Also the owner of several other flats throughout the city, with a handful in Govanhill. No doubt used for money laundering. Suspected of ordering a double killing in Shettleston a couple of years back, not that we could pin anything on him. Nasty piece of work.'

'And who's the woman?'

'Fiona Balfour. His girlfriend. Fiancée, actually. Due to get married at the end of November.'

'Blimey.'

Balfour? The name rang a bell.

'You did the right thing moving her, by the way. Good thinking.'

'I did what I needed to do.'

He looked at her uncertainly. What had he expected, a meek "thank you"?

'Someone's done us a favour, really,' he said now. 'Another scumbag in the ground. Shouldn't be too hard to find out who did it. A bit of intel work should produce something before long. Nice straightforward case, I reckon.'

'You think?'

He looked at her in surprise. 'What do you mean?'

'The woman,' she said. 'Why was she here? Why involve her? Think about it, Graeme. She was strapped to her fiancé's corpse — yet apparently unharmed.'

He scowled, then shrugged, and she could see he wasn't interested in even thinking about it. 'Give her a fright, maybe? Could be a way of telling her not to talk.'

'Why not just shoot her too?'

'Maybe she'll have the answer.'

'I wonder . . .'

He peered hard at her, fists back on his hips. 'Always have to complicate things, don't you?'

'I suppose I do,' she said, smiling a little, eyes away towards the tent behind the car.

'Why are you still here, anyway? You're not working.'

'Actually . . . about that, Graeme,' she began, turning her body so she was facing him. She beamed.

'Yes?'

'You're a busy man, aren't you?'

'What of it?' Defensive now.

'Let me take the case off you.'

'Are you being serious?' Eyes widening in disbelief.

'It's going to be complex. Tricky. This is no gangland execution, and you know it.'

He licked his lips, thinking about it, she could tell. His eyes moved to the tent, where Marcus and the photographer seemed to be discussing angles.

'No,' he said sharply. 'It's my case.' He smiled unpleasantly. 'Once that young lady starts talking, I'll have it wrapped up in a couple of days. You see if I don't.'

CHAPTER FIVE

Tuesday 25 October
3.34 p.m.

Lola had spent the day in the suffocating witnesses' room at
the High Court, waiting for a call to give evidence relating to
an armed robbery she'd worked on nine months before. The
call didn't come until three, by which time she was hot, tired
and bored. She delivered her evidence, which was routine,
and was released into the fresh, sunny afternoon.

Outside the building, her phone pinged. A voicemail
from Izatt. She listened with eyebrows raised and a growing
smile of grim satisfaction.

'At last,' he snapped, when she called him back. 'Are you
free now?'

'Where is she, Graeme?'

'Here at her sister's in Shawlands. Can you come?'

'Of course. Give me the address and I'll be right over.'

Fiona Balfour's sister had a top-floor tenement in one of
the tight, one-way streets running south from Pollokshaws
Road. It took Lola an age to park, and Izatt was all but tap-
ping his watch when he opened the door to her.

A nervy-looking woman with a dark blonde frizz of hair came forward to meet her.

'Catriona Balfour,' she said, before Izatt could introduce her. 'Fiona's my sister.'

Catriona was a small woman, thin in a strong, wiry way. She wore black jeans and a black shirt. Her wide-set eyes were strikingly blue, shining as if they had their own light.

'I recognise you,' Lola said with a smile that wasn't returned. 'I've seen you on TV.'

Izatt looked surprised. *Hadn't he clocked who she was yet?*

'How's your sister doing?' Lola asked her now.

'She's . . . okay. She will be, anyway. I hope.'

Izatt cleared his throat irritably. 'Kitchen,' he said sharply. She followed him and he closed the door after her.

'What's up, Graeme?'

'Fiona won't talk,' Izatt said, eyes averted. 'Not to any of us. I told her she was at risk of hindering our enquiries, which is when—'

'She asked to see me?' Lola said.

'Yes.' He wasn't happy. 'What exactly did you say to her on Sunday morning?' he demanded.

'I said I'd help her, that's all. I told her she was safe with me.' She shrugged then added, pointedly, 'I was *nice* to her.'

Izatt scowled.

'She was drugged, I take it?' Lola asked.

'Ketamine. Reckon it was administered intravenously, and a good dose.'

'And Rennie?'

'Evidence of a substantial dose, though we don't know when he died. Pathologist says it could have been within two hours either side of midnight.'

'How's the enquiry going, Graeme?' she asked, meaning it to sound genuine.

'Slowly.'

'Expect there's a lot of ground to cover, isn't there?'

'Her sister says the relationship was rocky. Who is she, by the way? Seemed like you knew her.'

'She runs the MyLife Centre in Bridgeton — the women's refuge.'

'Yeah, she told us that.'

'Haven't you seen her on the news? She's a very dynamic young woman. Pretty vocal too. Political.'

'Ah. One of those.' Graeme all but rolled his eyes.

'One of those *what*?' Lola raised her eyebrows. 'Women? *Feminists*?'

'You know what I mean.'

'Aye,' she said. 'I think I do . . . She's made a difference to lots of women's lives, Graeme. Helped them sort themselves out, helped them deal with the rotten sods they've got landed with.'

'And yet her sister ended up with a character like Rennie.'

'Aye. Interesting, isn't it? Rebellion, perhaps? What did Catriona Balfour say about him?'

'She obviously didn't approve one bit. Said he was involved in "a lot of nasty business". Says she's been on at Fiona to leave him for a year.'

'They were due to be married in a month.'

'They weren't though. That's the thing. Not according to your lady activist out there. Something changed pretty recently. Fiona told her sister three weeks ago that she was planning to leave him but she was "scared of what he'd do". Seems that Rennie hadn't a clue. Catriona says she suggested a plan to get young Fiona out of the flat and into a new place while Rennie was out of the country.'

'A jailbreak?'

'Something like that. Fiona refused. Said she would do it in her own time. There wasn't only Rennie's rage to be wary of. There was his mum too. When it comes to matriarchs, Rita Rennie's the real deal. Word is she had people watching the place. "Looking out for her boy's interests."'

'Jeezo.'

'Anyway, on Saturday, Catriona knew her sister would be on her own, because Rennie was going to Amsterdam. She tried to get hold of her in the evening, but no answer. Kept trying. Again, nothing. So she turned up at her flat. Let herself in with a key her sister had given her — and found the place empty. Lights were blazing, TV on, dinner for one baked dry in the oven. Pollokshields' version of the *Mary Celeste*.' She called it in, but it hadn't even been twenty-four hours, so . . .'

'Saturday night?'

'The night before you found them in the park.'

'Rennie was due to go to Amsterdam, but never left the country?'

'No. Checked in for his flight in the morning but never made it to the airport. It was his BMW in the park. We're looking at CCTV to try to work out his movements.'

'So it looks like they took Fiona sometime during the evening? Interrupted her cooking. So, what — mid-evening-ish?'

'Hard to say. Maybe she knows, maybe she doesn't. Either way, she isn't playing.'

'Think what she's been through, Graeme.'

'It's not trauma. Not entirely, anyway. I think she's frightened.'

* * *

3.57 p.m.

Catriona Balfour was still in the hallway, arms folded, eyes down. When she looked up her expression was cold.

'Through here, is she?' Lola asked.

Catriona nodded and went silently ahead of her, leading down a short passage to the back of the flat.

She rapped on a door. 'Fi, it's me,' she said softly. 'DCI Harris is here to talk to you.'

Silence, then a muffled voice. Lola couldn't make out the words, but Catriona apparently could. She turned to Lola. 'She's ready,' she said, then turned the door handle and stood aside.

It was a nice room, high-ceilinged. Sunshine came in at an angle, lighting one wall and landing diagonally across a dark green armchair. Fiona Balfour sat on the bed, propped against pillows, knees up to her chin. She was dressed in jeans and an oversized green woollen jumper. The expensive kind. Possibly hand-knitted.

'Hello, Fiona.' Lola made a show of looking for a seat and indicated the armchair. 'Mind if I sit down?'

A nod.

'Been a long day.' She made herself comfy and smiled mildly at the woman on the bed.

Fiona was even slighter than Lola remembered her. She noticed her hair. It had been lank and muddy on Sunday morning, but now she saw it had been beautifully — and expensively — cut and coloured, perhaps as recently as a few weeks ago. Lola had been a hairdresser in her teens and knew you could tell a lot from a person's hair. This was no ordinary style. It would have taken a skilled stylist at least half a day, and cost two or three hundred pounds, easily.

The young woman's face told a different story. It was thin, taut and tired, and there were shadows under her eyes and lines round her mouth. Not a smoker. A worrier. She was twenty-six, Lola knew, but she could pass for thirty, or older. What she'd been through would age anyone . . . But Lola didn't believe just one incident had done this to her. She was looking at a deeply anxious young woman.

'I'm glad to see you,' Lola said now. 'How are you feeling?'

The eyes — the same blue as her sister's, but duller somehow — dropped.

'You asked for me.'

A small nod. Brief eye contact again.

Lola waited. At last the young woman said, 'What happened to me?'

Lola took her time, thinking about how to reply. 'We don't know yet. We hoped you might be able to help us shed some light on things.'

'But I can't. I *can't.*'

Her eyes were full of anguished appeal. Lola got the impression the words were genuine.

They sat in a companionable enough silence, eyes meeting from time to time, as if each was waiting for the other to speak.

Fiona Balfour cleared her throat. 'Why not me?' she said in a near-whisper.

'What do you mean?'

Eyes on her knees again. 'Why didn't they kill me too?'

'We don't know.'

An incredulous expression, eyes disbelieving, accusing. 'Really? *You* were there. You must have seen something. Some kind of . . . indication.'

'I don't think I did.'

The woman didn't believe her. Lola could see her withdrawing in disappointment.

'Maybe you remember bits and pieces,' Lola said tentatively.

'I don't.'

'What about the night before? Saturday evening?'

The young woman watched her. 'A few things.'

'What's the last thing you do remember?'

She appeared to be thinking about it, but her eyes belied her. Lola got the impression she was playing for time.

'I'd been shopping,' she said. 'I walked to the Sainsbury's at the end of the road and got stuff for dinner. I knew — I *thought* — it was just going to be me, because . . . because Sean was away. I remember coming up the stairs to the flat. Going into my pocket for my keys, and . . . And then—' her eyes met Lola's with defiance — 'it's a blank.'

Lola said nothing for several seconds. The young woman held her gaze.

'What is it you don't want to tell me, Fiona?'

A tiny intake of breath.

Lola waited, but no answer came.

'Do you know who did this to you and Sean?'

'No!'

More silence. More waiting.

'Who are you afraid of, Fiona?'

'I'm not afraid.' Defiant, but utterly unconvincing.

'I think you are.' Lola watched her. 'You look how I do when I'm worried to death about something. I know it, love. I've been there.'

Suddenly the young woman's face crumpled. She started to cry.

'You asked for me and I came,' Lola said. 'You want to trust me, so *please do*.'

Fiona shook her head and sniffed back her tears. She lifted her chin and was composed once more. 'I thought you'd explain what happened to me,' she said. 'That's all.'

'And I've told you I can't,' Lola said, but very gently. 'I'm sorry I can't help you. Really, I am.'

CHAPTER SIX

5.10 p.m.

'You're right that she's frightened,' Lola told Izatt, back in the kitchen.

'Find out why?'

'No specifics, no.'

Izatt huffed and rolled his eyes. 'Waste of bloody time.'

'I don't think so. It'll take time, that's all.'

'Do you think she knows who did it?'

She thought about it, arms folded, gazing out of the kitchen window at the quad behind the tenements. A woman was bringing in washing from a whirligig washing line. 'I don't know. I think . . . I think she suspects *something*. Something she can't quite bring herself to believe.'

'Oh?'

'She wanted *me* to tell *her* what happened,' she said. 'As if I could put her mind at ease.'

'"Her mind at ease"? Her boyfriend was *shot dead*!'

'I know. But that's the impression I got: she was looking for reassurance.'

They watched each other, Izatt looking pissed off.

'What's Rennie's mum saying?' Lola asked. 'If Catriona thinks she was — what was it, "looking out for her boy"?'

'Not a lot. Rita's a piece of work. You should meet her.'

'I'd like to. Maybe I could—'

'Forget it,' he said sharply. 'I was talking generally. I don't need any more help.'

She thought fast. 'Why don't we talk to Elaine Walsh? She might think it's worth us teaming up.'

'No, Lola!'

'Why not?'

'I said no.'

'Right you are.' Izatt and Detective Superintendent Elaine Walsh had a tricky relationship. Mainly because Elaine had the measure of him. Lola smiled and reached for the door.

Catriona was waiting for them in the hallway. She looked riven with anxiety, hands opening and closing at her sides, her eyes gleaming like sapphires. 'Do you think they'll come back for her, whoever did this?' she asked Lola, ignoring Izatt, who loomed menacingly at Lola's shoulder.

Izatt answered before Lola could speak. 'We have no reason to think they will, Ms Balfour. Unless you know something we don't, that is . . .'

Catriona lifted her chin. Her eyes widened. Lola recognised in them the same defiant manner she'd seen in Fiona. It struck her that the sisters had found themselves besieged, but seemingly determined to fight their own battles.

'Is something specific bothering you?' Lola asked gently.

'No.' A sharp rejection of the suggestion. 'What exactly did Fi say to you?'

'Not a lot,' Lola said. 'She said she wants to understand what happened to her.'

'We need to go,' Izatt said, putting an unwelcome hand on Lola's arm, making her muscles tense and her skin creep. 'Come on, DCI Harris.'

At the door, Lola turned and swapped glances with the young woman with the avid eyes. She had something to say,

Lola knew it. And she suspected very strongly that she didn't want to say it in front of Izatt. Every fibre of her being urged her to remain.

'DCI Harris . . . ?' Izatt said, irritated.

She took a last look at the agitated young woman, then followed Izatt out into the close.

You had to pick your fights. You also had to bide your time.

CHAPTER SEVEN

8.44 p.m.

Cat Balfour got back to the flat and was relieved to find Fi still asleep in the spare room. She'd felt bad leaving her, but the call had been an emergency. A man had found out his wife was staying in the Langside safe house and had gone there to retrieve her — or so he intended. The volunteer on duty had called the police, who'd promised to come as soon as they could, but the man had begun hammering on the windows and the volunteer was panicking. Could Cat come and try to help calm things down?

She'd arrived at the house — the end of a red sandstone terrace — to find him pacing, muttering to himself and occasionally banging a fist off the iron railings that separated the small garden from the pavement.

'The police are on their way,' she told him, as she got out of the Fiat. 'You might want to head off for your own good.'

'And who the fuck are you?' he spat, coming to a halt and looking at her with an expression of rage. He was a short man, stocky and bow-legged with thick black hair and strong eyebrows. He reminded Cat of an angry bull terrier.

'Catriona Balfour,' she said calmly, locking the car. 'I manage the charity that runs this place. Who are you?'

'Why?'

'Because if you don't tell me, I won't talk to you. That's the way it is.'

He scowled and scuffed his feet irritably on the pavement. 'Name's Tam.'

'Right, Tam. You're scaring the women and you need to go.'

'I'm going nowhere. My fucking wife's in there.' He jabbed a finger at the house. 'I want her back.'

'That's up to her, don't you think?' she said with a shrug.

'How am I supposed to know, when she won't even talk to me?'

'Again, it's her choice. Walk with me.'

'*Whit?*'

'I said, walk with me. We'll take a turn round the block. You'll feel better.'

He stared in disgust.

'What's wrong? Are you worried I'll bite or something?'

He looked unnerved now, wrong-footed. She caught a glimpse of a blind twitching behind his shoulder.

'I know what this is,' Tam said now. 'This is some mind trick, isn't it? You're going to trap me.'

She put her hands up, in mock surrender. 'Tam, you got me. That's right, I'm Dr Freud and the FBI combined. Look . . . just a short walk. Let me get to know you.' She nodded at the cigarette packet he'd taken out of a jacket pocket. 'And you can give me one of those smokes while you're at it.'

He stared at her, then, like an automaton, held the packet towards her. She took a cigarette and they went through the niceties of Tam lighting hers before his own.

Cat inhaled deeply and smiled. 'Feels better. Stressful day.'

'What've you got to be stressed about?'

Apart from dealing with arseholes like you?

'You wouldn't believe it if I told you,' she said aloud.

'Try me.'

'All right. Someone tried to murder a member of my family,' she said. 'She's in bits. I'm looking after her.'

'Whit? Seriously?' He stared, eyes wide.

'Come on, walk,' she said, and made to set off.

He came, obedient now. They walked to the end of the road, smoking and talking. By the time they were round the block, she knew all about Tam, his wife, their son.

They were outside the house again. Still no police. He eyed the building, and she watched the rage build in his expression again.

'She's not coming out,' she told him gently. 'And you being here — it's not going to help. Go away. Stay away. Talk to your solicitor. And take some care of yourself.'

He started to cry. Tears of impotent frustration and undirected anger.

'Go home, Tam.'

He nodded, sniffing hard, then went back into his jacket for his smokes. 'Want another of these?'

'No,' she said. 'But thanks.'

He nodded, then went on his way, head down, shoulders up, hurrying between the shadows.

The police car was there two minutes later.

'All sorted,' she told the community officer breezily. 'I doubt he'll be back.'

She'd gone inside and talked to the volunteer and to Tam's wife, offering her the chance to move to a flat they used in Govan, where there was a spare bed. A cup of tea and a soothing chat, and the woman, Veronica, said she'd stay here.

Now, home and armed with coffee, she tried to make headway with a funding application, and was just about to give up when Fi appeared in the living-room doorway in a dressing gown. She looked sleepy and confused as she stood by the door, squinting at the TV.

'What you watching?'

'Oh, nothing,' Cat said, putting her laptop on the floor. 'You can turn it over if you want.'

'No, this is fine.' She sat at the other end of the settee, curling her slight frame into a protective ball, and frowned at the TV, where a beauty therapist was making spaghetti bolognese for a blind date in a tiny kitchen and cackling as she splashed sauce down her top.

Cat turned down the volume and sat forward, hands on her knees.

'Feeling any better?'

'I'm okay.' Fi's eyes didn't move from the quietened TV.

She didn't look okay. She had the look of any number of Cat's clients over the years: shell-shocked and fragile, and ready to spook at anything.

'How did you get on with the inspector earlier?' Cat asked her. 'The woman? Was she kind to you?'

'Yeah. She was.'

Cat had formed a good impression of the inspector when she arrived. There was an almost motherly solidity to her: a no-nonsense humanity that was both appealing and disarming, and which, she suspected, could be dangerous if you had something to hide. They'd only spoken briefly, but Cat had found her reassuringly calm and focused. Thoughtful too; the way her green eyes narrowed as she listened, nodding gently and smiling a little to show she understood, all the time playing with the silver locket that hung round her neck. In fact, she seemed exactly the kind of person Cat would value as a volunteer at the MyLife Centre — even as a trustee. Relations with the police hadn't been great, thanks to a recent incident, but she had hopes they were improving.

'What did you talk about?' she asked Fi.

'Not much. I thought she might tell me . . . well, *something*. Anything that would help me understand what had happened. She couldn't. Then she accused me of holding stuff back — as if I knew, but was holding back for some reason. Waste of time.'

They sat in depressed silence.

'There's soup if you want some,' Cat said. 'I could—'

'Not hungry.'

'A drink, then?'

She agreed to a cup of tea, though barely seemed to notice when the mug appeared on the coffee table. Fi had taken possession of the TV remote, and the volume was back up. Cat reached uneasily for her laptop and tried to work. It was no good. She was a mass of tension, and unable to concentrate. Staring blankly at the text on the screen, she willed herself to relax, to think what she'd do if Fi wasn't Fi, but some other traumatised woman — a stranger at the shelter, on the run from a disastrous relationship.

Allow her space. Don't pester her. Give her a sense of safety and she'll talk when she's ready.

She began to type, writing meaningless sentences she knew she'd end up deleting later.

On the TV, the blind date had been a disaster, and the programme ended. Adverts blared.

Fi turned the sound down and asked, a little slyly, 'Who phoned?'

'When?' Cat kept her eyes on her laptop, heart sinking.

'Earlier. I heard you in the kitchen. You told someone to "leave us alone". Who was it?'

Never shy from the truth. Always be as honest as you can.

She slowly closed the laptop and put it on the floor.

'It was Rita,' she said. 'She phoned yesterday as well.'

Fi stared at her. 'What does she want?'

'To know where you are. She wants to talk to you. Her and Gerry.' Gerry was Sean's older brother. 'I said you were staying with friends outside the city. She wanted to know where. I said it wasn't any of her business.'

'Oh, God . . .' Fi covered her face with her hands and started to cry. 'What am I going to say to them?'

Cat moved along the settee and put an arm round her sister and pulled her into an embrace.

'Nothing. They're over and done with.' *Like Sean*, she wanted to add. 'You're going to move on. You're going to live a wonderful, happy life.'

'What if she comes here?'

'She won't. She doesn't know this address.'

'She knows the phone number. She rang on the land-line, didn't she? She'll be able to use that to find the address. She could find us here no problem.'

Cat didn't answer. Just held her sister tight and closed her eyes, as if to deny the storm clouds she'd already glimpsed, massing in the near distance.

CHAPTER EIGHT

Wednesday 26 October
1.07 p.m.

'It was you that found Sean Rennie's body, wasn't it?' a voice asked her.

Lola turned a surprised expression on the man who'd spoken. They were neighbours in the queue to pay for food in the canteen at Gartcosh, the high-tech home of the Scottish Crime Campus, east of Glasgow — home, too, to a better class of lunch. He was an older chap, wiry and tanned. She didn't recognise him and his ID badge had swivelled back to front. 'Depends who's asking,' she said drily.

'Bill Delaney,' he said, beaming. 'DCI in Livingston. I'd shake your hand if I wasn't holding this tray. Nasty wee fella, Sean Rennie. Came across him a decade ago. Nice to know he won't be bothering us anymore.'

'Aye, well,' she said, noncommittally. The queue moved. Lola and Delaney moved with it.

'Took a fella's eye out over a deal he missed out on. Not in the heat of the moment either. Waited for him. Jumped him from behind. Knocked him out, tied him up, then used a screwdriver. Took his time. Enjoyed himself, I reckon.'

Lola nodded, processing the image.

'His dad Mickey was a nasty bastard too. As for the mammy . . .' He made a whistling sound.

'Never met her,' Lola said.

'Shouting her mouth off in today's *Chronicle*, if you're interested.'

Lola was but didn't want to show it, for reasons she couldn't quite pinpoint.

'Any idea who might have done for him?' she asked, trying to sound only mildly interested.

'Hard to say,' he said. 'Any number of possibilities. Drugs, it'll be. Always is.'

She leaned in a little and said quietly, but pointedly, 'Whoever did it tied his fiancée to his corpse so she'd wake up and see him shot in the forehead and not be able to escape. Does that sound like a drug murder to you?'

Delaney pushed out his bottom lip and shrugged. 'Nasty people do nasty things.'

'Aye, well . . .'

She was relieved when it was her turn to pay.

Detective Superintendent Elaine Walsh was already installed at the far end of the canteen, with a view over a courtyard where a metal sculpture turned slowly in the breeze. The Crime Campus was immense, managed with cutting-edge technology and protected by the tightest security. It was architecturally self-conscious, built in the shape of a pair of chromosomes, and had already won awards.

Elaine had apparently finished her lunch. She moved her tray aside to make room for Lola to settle opposite.

'Goat's cheese tart?' she said, glancing at Lola's tray. 'I hear it's good.'

Neither of them was based at the campus, but when Elaine realised they would both be attending a child protection training session here, she'd suggested they have lunch in the canteen and use the opportunity to go through the motions of Lola's annual appraisal — a tick-box exercise that would no doubt descend into a gossip.

Lola liked Elaine a lot. She was quiet and reserved, and wore her seniority lightly. With her tidy bob and her understated tailored suits, she could be a family lawyer or the manager of an estate agency. You'd never think she'd brought countless murderers, gangsters and drug dealers to book. You certainly wouldn't imagine she'd spent two years seconded to the CIA, working in Langley, Virginia, on a project to improve covert intelligence links between Scotland and the States.

Elaine had worked for a number of years at G Division before being promoted and moving to Stirling. Her recent return to Glasgow had seen Graeme Izatt, who'd temporarily held the superintendent's role, a mere DCI once more — to his displeasure.

'How are you doing?' Elaine said now. 'No nightmares after the Rennie thing?'

'No.'

Elaine watched her carefully, then nodded, satisfied. She let Lola get started on her tart and concentrated on the slowly revolving artwork outside.

'And how's your man?' she asked now, in a very low, very gentle voice.

'He's not my man,' Lola said, matter of fact. She shrugged. 'He never was. Not really. We're friends now, that's all. The sooner I get used to the idea the better.'

Elaine nodded, going along with it. 'He's started his treatment, hasn't he?'

Lola nodded. 'He starts the second cycle tomorrow. There'll be three in total.'

Joe, the love of her life but firmly married to another woman, was having treatment for cancer. Earlier in the year she'd managed to ditch him and had set about "moving on", only for him to turn up on her doorstep with his devastating news. She'd let him in — of course she had — and the pair of them had sat on her sofa, weeping in each other's arms. Now, watching him go through the various stages of treatment, seeing him at his most vulnerable, hearing the fear in his voice every time he spoke — it was eating her inside.

'You've a heart of gold,' Elaine told her now, studying Lola's face.

'Have I?'

'You don't need me to tell you that. I just wish you had a bit more self-belief.'

'I have to support him, Elaine,' she said, and used a serviette to quickly wipe away the tears that had sprung in her eyes.

The truth was that she hadn't heard from him for several days now. Nearly a week, in fact. Two days ago, jangled from the find in Pollok Park, she'd broken their rule and texted him, asking how he was and saying she was having a stressful day.

He still hadn't replied. It was taking every last reserve of her willpower not to text again. Not to worry that his health had taken a turn for the worse.

She put down her knife and fork and pushed her plate aside. Elaine had paperwork in front of her. 'I booked a room upstairs, but I thought we could just do it here. What do you think?'

Lola glanced behind her. The place was thinly populated. She said here was fine.

They talked about the past year. About successes and challenges. Elaine asked how Lola was finding the temporary promotion, and whether it had put strain on her relationship with Izatt.

Lola had staffing problems to thank for her bump up the ranks, but she also owed a debt to Assistant Chief Constable Clive Reid, a man of no mean reputation, who'd taken a special interest in her career. He'd personally recommended she be given the opportunity of a temporary promotion to DCI, given her "clear talents as a detective and a leader". Izatt had been tasked to communicate the good news, and had done so with a face like thunder. It had taken all Lola's self-composure to maintain a poker face. She was now the same rank as the man who'd spent months trying — but largely failing — to lord it over her.

'No strain on my part,' she said.

Elaine made a knowing face.

Lola thought fast. Since the visit to Catriona Balfour's flat yesterday afternoon, she'd been stewing about Izatt's refusal to let her any closer to the case. True, she had enough on her plate as it was, but the meeting with Fiona Balfour had worried her a great deal. As had Izatt's dismissal of Lola's offer of help — that, and the way he'd reacted when she'd suggested they talk to Elaine about it.

'I told DCI Izatt I wanted to help with the Rennie case,' she said in a rush, before she could stop herself. 'He said he didn't need me.'

Elaine smiled sourly. 'He did, did he?'

'I said I was worried there was something strange going on. Why on earth did Rennie's killer tie his fiancée to his corpse, yet not harm her? And why won't Fiona Balfour talk to Izatt? So I suggested we come and talk to you. See what you thought.'

'And he said, "no chance"?'

'Pretty much.'

'Why do you think he said that, out of interest?'

She took a deep breath. 'I think he feels threatened. Three weeks ago he was a detective super and I was a lowly DI. Now we're the same rank. It's understandable.'

'That's not the reason,' Elaine said plainly.

'Isn't it?'

'No. The reason he doesn't want you to discuss it with me . . . is because I've already suggested he bring you into it.'

Lola stared and kept her mouth shut.

'To which he replied,' Elaine went on, 'that he didn't need you. He was adamant. When I pushed him, he asked me for a week to make progress, and I agreed to that, though I'm starting to doubt myself.'

So that explained that . . .

'I agree with you that there's something strange going on,' Elaine said. 'Graeme has a number of qualities, including bloody-mindedness. But he isn't good at *strange*.' Elaine smiled. 'You are, Lola. You're *very* good at strange.'

'What do you want me to do?' Lola said, her heart racing.

'Nothing. Just wait. Though I half-suspect Graeme might be getting in touch with you.'

'Oh?'

'Catriona Balfour has spirited her sister away somewhere, and won't tell Graeme where.'

'Spirited her away?'

'Last night, apparently. "Worried for her safety", "doesn't trust the police" *et cetera, et cetera.*'

'I see . . .'

'I even offered to speak to her. He didn't like that.'

'I could try to have a quiet word with Catriona . . .'

Elaine eyed her for a minute, then leaned forward and said, meaningfully and quietly, 'So long as *I* don't know anything about it. *Understand?*'

Lola gave the lightest of shrugs.

Elaine gave a satisfied nod, then turned her attention to the papers before her.

'Right,' she said with mock cheer, 'let's get this appraisal signed and sealed for another year, shall we?'

CHAPTER NINE

3.30 p.m.

The most direct route from Gartcosh, east of the city, back to HQ in Govan was by the motorway. Instead, Lola took a deliberately circuitous route, winding down through Glasgow's eastern suburbs until she found herself in Bridgeton. She parked on James Street, across the road from a discreet doorway that Google Maps suggested was the entrance to the MyLife Centre, the refuge run by Catriona Balfour.

The neighbourhood, run-down and lightly littered, seemed relatively quiet. A man appeared, zigzagging drunkenly along the pavement, then stopped to leer in at her, waving with a toothless grin.

She waved back, at the same time activating the car's central locking.

She googled the centre's phone number and dialled as the man wobbled off.

Yes, Catriona was around today, a diffident-sounding older woman told her. Who was calling?

'I'm from the police,' Lola said. 'It's nothing to worry about. Just routine.'

'And you say you want to pop by?' A note of strain in the woman's voice now.

'Just to say hello. Nothing official. I won't take up too much of her time.'

'I suppose it's all right. Could you come after four? Just ring this number when you're at the door and someone will come down.'

She got a takeaway coffee from a café and then went into a newsagent's for a paper before returning to the car.

The chap in the canteen at Gartcosh had been right: Rita Rennie was indeed mouthing off in today's *Daily Chronicle*. All over the front page and half of page two, in fact.

The piece was by Shuna Frain, an old sparring partner of Lola's, along with another reporter whose name she didn't recognise.

Mum Brands Police Efforts Woeful, the headline read, beside a close-up photo of Rita's face.

The woman looked bitter and angry, glaring at the photographer through strands of her dyed-blonde fringe, eyes like chips of malachite behind mascaraed spider's legs. The article said she was in her fifties, but Lola suspected she was at least a decade older than that. She'd had work done, judging by the shape of her eyes and the tightness of her jaw. Her coral-painted lips, curled back in a snarl, were improbably plump. The gold cross at her throat caught the light and gleamed. Lola felt she would be pleased with that detail.

She read:

> *Rita Rennie, 53, of King's Park, has today branded as 'woeful' police efforts to catch her son's killer.*
>
> *It's three days since Sean Rennie, 30, of Pollokshields, was found shot dead in the city's Pollok Park. Rennie, a property developer, was due to wed fiancée Fiona Balfour in two weeks' time. Fiona, 26, was found nearby but unharmed in the early hours of Sunday morning. She has since made a full recovery.*

> *'Sean was such a good boy,' said Mrs Rennie, 'but the police have always had it in for him, because of who his dad was.' Rita's husband was Mickey Rennie, who died in a shooting incident in Castlemilk in 2005. 'They called my husband a criminal but it was never proved,' Rita explained. 'They never found his killers either.'*

Dead gangsters were always good boys, according to their mums. Lola scanned the article, shaking her head in distaste.

The article stated that Sean Rennie had left behind an older brother, Gerry, and two sisters, Bernie and Terri. Gerry was quoted, swearing revenge on whoever had murdered "Our Sean", calling his younger brother "one of the good guys" and his "hero".

It ended on an interesting note:

> *Asked if she had a message for her son's killer, Rita was quick to answer.*
>
> *'There's someone out there who's got a reckoning coming to them,' the grieving woman warned. 'I say to that person: you think you've been very clever, but you'll pay for what you've done.'*

Such an irresponsible thing to print. Did Shuna Frain and her colleague — and their editor — really want their newspaper turning into a message board for gangsters?

The clock on the dashboard said it was time to go. She folded the paper and reached for the door, when her phone buzzed in her jacket pocket. She pulled it out and her heart jumped when she saw a text from Joe.

Can meet you tonight. Same place as last time at 8?

She typed back: *Yes. No problem.*

Spirits lifted, she got out of the car and crossed the road.

* * *

4.04 p.m.

'You wait in here, hen,' Jeanie told her, all reassuring smiles. Jeanie was an older woman, sixty-something, working-class, motherly. 'Would you like a cup of tea or something? A wee biscuit?'

'I'm fine, thank you,' Lola said, picking a seat.

'I'll leave you be then, hen. Catriona'll be along in a wee minute.'

The door closed softly. The room was tiny and windowless, with low, soft seats. There were innocuous prints of watery landscapes on the walls and an array of magazines on a little table. There was a box of tissues too.

This must be the first place they brought you after you came over the threshold, Lola thought. You'd left your abusive partner and made your way — through the night, probably — to this nondescript building. You rang the bell and showed your face to the little camera on the door. Then a nice friendly lady, probably much older than you, brought you in here and made you a hot drink. Lola wondered how many frightened women had been in here over the years. How many were being helped now? Did they stay here? Were there bedrooms somewhere in the building, or did they find you a room somewhere else? Did you feel safe here, or like a frightened animal, hounded away from your home and into hiding?

The door opened, making her jump.

'It's *you*,' Catriona Balfour said when she saw Lola. She seemed genuinely surprised.

'Hello, Ms Balfour,' Lola said, rising.

'Catriona, please.' She came into the room and let the door close behind her. She was wearing a grey wool suit and had her curls tied back. She looked businesslike but wrung out, as if she hadn't slept. 'Jeanie said it was the police, so I assumed it was one of our local community constables, now they're trying to make an effort.'

'"An effort"?'

46

'We haven't always had a good relationship with your colleagues,' she said, making a face. 'You might have heard what happened a couple of years ago.'

'Remind me . . .'

'A young woman left her abusive boyfriend, came to us covered in bruises. Two fingers broken on one hand. We got her sorted, set her up with accommodation. Then we persuaded her to report him. Turned out the boyfriend's best pal was one of your lot: a constable based just down the road. He got the address where we'd taken her and passed it to the woman's ex, who went round and attacked her all over again. Cut her up pretty badly.'

'I do remember,' Lola said dismally. 'The officer lost his job, and rightly so.'

'There's a new superintendent here now. She's trying hard.'

'I'm glad to hear it.'

Catriona nodded then her eyes narrowed. 'So, why are you here?'

'I was just passing,' Lola lied with a smile. 'I remembered where you were and . . . I wanted to ask how Fiona was doing, that's all.'

The woman raised a sceptical eyebrow. 'So, you're not here to find out where I've taken her?'

'Where you've taken her . . . ?' Lola said, feigning inno-cence. 'I'm not sure I—'

'Don't give me that.' She folded her arms. 'That is why you're here, isn't it?'

'Would you tell me if I asked?' Lola said.

'Unlikely.'

'We want what's best for Fiona,' Lola said gently. 'We all do, don't we? You most of all.'

'Yes.' Catriona's expression changed subtly. She seemed momentarily choked. She cleared her throat. 'What else would you expect?'

'Nothing less,' Lola murmured. 'I've a younger sister myself. It's a special bond, isn't it? You love them dearly, though they do their best to drive you round the bend.'

'Something like that.' She took a seat opposite Lola. Catriona was so different to her sister, Lola thought, with a head of thick curls where Fiona's hair was straight. Where Fiona was slight and feminine, Catriona appeared lean and athletic. What they shared was a nervous energy that made them seem edgy, as if they might bolt at any moment.

'You've achieved so much — with the centre, I mean,' Lola said now. 'You set it up from scratch, didn't you?'

'Yes. Ten years ago. It was an effort, but it worked.'

'Do you house people here?'

'Not here, no. These are our offices — we offer counselling and train volunteers here. We've a number of safe houses around the city. Six just now, a seventh coming. Bought and run with a modicum of government funding, plus donations. A few legacies.'

'You're planning to grow?'

'We have to. There's a pandemic of domestic abuse in this city. In this country.'

Lola nodded. 'These safe houses,' she said gently. 'Where are they?'

A cynical smile appeared on Catriona's lips. 'Fiona's not in one of the safe houses,' she said. 'But nice try.'

Lola relented.

'You're not even working on this case, are you?' Catriona said, frowning. 'Mr Izatt said he'd only called you in yesterday because . . . because you found Fi, and he thought she'd talk to you.'

'I'm not, no,' Lola said. 'But, let's just say it feels somewhat personal — because I found her. I want to know she's okay.'

Catriona appeared to process it. 'Yes,' she said at last. 'I understand that well enough.'

'How is she doing?'

'She's . . . okay.'

'It'll take her a good while to get over it,' Lola mused.

'Over Sean dying, you mean? She didn't love him anymore. She was planning to leave him. She was going to tell him this week, as it happens. Funny how things turn out.'

Yes, Lola thought to herself. *Very funny.*

Aloud, she said, 'I meant, it'll take her time to get over what happened.'

'Maybe. Maybe not. Fi's unusual. She feels things very deeply, but she bounces back with amazing resilience.'

'Tell me about her.'

Catriona watched her carefully, as if deciding whether to trust her. 'She's a very loveable person,' she said at last. 'Well, she was. Lately . . . well . . . The thing about Fi is, she doesn't always make good choices. I think she's one of those people who life is too harsh for, so she chooses to live in a world of her own, where everything's lovely and if you just think the best of people, then everything will be fine.'

'Does she work?'

'She did.' Catriona gave her a dark look. 'She was a teaching assistant at a school in East Renfrewshire. She loved everything about it: her colleagues, the kids. She helped run a club for parents who wanted to help their children learn. Then Sean made her give it up. He told her he made more than enough money, and that he wanted her to make a nice home for the two of them — and anyway, soon they'd be married, and she'd have children of her own. Fi was convinced. You can imagine how I felt about it. I work with abused women every day. Let me tell you, the bruises and broken bones are only the tip of the iceberg. The real damage is from control and coercion. Years of demeaning words, endless criticisms, being told you're worthless and weak. That you can only survive because he's there to protect you.'

Lola nodded.

'Fi's a beautiful girl,' Catriona went on. 'Sean wanted a trophy he could show off, but I think he also wanted to recreate the rock-solid family unit he'd grown up in. You know about the Rennies?'

'Yes,' Lola said, not committing. 'Tell me, what did the rest of your family make of the relationship?'

'Both our parents are dead, and neither of them had siblings. It's been me and Fi against the world since I was twenty-three and she was seventeen. That was the idea, anyway.'

'Her friends?'

'Three guesses what happened to them once Sean came along.'

'She doesn't see them anymore?'

The young woman shook her head. 'When she was still working she saw people at the school, but . . . not now.'

'Did you try to intervene?'

'Of course! But if I'd pushed any further, I might have pushed her away for good. It's very hard to support someone in that situation. I've learned a lot about myself the past couple of years.' She added, darkly, 'Not all of it good.'

Lola nodded. 'How did they meet?'

'At a sports bar in town. You know the kind of place. Screens everywhere. Loud music. Waiters walking around serving tequila shots. She was with some colleagues. Sean Rennie was out with his brother and some mates. Love's young dream.'

The young woman's eyes flitted to the clock above Lola's head and Lola realised time was short.

'You're very worried about her, aren't you?'

'Of course.'

'Because of Rennie's family?'

Catriona said nothing, but her eyes hardened.

'Where is she, Catriona? Tell me and I'll do what I can to help you. To help Fiona.'

Lola watched the woman's eyes as she weighed the risks.

'But how can you?' she said after a few moments. 'This isn't even your case.'

'And yet here I am.'

'Did DCI Izatt send you?'

'No. As a matter of fact, he has no idea I'm here.' She gave a grim smile. 'And I expect he'll be less than pleased when he finds out.'

'Then . . . ?'

'My superintendent told me you'd taken your sister away and that you hadn't told DCI Izatt where. I thought I'd pop by and see what I could find out.'

50

'For your superintendent?'

'No. *For Fiona.*'

The chin lifted again.

'Catriona, you might think you're helping her, but you could be putting her in more danger.'

More silence. More weighing.

'There's something you need to understand,' she said finally. 'Something Fi's been living with.'

'Go on.'

'It sounds crazy, I know, but for a long time Fi's had this idea that . . . well, that someone's out to get her.'

'*Out to get her?*'

'Yes. Someone who wants to do her harm.'

It explained the fear in Fiona Balfour's eyes the other evening.

'You say it goes back a long time. Longer than—'

'Than Sean? Yes, a lot longer.' A deep breath. 'She believes someone wants to kill her. But the thing is, she has no idea who. So, you see, she's already come to the conclusion that the attack on Sean *wasn't about him at all.* That it was about *her.*'

They sat in silence while Lola took it in. 'And do you think there's anything in it?'

'Possibly.'

'Where is she, Catriona?'

Catriona Balfour watched her warily.

Eyes down, then, at last: 'I asked a friend to take her in.'

'I see.' Lola hid the wash of relief. 'And where does your friend stay?'

'Ayrshire. It's a farm in the middle of nowhere.'

'And this friend is someone you trust?'

'One hundred per cent. I've known Tom since university. He and Diana are wonderful people. There's a cottage on the land. Fi's staying there. She's happy about it because she loves kids, and Tom and Diana have got five.'

'Thank you for trusting me, Catriona,' Lola said. 'Will you give me the address?'

The young woman inclined her head, eyes averted again, her discomfort evident.

'It's vitally important that we help you keep your sister safe. Do you understand?'

A pause that lasted an age. Then, quietly, unhappily: 'I understand.'

CHAPTER TEN

8.16 p.m.

She'd arrived at the bar early, got herself a lemonade and found a corner at the back of the pub. From there she texted Joe to tell him where to find her.

He didn't reply, but he was probably driving.

It would be the first time they'd seen each other since he'd begun his treatment.

He'd still been having tests when he first told her he was ill, but had known from early results that it was likely to be non-Hodgkin's lymphoma. The remaining tests had been to help the doctors plan his treatment, and to check that his body, and specifically his heart, would cope with the chemotherapy.

In the weeks that followed, with the help of the internet, Lola had become a lay expert in lymphomas and how they were treated. The prognosis seemed hopeful, and good news followed when it was confirmed his lymphoma was at an early stage. He would have three twenty-one-day cycles of a chemotherapy regime known as 'R-CHOP', which was known to work well, despite being harsh. He'd lose hair, feel sick and probably need to take time off work.

They'd been in touch when he started the first cycle, by text message, and once talked on the phone. There were rules, though: ones she'd insisted on right from the off, seeing they were now "just friends". There could be no "love yous", no kisses on text messages, no fond reminiscing or regrets expressed for what could have been. He'd accused her of being hard on him.

She wasn't though. She was being hard on herself.

The first cycle had gone to plan. Joe's wife Marie had driven him to the hospital, waited with him and driven him home several hours later. There'd been no texting that day. His nausea had kicked in a few days later. And then, to his horror, though he'd known it would happen, his hair had started to thin and came out in clumps in the night. That was when he'd phoned her, during a break from work. She'd stopped in a lay-by to talk to him. He wept for fifteen minutes, and she joined in.

Time had flown by, the doctors were pleased with how his body had coped with the treatment, and his second cycle was due to begin any day now.

She thanked God for a taxing, all-consuming job that distracted her for some of the time, at least.

Her thoughts turned to the phone call she'd made to Graeme Izatt from the car.

'Don't shout at me,' she'd said, eyes squeezed tight, when he answered. 'I've been to see Catriona Balfour.'

'You've *what*?'

'I know where she's taken Fiona. *And* the reason why.'

'Lola, for fuck's—'

'I said, *don't shout at me*, Graeme! I shouldn't have done it. But I was passing through Bridgeton and I saw the place and I—'

'And you thought you'd pop in, did you? I'm not happy about this, Lola, and I'll be talking to Elaine.'

'Fiona believes *she* was the intended victim,' she went on quickly, 'not Rennie. She's been convinced for several years that someone's out to get her. Catriona's terrified she might be right. Now,' she said, eager to get the conversation over and done with, 'do you want this address or not?'

Her phoned buzzed on the table before her. She grabbed it, then her heart stopped.

Can't make it. Will try to talk to you soon. Sorry. J.

CHAPTER ELEVEN

Thursday 27 October
9.05 a.m.

'You had no business doing that, DCI Harris,' Elaine Walsh said coolly, though her eyes communicated a subtly reassuring message. One that Graeme, sitting beside her, would fail to detect.

'I'm sorry, boss,' she said, eyes down, playing meekly along. 'It was a spur-of-the-moment thing.'

Izatt was a picture of pissed-off fury, fists on his knees and hunched so far forward he almost touched Elaine's desk. 'I'm sorry, Graeme,' she said. 'I was only trying to help. And I did get the information you needed, didn't I?'

'Never do this again, Lola,' Elaine said to her, finger up. 'Maverick nonsense can derail an investigation and sabotage a prosecution case.'

Lola nodded.

'What's to be done?' Izatt demanded of the superintendent. He still hadn't made eye contact with Lola.

She made herself remain expressionless as Elaine studied her thoughtfully. 'Give us a minute, would you?'

'Boss.'

'But don't go far.'

Outside the room she checked her phone. She'd texted Joe after he'd called off meeting her the night before. He still hadn't replied. She'd lain awake for hours, worrying that his health had taken a nosedive and that he was too tired or weak to text, or that he didn't want to worry her.

Ignoring the anxiety fluttering inside her ribcage, she returned to her desk, steeling herself for DS Aidan Pierce's speculative gaze. He'd swaggered in earlier, in one of his beautifully tailored Italian suits, a pair of shades perched on his perfect hair, all smiles for Marcus McVittie and Jonno Gillies. The DCs were good lads really, assiduous and committed, but easy meat for the division's most toxic detective.

Pierce was there now, hunched over his laptop, Marcus at his side, the pair of them sniggering at something on the screen.

He glanced up as Lola came in, a look of dark amusement in his eyes. She nodded pleasantly to him and he looked away.

She couldn't stand him, and the feeling was mutual. He'd done his best to upend the big murder investigation in the summer, pushing her almost to breaking point, then putting in a grievance against her. But he'd picked a fight with the wrong woman — as he soon found out. Now he was on an improvement plan, one Lola herself was overseeing. Much to his ill-disguised disgust.

'Morning, boss,' came a breezy voice from behind her.

'Morning, Kirstie!'

DC Kirstie Campbell made her way from the kitchen to her desk, a picture of cool and tidy calm, with her blonde hair clipped neatly back from her pale, serious face.

'Is everything . . . ?' Kirstie seemed to remember who was sitting only a few desks away and stemmed her question.

Lola had barely sat down when Elaine's voice called down the office: 'DCI Harris — a few more minutes of your time, please.'

* * *

She'd expected to find Graeme still seething in his seat, but he was nowhere to be seen.

'Away to lick his wounds,' Elaine said, answering her unspoken question.

'Did it do the trick?' Lola said.

'Depends on the trick. Take a seat.'

Lola did as she was told.

'He was *this* close to making a formal complaint,' Elaine said, pinching her finger and thumb in front of her face. 'I managed to talk him out of it.'

'Thanks, boss.'

'He's angry, Lola. You — *we* — overstepped the line there.'

'But it worked.'

'Graeme wanted me to tell you to back right off. To "remind you of your position" as a temporary DCI.' Elaine sat back in her chair, eyes narrowed. She shook her head. 'You're a bad woman, Lola,' she said, a conspiratorial gleam in her eye. 'I suppose that makes two of us.'

She began to chuckle.

'Catriona Balfour doesn't trust Graeme,' Elaine said. 'Nor the police in general. But she trusts you. I wonder why.'

Lola said nothing. She could have offered several reasons, but suspected Elaine didn't need to hear them.

'Graeme went to the place in Ayrshire last night, mob-handed, and of course Fiona Balfour refused to give him the time of day. Another reason why he's seething. Fiona trusts you though, doesn't she?'

Where was Elaine going with this?

The superintendent watched Lola quietly for several seconds, then said, apparently apropos of nothing, 'The Clyde Fisheries fraud case.'

'What about it, boss?'

'Pass it to DCI Izatt.'

Lola stared, suddenly comprehending a lot, including why Izatt had done a vanishing act.

'Boss . . . What are you—?'

'What am I saying? I'm saying, Lola, that the Rennie case is yours.'

CHAPTER TWELVE

9.35 a.m.

Losing no time, Lola confirmed her team, securing Elaine's permission to bring Kirstie with her from the fraud case onto this one to make a complement of three DCs.

'You happy to keep DS Pierce?' Elaine asked her pointedly.

'Of course,' Lola said, meaning it. 'It'll be useful to see how well he's developing first-hand.'

Elaine looked cynically amused.

'You'll have a new DS as well. Anna Vaughan. She's due to start on Monday, but she might be willing to come in over the weekend to get up to speed on the investigation.'

'She the one from London?'

'That's her. DCI Izatt was due to meet her today. I'll ask him to explain you're taking over. She's done the conversion course, so she should be ready for our peculiar Scottish ways. Plays tennis. Husband's a lawyer. They've bought a villa in Dumbreck. Very impressive young woman, so I hear.'

Lola groaned inwardly, but said nothing.

'Graeme's very sore about it, Lola,' Elaine said when it was time to take her leave. 'Try and talk to him today. Gee him up a bit. We don't want him nursing a grudge.'

'No problem, boss.'

She phoned him straight away, asking to meet as soon as possible. He muttered something about an appointment in town, then agreed to meet her at half eleven. Next she pulled her team into a meeting room, enjoying the look of barely concealed horror on Pierce's beautifully groomed features. She tasked him with preparing a report on everything that had been done to date and to identify any hot, warm or even cool leads.

Then she rang Catriona Balfour and told her the news.

* * *

1.37 p.m.

'If you wait till evening, I can take you there myself,' Catriona had told her.

But Lola couldn't wait.

'In that case, don't take any notice of the GPS,' Catriona warned her. 'It'll take you into a burn.'

Lola didn't know Ayrshire very well, apart from the windswept coastal towns where she'd spent many a bracing childhood holiday. The place she was heading to today was well inland, in the high rural wilderness that stretched beyond Beith.

It was a pleasant enough drive, and a chance to decompress after a stressful morning — one that had ended with her trying to mollify a disgruntled Izatt. She didn't particularly consider it her job to appease a bruised male ego, but such things had to be done.

The roads twisted and became narrower and more shadowy. She went wrong twice, having to make awkward turns between looming hedges, but finally found the place: a half-concealed driveway entrance, and a simple, hand-painted sign that read *Ladymere Farm*.

The drive wound through dense woodland for a quarter of a mile, its potholes testing the Audi's suspension almost to the limit. Then it emerged into space and light, and she found herself amid a ramshackle collection of low buildings, seeming to straggle in all directions. There was a silver people carrier parked near a crumbling barn. She stopped beside it, then checked her phone. Still no message from Joe, but there was no signal out here.

A chaotically dressed child, aged about three or four, was staring at her from the doorway of the house across the muddy yard. A young woman appeared at its side and gazed too, before bending to whisper to the child, who nodded compliantly and disappeared back inside.

'Are you from the police?' the woman called, coming across the yard, rubbing her hands on her corduroy trousers.

'That's right. DCI Harris,' Lola said, crossing the yard, being careful of her footing. 'Ms Croy, is it?'

The woman nodded. She looked every inch the farmer's wife, with her ratty woollen sweater and half-pinned-up, slightly mad hair. Lola would have been fooled, had Catriona Balfour not already told her that Diana Croy and her partner Tom Mackenzie were graphic designers, playing the part of rustics while taking advantage of the endless possibilities of video conferencing and remote working. The property had several acres of fields and woodland, but none of it was currently farmed. There were, Catriona had said drily, "big plans", including chickens, sheep and horses — and, in time, yurts.

'Have you got some sort of ID? Only . . .' She looked embarrassed.

'Of course.'

Diana Croy squinted at Lola's card for several seconds. 'And it's just you, is it?'

'Just me. I understand you had quite the visitation yesterday.'

'That's right. It was very unpleasant.'

'I'm sorry.'

She nodded, but looked unconvinced. 'Come with me.'

The child had reappeared, along with a smaller sibling, and the pair of them watched, fascinated, as their mother led the visitor away around the side of the house.

'How do you know the Balfour sisters?' Lola asked, as they passed outhouses and entered a second, smaller yard lined by disused stables.

'I don't really. Tom — my partner — he knows Catriona from university.' She glanced back at Lola over her shoulder. 'Oh, not like that. Catriona's gay, if you hadn't realised. We're just along the track here.'

About fifty metres beyond the stables, facing a field of brown grass and backing onto woodland, was a little cottage, white-fronted and old, a door in the middle and a sash window on each side.

Diana Croy rapped an iron knocker and called brightly, 'Fi? The police lady's here for you.'

No one had called Lola a "police lady" for some years. She wanted to smile, especially hearing it from a woman a good deal younger than herself.

Sounds from inside the cottage, then a key grating in a lock. The door inched open, and Fiona Balfour peered out into the daylight.

Lola controlled her desire to gasp. The girl looked not only tired and thinner than before — she looked frightened to death.

CHAPTER THIRTEEN

1.55 p.m.

'Not a bad setup,' Lola said, looking round the bright little kitchen, which was antiquated and untidy but well-stocked.

'They're very kind, really,' Fiona said, prising open a second tin in her hunt for teabags. 'The children are sweet. There's good internet in the house, but none out here. Not even 3G.'

'My colleagues descended on you last night, I believe.'

She nodded, eyes down, expression darker.

'Must have given you a fright. That why you didn't want to talk to them?'

Another nod. Eyes still averted.

'Well, as I say, I'm in charge of this case now. You'll be dealing with me, or with one of my team, who will be operating under my instructions.'

Lola let the young woman busy herself filling the kettle and finding mugs.

'I have to say, I'm a bit worried about you being out here on your own,' Lola said, when the kettle was boiling.

'I don't mind. I'm safe.'

Lola nodded, waiting for her moment.

'Safe from what, Fiona?'

Fiona turned her back and busied herself with the kettle and cups. 'Cat told you,' she said at last, a nervy glance over her shoulder. 'About me, I mean. That I think someone's got it in for me.'

'She did. Who do you think it is? And why are they doing it?'

The young woman went to a little fridge for milk.

'Just black for me, thanks,' Lola said quickly. 'And you can leave the teabag in.'

Fiona brought the two mugs to the table and sat opposite Lola.

'I don't know,' she said, making the minimum of eye contact. 'I . . . Well, I *thought* I knew. But, then . . .'

'When did it start?'

'Oh, *ages* ago.' She was up again, as if driven by nervous energy, rummaging through cupboards. Lola watched her, and wondered what the young woman was trying to avoid telling her. She came back with an unopened roll of currant shortbread biscuits.

'When you say "ages ago", when are we talking about?'

'I was at university in Glasgow, doing law. I never finished that degree, though. I dropped out and went to a local college instead and trained as a teaching assistant.'

'You're twenty-six now, aren't you? So, this would have been — what? Seven years ago?'

'Eight. It'll be eight years next month.'

'Tell me what happened.'

She focused on picking open the roll of biscuits. She offered one to Lola, who refused, then extracted one herself and nibbled unenthusiastically at its sugary, scalloped edge.

'Fiona . . . ?'

She put the biscuit down and looked Lola in the eye.

'Someone got into my room in halls, and went through my stuff when I was out and . . . *did* things.'

'What "things"?'

'He put a condom on a candle. He put my underwear on a giant teddy I'd had since I was a kid. He sort of . . . dressed it up.'

'"He"?'

'Yes. I thought it was a guy — a medical student — called Alistair. Ali.'

'Surname?'

'Howe — H-O-W-E. Oh, but it wasn't him,' she said sharply. 'You can't speak to him or anything. I said I *thought* it was, but . . . It turned out he couldn't have done it. He'd been with people, you see? They swore on it.'

'Did you report it to the police?'

'No.' She looked down at her hands cradling the mug. 'My friends said I should. Catriona thought I definitely should, but . . . a girl on his course came and spoke to me and warned me it'd ruin his career. I told the warden at the halls and she told the student services people. They wanted me to get counselling. They moved me to another hall, but . . . Well, all my friends were back at the other one, so . . . as I say, I ended up dropping out.'

'I'm sorry,' Lola said.

Lola watched the young woman for a reaction, but she merely sat and eyed Lola back, with a kind of exhausted resignation. 'Why did you think it was this Alistair Howe?'

'I'd been seeing him. Only briefly. I broke it off and he didn't take it well. He sent some texts. Threatening ones. Well, you wouldn't think they were threats, unless you knew to read between the lines, if you know what I mean.'

Lola knew.

'The moment I walked into my room, I thought, *Ali did this*. It was like an instinct.'

'But he had an alibi.'

'Yeah.'

'Credible, do you think?'

'He'd been at a dinner. There were quite a lot of people there, and they had no reason to lie. They weren't, like, a clique or anything.'

'So, who else could it have been?'

'I have no idea.' She looked Lola in the eye and shook her head. 'Honestly. It was just so . . . *weird*. My pal Emma, she said maybe whoever it was had got the wrong room. I mean, all the doors looked the same. Or maybe it was a random thing. Some weirdo who liked touching women's underwear. I never believed that, though. It was so deliberate. So personal.'

'Your sister told me you've thought for some time that someone wanted to hurt you.'

Fiona nodded.

'Based on this thing that happened in your room in halls?'

'Yes. But, that was only the start of it.'

'What do you mean?'

Nothing for a moment.

'It's mostly just weird stuff. Like a sixth sense, you know?'

'Like what?'

She took a deep breath. 'A feeling someone's watching me. Usually in crowded places. On an escalator in Buchanan Galleries once. And in Kelvingrove Park. It's like I know there are people all around, moving about, but then my subconscious tells me one of them *isn't* moving. That he's standing stock-still and staring at me. But then when I turn to look, he moves and he's just part of the crowd. It's . . . creepy.' She gave a little shudder.

'You could have imagined those things, couldn't you?'

'Yes, I know that,' she said, indignant. 'But a few months ago something happened. Something *real*, I mean. It was at the end of July. The trains were off — a strike or something. I took the Subway to Shields Road instead. It's a twenty-five-minute walk, but it was a nice night and it was light, and there were people about, so I didn't mind. And . . . well, I was a bit drunk. I'd been for cocktails with three of my old colleagues in Princes Square. Sean wasn't happy about it, but one of them was getting married, so . . . Anyway, I walked up St Andrews Drive, and I was going to cut through

Maxwell Park, but it was twilight by then, so I thought better of it. I walked round the outside instead, past the Burgh Hall. That's when I realised there was a car following me. It was so quiet. It must have been electric. But then a tyre went over some broken glass. It was crawling after me, and the thing is — even though it was getting dark, *it had its headlights off.*'

Lola felt tiny fingers run over her shoulders.

'The car was getting closer and I started to walk faster. It was on my left, and there was a hedge to my right, so I had no choice but to keep going. Then it was beside me. I looked to try to see who it was, but the windows were tinted. Then its headlights came on and it screeched off round the corner. I thought it must just be lads, maybe drug dealers. Or maybe someone wanting to pick up a woman . . .'

Lola sensed the "but" before it came.

'But when I got to the junction, he was there again, a bit further along Terregles Avenue. Only he'd turned the car round and it was pointing my way, waiting for me, and the lights were off again. I stood there at the corner, and I didn't know which way to run. I was petrified! It was like facing a dog that's going to attack you the moment you move. There was nobody about. I thought about calling out, in case someone in one of the big houses might hear me. But I just needed to get home. I thought, if I could make it across the road, to the footbridge over the railway line, then I'd be on Fotheringay Road, and it'd only be a short walk. So I took a deep breath and stepped into the road. I was near the other side when his lights came on and he drove at me, *right at me*, swerving onto the wrong side of the road. I screamed and jumped forward onto the pavement by the railing. He came up on the pavement, then reversed, as if to get a better shot at me, and I just *ran*. I ran like crazy. I got to the footbridge just as he rammed into the bollards either side of the bottom step.'

'Did you report it?'

She was looking at her hands again, then shook her head.

'Sean told me not to.'

'He did, did he?'

The young woman peered up at her, a little shamefaced. 'Sean had a few things to hide.'

'I'm sure he did, love,' Lola said drily. 'Could you describe the car?'

'Big. Black. A BMW, maybe, though it could have been an Audi or a Mercedes. Expensive, anyway.'

'Registration?'

'Sorry, no.'

'Do you know if the car stayed around or if it drove off?'

'I think it drove off. Sean went out looking for it. His brother Gerry came over to help. They were gone half an hour. I kept looking out of the bay window in the living room — it faces towards the park and the Burgh Hall. I stood there for ages in the dark, but I didn't see anything.'

'The end of July? Do you know the exact date?'

'I could work it out. We arranged the cocktails on WhatsApp so I'll be able to find the messages if I look back. D'you want me to look?'

'In a wee minute. What time of night did this happen?'

'I got back to the flat at ten twenty. I checked the time.'

'And you first noticed the car following you at about what time?'

'I'd say, twenty minutes before that, so . . . about ten.'

Lola looked at her notes. 'You said he was a medical student, this Alistair Howe. He'd be qualified now. Any idea where he is?'

The young woman shook her head. 'Why?'

'Because I'm going to talk to him,' Lola said.

'Oh, but—'

'"Oh, but" nothing. Your fiancé was murdered. You were tied to his body. This is serious. Do you understand? I doubt I could check his alibi for the underwear incident, but I can check where he was one evening in July — and for last Saturday evening, of course.'

The young woman gave a little nod. She looked drained, and on the verge of tears. Lola, about to launch into a new line of questioning, paused.

'It's a lovely afternoon,' she said, eyes on the kitchen window. 'The trees are all reds and golds. Why don't we take a wee walk? We can stay close by.'

Fiona thought about it, then acquiesced.

'That's good,' Lola said, rising, all smiles.

* * *

3.01 p.m.

The young woman's waif-like appearance worried Lola, so she was pleased to see her putting on a decent winter coat together with a woollen scarf.

Outside, the air was fresh, unwarmed by the thin sunlight leaking across the fields.

Diana Croy, in her role as farmer's wife, was chopping logs behind the farmhouse, and making a decent fist of it, from what Lola could tell. She lifted an arm and waved.

Lola led the young woman away from the house, along the edge of the wood, where leaves made a brown carpet over the muddy ground.

They trudged on, their breath going before them in clouds. Lola considered the likelihood that Fiona had a mortal enemy who'd enacted a bizarre punishment on her and her fiancé. In the kitchen it had sounded, well, at least *plausible*. But out here, in the cold, milky light of day, it seemed ridiculous. Outlandish and paranoid.

'Do you know about Occam's razor?' Lola said, once they'd gone a little way.

'I've heard of it.'

'The idea is, you get rid of the noise and what's left is the simplest explanation — it often turns out to be the right one.'

'Meaning?'

'That the attack was targeted at Sean, and that your involvement was incidental.'

'Incidental?'

'Yes.'

Fiona stopped and stared at Lola, confusion visible in her expression.

'What is it?' Lola said.

'I could believe that if I'd been with Sean, so that when they took him they had to take me too. But we weren't together. He'd gone off early in the day. He went to see his brother, and he was going from Gerry's direct to the airport to fly to Amsterdam. I spent the afternoon on my own. Whoever came for me did so deliberately. Don't you see that?'

Fiona had a point.

'Do you remember anything more about that evening?' she asked.

'No. Oh, God . . .' She gave a gasp of frustration and put the heel of one hand to her forehead. 'I can't recall anything beyond letting myself into the flat. It's horrible not remembering.'

More likely a blessing, Lola thought.

'Sean wasn't a nice person,' Fiona continued. 'I know that now. For months I told myself he was. The stuff he got up to — he told me not to worry my head, so I didn't.'

'But then you decided to leave him. Why was that?'

She stopped again, frowning, eyes on the mulchy ground. 'I don't think I should say anything about that.'

'Why not?'

'I think . . . I'd prefer to have a solicitor with me. I don't want to . . . I don't want to incriminate myself.'

'A lot of stuff is likely to come out,' Lola said. 'Just so you're aware. You'll be asked to testify about what happened to you and Sean. But you might also be questioned about Sean's business dealings.'

She said nothing. Someone had advised her well, Lola realised. Her sister, perhaps.

'We'll be talking to all Sean's contacts. Going through his devices, looking at online accounts. At his financial affairs too.'

The young woman said nothing. They walked on in tense silence.

'Have any of his family spoken to you?' she said, and detected a further stiffening of the muscles. 'What about Sean's mum, Rita? You must have spoken to her.'

She shook her head.

'Really? I find that very odd. Why wouldn't you—'

'Please — I don't want to talk about them.'

They'd come to a fence with a stile. 'I'm tired,' Fiona said. 'I'd like to go back now.'

CHAPTER FOURTEEN

5.47 p.m.

'I preferred the fella,' Rita Rennie said, when Lola told her why she and DC Kirstie Campbell were there, and that she was now in charge of the investigation into her son's murder. 'Needs a man, this kind of thing. One with a strong stomach.'

'Mrs Rennie, my stomach is very strong indeed,' Lola said.

The three of them sat at a marble-topped table in the gaudy, overheated conservatory built onto the back of Rita's semi-detached house in King's Park. A mere semi it might have been when the Rennies moved in, but it had been extended at the side, at the back and up out of the roof, then rendered, and the render painted lilac. Lola knew that Rita had bought the house next door as well, and that one of her daughters lived in it. Together, the attached houses looked like an overblown cake on this ordinary residential street. Add in the black railings and security gates tipped with gold spikes, and the several aerials and dishes positioned on the gable end, and it had the feel of a military compound in some semi-exotic location. LA, maybe, or perhaps Dubai.

Rita Rennie hunched forward over the table, eyeing Lola suspiciously with her hard green eyes and taking regular, thoughtful drags from a pink cocktail cigarette with a gold filter. She ignored Kirstie almost completely, keeping her gaze locked balefully on Lola, who tried not to wince as smoke crept into her nostrils.

'I read yesterday's *Chronicle*,' Lola said now.

'What of it?'

'Who's got a "reckoning" coming to them, Mrs Rennie?'

The woman sucked at her cigarette, eyes never leaving Lola's face.

Lola waited, patient and implacable.

'Whoever killed my little boy,' Mrs Rennie said.

'And you think you know who that is, don't you?'

More seconds of baleful resistance. Then: 'Now, why do you ask that, I wonder . . .'

'Because I can read between lines, Mrs Rennie. I think you've a very good idea who killed Sean — or who arranged it.'

Rita tapped her cigarette on the edge of a brown glass ashtray, dislodging an inch of ash, before lifting the gold filter once more to her plumped coral lips.

'Mrs Rennie,' Lola said sighing, 'I'm going to find out who killed your son, whether you help me or not. Now, can we stop messing about and talk?'

The woman looked surprised and darkly amused. Possibly a little impressed as well.

'I think I'll keep my powder dry for now, thank you, Ms Harris.'

'Tell you what — why don't we dispense with the formalities? We're two women with one goal here. I call you Rita, you call me Lola.'

'As you wish, *Lola*.' A tiny smirk of the lips. '*Were* you a showgirl?'

'No. I was a hairdresser for a while. Then I joined the police.'

'Born where?'

'Govan. And I was raised a Catholic, if that was going to be your next question.'

'It wasn't.' A husky laugh. 'I knew it the moment I saw you. Takes one to know one.' Her eyes slid briefly to the painted porcelain figure of the praying Madonna on the windowsill to her right.

'I'm lapsed, before you ask,' Lola said. 'Long since.'

'Kiddies?'

'None. Not married.' She glanced at her own left hand. 'But I'm sure you had that one worked out already too.'

'Probably best.' Another throaty chuckle that rattled with decades of cigarette smoke. 'Men'll only break your heart.'

Lola said nothing.

She decided to try a different tack. 'Tell us about Sean,' she said. 'Tell us what he was like.'

The woman's expression became tragic, the corners of her mouth drawn down. Tears welled in the hammocks of her lower lids.

'He was my baby. My youngest.' She sniffed. 'I'll never see him again. Never speak to him or hear his voice.'

Lola left a respectful pause.

'Did Sean have a lot of friends?' she asked now.

'Oh, he had friends.' Rita sucked at the cigarette, her eyes peering hard at Lola once again. 'Enemies too. That's what you really want to know, isn't it?'

'I'm afraid it is.'

The woman talked about her boy, about the difficult birth thirty years ago, how his dad Mickey had doted on him — and how heartbroken Sean had been when Mickey was shot and killed. She talked about Sean's siblings, about Gerry — her "rock" — and about Bernadette and Therese, each with families of their own.

Rita talked on, finishing one cigarette and lighting another. She never once mentioned the woman her son had planned to marry — an omission that screamed for attention.

'And what about Fiona?' Lola said, when the moment felt right.

'What about her?' A colder tone. Sharper.

'That poor girl's been through an ordeal. You must have spoken to her.'

The woman's eyes narrowed. She said nothing.

The noise of a door banging emanated from the house. The woman glanced at the French windows that connected the conservatory to the house.

'Ma?' A male voice. 'Where are you?'

'Out back, son,' Rita Rennie cried, her voice cracking and precipitating a coughing fit.

A man filled the gap in the French windows. He was tall and stocky, handsome in denims, and very Irish-looking, with dark hair and his mother's green eyes.

'Who's this?' he demanded.

'We're police detectives, sir,' Lola said, rising. 'You're Gerry Rennie?'

'Aye, that's right.'

Lola introduced herself, extending a hand. He looked at it but didn't take it. He came into the conservatory and turned to his mother. 'Ma, I told you — *never* talk to these people without me.'

'I can handle myself,' Rita said. He put a hand on her shoulder. Rita reached up and patted it.

'Well?' Gerry Rennie said now, turning fiercely on Lola. 'Have you found out who killed my wee brother?'

'Not yet, Mr Rennie.'

He muttered something. Lola caught a word.

'Sorry — "games", Mr Rennie? Who's playing games?'

Rennie swore under his breath.

'Gerry, no!' his mother warned him sharply.

'No, Ma. Enough's enough.'

'What's enough, Mr Rennie?' Lola asked.

'Gerry, I said no.' Rita started to get up, wheezing as she did so.

Gerry Rennie covered his face with a hand and started to sob. Big, angry, heaving sobs that shook his whole body. A second hand went to his face and he started to shake his head, as if in shame.

'Oh, my boy,' Rita Rennie said, and leaned in to her son's tall frame, embracing him. 'We'll deal with this. We'll do it *our way*.'

He let her hold him, his hands still over his face, and the two of them rocked back and forth.

Lola glanced at Kirstie, who was impassive and calm. She wondered if, beneath her cool exterior, Kirstie had just come to the same conclusion she had.

'Rita, Gerry?' she said, firmly. 'Sit down, would you? Just for a minute.'

They did so, as if too overcome with emotion to defy the request.

Lola thought quickly, weighed the words she could use, tried to anticipate their impact: whether they'd elicit honest responses or merely throw up new walls.

'You think Fiona Balfour did this to Sean, don't you?' she said. She watched them intently. 'You think she arranged his murder. It's Fiona who's got a "reckoning" coming, isn't it?'

They stared. Then Gerry Rennie turned to his mother. 'Ma?'

'Say nothing,' Rita snarled.

'Mrs Rennie — Rita — *please*. Help me to understand.'

She looked at Gerry Rennie, trying to read the pain in his eyes, appealing to him to speak.

'You need to leave,' Rita said. 'Now.' She turned to her son. 'Gerry, show them out.'

CHAPTER FIFTEEN

6.52 p.m.

Cat phoned Ladymere Farm as soon as she got home. She was headachey and frazzled thanks to a stressful drive from Edinburgh, but Fi remained at the forefront of her mind and she knew she wouldn't relax until she'd checked in with her.

Diana answered the call then nipped out to the cottage to bring Fi to the house phone.

Cat kicked off her shoes while she waited, then saw that some post was caught in the flap of the letterbox. She tugged the envelopes free and glanced at them as she went into the kitchen before dumping them on the counter.

Fi came on the line as she was running a glass of water. Yes, she was perfectly okay, Fi told her. She really didn't need to worry. And yes, the inspector had been to see her, and she was *so* much nicer than DCI Izatt.

'She's going to speak to Ali Howe,' Fi said.

'Ali Howe? But that was *years* ago!'

'She wants to know where he was the night the car came after me. Remember?'

'The car . . . ? What? She thinks it might have been *him*?'

'He won't thank me,' Fi said now.

'Yeah, well, who cares what he thinks?'

'It wasn't him though, Cat — the stuff with the underwear.'

'He treated you like shit on other occasions. Call it karma.'

She poured herself a glass of water, clamping the phone in the crook of her shoulder, while Fi outlined the rest of her meeting with DCI Harris. At first Cat had been pleased to have a capable woman in charge instead of the shambling, careless idiot who'd dealt with the case thus far. But now she was having doubts. She'd told the inspector that Fi believed she was the target of a vendetta in order to illustrate her sister's paranoid and fearful state of mind, not because she thought it was something the inspector should take seriously. Irritated, she began to tear open the mail, immediately giving up on the first: a flier for a candidate in a forthcoming by-election.

'She wanted to know why I decided to leave Sean,' Fi said now.

'And what did you tell her?'

'I said I didn't think I should say anything about that without a solicitor present.'

'Good!' So some of the advice provided by Cat's solicitor friend Robyn had hit home.

She tore at the second envelope. A quote for another year's contents insurance. She put it aside.

'I'm scared, Cat.'

'Don't be. You're safe where you are.' She started on the third, and last, envelope.

'I know. But it's so quiet here.'

'That's why I sent you there. I—' Her words caught in her throat as she pulled a photograph from the envelope and took in the image.

'Cat — are you still there?'

'Yes,' she said now, getting herself quickly under control. 'Yes, I'm here.'

She stared at the image in her hand.

'I'll come and see you at the weekend,' she managed. 'Maybe on Saturday evening. I'd come tomorrow night but I promised I'd meet the trustees ahead of the AGM next week. I'll bring pizzas. We can heat them up and watch a DVD. *Ocean's Eight*, maybe. I know we've seen it before, but we both liked it.'

She rang off and stood in silence, an icy feeling washing over her as she looked at the photograph. There was no message with it. She checked and double-checked inside the envelope.

The picture was a telephoto close-up of Fi, in a street somewhere, her head back, laughing, as a man leaned in, apparently to kiss her neck. The man wasn't Sean Rennie, but Cat recognised him all the same.

It was Sean's brother Gerry.

'Oh, Fi,' she murmured, in rising horror. 'What have you done?'

She jumped as her phone began to ring in her hand.

CHAPTER SIXTEEN

6.59 p.m.

'It's Rita Rennie, isn't it?' Lola demanded when Catriona Balfour answered the phone.

A pause. A long one. 'What is?'

'I knew there was something you weren't telling me,' Lola said, eyes on the traffic around them as Kirstie drove them back to HQ. 'Instead you told me stories about an unknown enemy.'

'I don't know what you're talking about,' Catriona replied, sounding breathless.

'You're a clever woman, Catriona. You know the risks of spinning lies when there's a genuine threat out there.'

More silence.

'Catriona? Rita Rennie thinks your sister had her son murdered, doesn't she?'

Quietly: 'Has Rita said as much?'

'She didn't need to. It's what she thinks, and it's what her son thinks too. That's what she was talking about in Tuesday's *Chronicle*. I'm right, amn't I?'

'Yes,' the woman said, after a moment's further pause.

'Why would she think that?'

'I don't know! Because she's mad with grief? Or just mad! Fi's naïve. Which is why she ended up with a lowlife like Sean Rennie.' She paused. 'Besides, even if she *had* managed to arrange it, why would she go through with it? She was leaving him, anyway. *She didn't need to have him killed.* Christ, I can't believe we're even talking about this.'

'Is that why you moved her to your friend's farm?'

A long silence, then, in a low voice: 'Rita phoned here. Several times. So did Gerry, and one of her daughters too. They were angry and upset and demanding to see her. Said they wanted to "get to the bottom of what really happened". They're *gangsters*, for God's sake. Wouldn't you keep your wee sister out of their way?'

'Has Fiona spoken to Rita since . . . ?'

'No.'

'I'll be going to see Fiona again tomorrow. And I'll be expecting her to tell me the truth.'

CHAPTER SEVENTEEN

7.47 p.m.

Lola was so sick with worry about Joe she couldn't eat her dinner. She'd texted him after leaving Rita Rennie's, saying bluntly that his text had panicked her and that she was worried about his health. Was he okay? According to the app, the text had been delivered.

But still no reply.

And so, after scraping the pasta into the bin, she did what she knew she absolutely shouldn't, and phoned him.

It rang twice then cut out.

She pulled the phone from her ear and stared at the screen, heart racing, mouth dry.

She dialled again. Straight to voicemail.

She went into her message app and typed: *Joe please answer. I'm frightened.*

Nothing.

For something to do, she put her plate and fork into the dishwasher, but her phone was in her hand again within a minute.

He was typing a reply: three dots doing a Mexican wave.

She waited, hardly breathing.

On he typed, on the dots waved.

'Please be okay,' she whispered aloud, dread making her tremble. 'Please, God . . .'

And then it came. She read it twice. Three times, barely comprehending.

Marie checked my phone. Can't see you anymore. Don't text.

Alone in her kitchen, Lola crumpled.

CHAPTER EIGHTEEN

Friday 28 October
6.35 a.m.

Johnny had brought her on a different route this morning.

'I thought we'd go to Bellahouston Park for a change,' he'd said when he arrived at the house, seeming subdued.

'Suits me,' Lola had told him, equally happy to avoid Pollok Park.

So, off they'd set on their "mild jog" warm-up, until they reached the playing fields on the far side of the motorway.

'What d'you think about trying another timed mile?' he asked her after some stretches. Yes, he was definitely subdued. Certainly not the bouncing, eager lad he'd been before they'd discovered a murder together.

'Let me get my breath back first,' she panted. 'You seem quiet, Johnny.'

'I'm fine.' He gave her one of his boyish smiles, but it looked strained. 'I didn't sleep very well. Haven't really been sleeping since . . . well, you know.'

Johnny wasn't the only one who'd slept badly. She'd got no more than a couple of hours herself, but it hadn't been the murder of Sean Rennie playing on her mind.

'You know I'm in charge of the case now?'

He frowned. 'What do you mean?'

'Remember DCI Izatt, who was in charge to begin with? I've taken it over from him.'

'Oh, right.' He nodded but looked none the wiser.

'Thank you for your statement, by the way. It's very clear.'

'That's okay. How's the girl?'

'She'll be okay.'

'I've been following the news. The dead guy was a gangster, wasn't he?'

'My officers will talk to you if there's anything you need to know,' she said, not about to be drawn.

'Okay.' He looked away, distracted. In fact, he looked as if he might be about to cry.

'It's hit you hard, this, hasn't it?' she said. 'Maybe you should talk to someone.'

He nodded, but his expression said he wasn't interested in anything like that. She watched his face carefully.

'Is something bothering you, Johnny?'

He looked at her in surprise.

'No. Why?'

'Sometimes, after a traumatic event, people remember things. Something you saw or heard at the time that seemed insignificant — it can come back to you. Only you might not think it's worth telling anyone.'

'No, nothing like that.'

'You sure?'

'Uh-huh.' He nodded, and gave her another, weaker smile.

'Let's get that mile over with, shall we?'

That cheered him up, and he took out his Garmin.

CHAPTER NINETEEN

8.45 a.m.

What with Joe and everything else, she'd forgotten she was due to meet DS Aidan Pierce at nine o'clock to discuss his "personal improvement plan". Pierce's uncle, the once-feared Assistant Chief Constable Clive Reid, had tasked Lola with personally ensuring his nephew got his act together. Pierce wasn't happy about it, but he had no choice. Uncle Clive had made it clear to Pierce and to Lola, that this was his last chance for a career with the police.

He was seven weeks into his development plan now. For the first few weeks he'd been grumpy but cowed, and crept about, keeping himself to himself and muttering; but as his bruised ego healed, he'd begun to push back in subtle ways. The smirking and whispering to his mates were the least of it.

He was already installed at his desk when she came in, looking suavely sullen and ready for a fight.

Logging in, she went into her inbox and groaned when she read the subject heading of an email from Graeme Izatt.

DS Pierce — issue, it said.

He'd sent it at eleven p.m. last night.

She clicked into it.

DCI Harris
     Had cause to speak to DS Pierce this afternoon re. inappropriate joking re. sexist subject matter & putting DC McVittie in diff. position. Please raise with DS Pierce during supervision with eye to resolution.
     Grateful for update.
     G.I.

'Well, thanks very much, Graeme . . .' she muttered.
A vengeful wee poke in the ribs. Just what she needed.

* * *

9.12 a.m.

The session, which took place in a meeting room on the first floor, started well enough. Lola asked Pierce to talk through his work during the past week, and to give his reflections on his interactions with colleagues and with members of the public. Things turned sticky when she presented him with the allegation from Izatt.

'I can't think what DCI Izatt was referring to,' Pierce said quietly, watching her with cool blue eyes from under perfectly trimmed eyebrows.

'DCI Izatt asked me to raise it with you. He clearly expected you to know what incident he was referring to. Are you denying knowledge of an incident relating to "sexist subject matter"?'

'"Sexist subject matter" . . . ?' he quoted, as if mystified, then shrugged lightly.

'Something you shared with Marcus McVittie, I believe.'

'Oh . . . *that*.' He screwed up his face and gave a sadly incredulous shake of head, as if he couldn't quite believe she was even putting this to him. 'Trivial stuff.'

'DCI Izatt doesn't seem to think so.'

He smiled at her, the sunny smile of a gleeful devil.

'You know, DS Pierce, that sexism will not be tolerated.'

'The definition is broad, DI Harris,' he said, the smile still there.

'*DCI* Harris, thank you.'

He made an expansive gesture with his hands. 'I apologise.'

It continued: Pierce behaving like a combative, too-clever youth, trying to manoeuvre her into the role of the coaxing, tolerant, problem-solving parent. More than once she had to stop herself talking to him as if he were a child. The transaction must be adult to adult, or nothing would ever change.

'What action can you take,' she said, when he'd exhausted every possible trick to get her to move on, 'to reassure DCI Izatt that you understand your behaviour was unacceptable and will not be repeated? And when will you take it?'

'I'm happy to express my regret to DCI Izatt,' Pierce said, in his quiet, careful voice.

'When?' she asked, pen poised on her pad, her disgust bubbling just under the surface.

'Oh . . . today, I expect,' he said, that sunny smile on his face again.

She wrote. When she looked up he was eyeing his smart-watch. 'Is that us?' he said.

'That's us,' she said.

He smirked and left the room.

CHAPTER TWENTY

12.40 p.m.

Lola arrived at Ladymere Farm feeling tired and crotchety. She'd hoped the drive might calm her down and give her a chance to think about the Rennie murder — to consider it from different angles. Instead she'd spent most of the forty-five minutes or so stewing miserably about Joe, imagining what had happened when Marie saw their messages on his phone.

Marie knew about Lola. She always had. The three of them had been at school at the same time, and Lola and Joe had been a couple before Marie came along. Marie had bided her time, waiting till Joe and Lola had one of their famous rows and were "on a break", then pounced and drawn him into her sphere of control.

Marie would have administered a dressing-down more toxic than the chemicals being pumped into his body to attack his cancer. The woman was manipulative and a bully. Over the years she'd worn Joe down, dampening his vital spark until he was docile and passive. *Hers.*

She imagined the atmosphere in that grim house on the narrow, sloping street in Muirend, Joe too big for its wee rooms, his character too expansive for Marie's overpowering decor. It was a stuffy little house, full of cushions and ornaments and photos in frames and fake flowers, and everything scented by plug-in air fresheners. It was Marie's house. Not Joe's. He was just kept there.

Lola still hadn't replied to his message from the night before, though resisting the impulse caused her almost physical pain. She felt entirely powerless — not only rejected, but without hope — and was tormented by the taunting voice in her head.

What if his health gets worse, and I don't know? What if he dies, and I'm not there? What if . . . What if I never see him again?

STOP IT!

She gave herself a mental shake and forced herself to get out of the car and breathe in lungfuls of clean, chilly air.

Diana Croy was standing at the top of the steps that led to the front door of the main house. She waved cheerily, as if Lola was a long-expected and welcome guest.

'Fi's in here with us!' she called out. 'Come round the side of the yard, though or you'll soak your shoes.'

Fiona was in a south-facing parlour at the back of the house, sitting on a rug with the two young children Lola had seen yesterday, amid a mass of wooden toys. A fire burned in a grate and light filtered in through grimy mullioned windows showing a distorted view of misty fields and the golden woods beyond. It was an idyllic picture. One Lola was about to disrupt.

The frail-looking young woman got up and faced her, hands at her sides, as if in quiet surrender. The children rose too and flanked their new friend, one of them reaching to take her hand.

'Hello, again, Fiona,' Lola said. 'Time for another chat.'

* * *

12.56 p.m.

Lola offered a choice: they could talk in the cottage or take another walk along the edge of the woods. She was pleased

91

when Fiona chose a walk. Outside it was sunny but cold. The air would help keep Lola sharp.

'Tell me about Rita Rennie,' she said.

The young woman was silent for several paces. 'She doesn't like me,' she said at last. 'She never did. Or trusted me. I thought she might, you know, as time went on, but two years went by and she still had no time for me.'

'Why is that, do you think?' Lola kept her gaze forward and her tone light.

'I don't think it was personal. She worshipped Sean. You've probably worked that out by now. She'd never have trusted any woman he was involved with.'

'Have you seen what she's been saying in the papers?'

Fiona nodded. 'She thinks I did it, doesn't she? That I arranged it?' She stopped and turned to face Lola full on. 'Well, I didn't. Of course I didn't! She's grieving, and imagining things.'

'It's a big thing to imagine — and a bigger step to imply it in the papers.'

'She knows I was planning to leave Sean.' They were walking again, eyes forward. 'I don't know *how* she found out — Sean himself didn't know — but somehow she did. Now they're determined to find me. They want to make me pay for Sean's death. They think it'll make them feel better. But it won't, will it?'

'Mother-in-laws can be difficult,' Lola mused, as if she was merely thinking aloud, 'but to accuse your daughter-in-law — *prospective* daughter-in-law — of arranging your son's murder, that's something else. There must be *some* logic behind it.'

'Ask her to explain it.'

Lola said nothing.

'Rita's the big matriarch,' Fiona went on. 'She's like something out of *EastEnders*. I liked her at first. I mean, she loves her family so fiercely. She loved Sean especially. He was her baby.'

She fell silent, eyes down, feet kicking at the yellow leaves on the path.

'Are you frightened of her?' Lola said.

'I was when I found out she'd rung Cat's place, but since I arrived here, well . . . it just seems so far away.'

Lola waited a moment before asking, 'How long had you been planning to leave Sean?'

'Not long.' Lola detected a shift in the young woman's tone. She'd been uncomfortable on this topic yesterday as well. 'A few weeks.'

'What triggered the decision?'

Fiona stopped and stared ahead of her, chewing her bottom lip.

She wasn't about to answer, Lola could tell. Not yet, at any rate.

Lola said, conversationally, 'Did you have Sean killed, Fiona?'

The young woman turned her head and stared in open-mouthed astonishment.

'Did you?'

'*No!* I can't believe you're even . . . Of *course* I didn't!'

'Then why does Rita—'

'I told you who did it!' she said, her voice rising and breaking. 'I told you yesterday. Were you listening to a single word I said?' She was angry now. Shrill with it. 'It's the man who's been after me all these years. The one who drove at me. But here you are — accusing *me*. Why on *earth* would I do that?'

Lola watched the emotions twisting and contorting the young woman's face. 'Well, now I have a problem,' she said eventually. 'Because I have three scenarios in my head, and not one of them makes sense — as far as I can tell.'

Fiona glared at her, waiting.

'First there's your theory: Sean was killed by an unknown man with a personal vendetta against you. This man has followed you for years, tormenting you for reasons you can't explain, showing himself only occasionally. Finally, he's

93

come for you. But it's not you he's chosen to hurt. Instead he's murdered your fiancé — who you were about to leave — and strapped you to his body. *Why?*'

'I think he meant me to die in the night. If you hadn't come along, I might have died of hypothermia.'

'Second,' Lola pushed on, 'Rita Rennie's theory. That you arranged Sean's death, possibly paying someone. But why would you? You were about to leave him anyway. Unless he did know you were leaving him, and he was trying to stop you. Is that it, Fiona?'

'No! My God—'

'And third,' Lola continued, 'is the accepted theory: the one that fits the narrative most comfortably — the one my seniors would prefer and the one the media will lap up, because it's the same old story: Sean Rennie was a bad man. He antagonised the wrong person, and got himself killed. The only problem with that is—'

'Me,' Fiona Balfour said.

'Precisely.'

Lola gazed around her, at the grassy fields, at the vast, pale sky.

'I'm going to send one of my constables out here to spend some time with you tomorrow,' she said. 'She's very calm and logical and sharp. I want you and her to talk, for hours if necessary, about every aspect of your life, probably going back as far as your schooldays.'

Fiona watched her.

'If there is someone in your past who has a vendetta against you, DC Campbell will find him. Meanwhile, I have to focus the majority of my resources on the third theory: that this was a gangland execution. We're hosting a press conference at four o'clock today, seeking further information about Sean's business dealings. No doubt you'll see it on the news. As far as the public are concerned, we're investigating the murder of Sean Rennie, which was likely connected to his business dealings, legal or illegal. We won't be mentioning the other theories.'

'Including Rita's? Are you just going to ignore her?'

'She isn't talking to us, but I'll go on trying. I mean to understand why she thinks what she does.'

Fiona lifted her chin and looked Lola hard in the eye. 'Do I look like a killer?' she asked. 'Do you really, honestly think *I* could have someone *murdered*?'

'I don't know,' Lola said. 'I'm being absolutely frank with you. I really don't know.'

CHAPTER TWENTY-ONE

3.12 p.m.

'I put them back. Of course I did!' Jeremy Warren, manager of the park, sneered. 'I wasn't about to leave them under the tree, was I?'

Lola said nothing, but gazed at the tidy line of six white-washed stones, each one roughly the size of a football, that made a tidy barrier between the road and the swathe of grass that stretched to the trees — where, only a few days ago, Lola had found a man dead.

'I asked that Izatt chap!' the man barked defensively. 'He said it was fine once your fellows had finished.'

She'd come with Kirstie to view the scene in the cold light of the afternoon. Cold it was, but beautiful too. Thin, lemony autumn sunlight bathed the park, and the trees glowed like the embers of summer. There were bouquets of fresh flowers and a couple of wreaths propped against the metal fence separating the fields from the road. While Lola dealt with Mr Warren, Kirstie was discreetly noting the names written on the accompanying cards.

'I wish people wouldn't do this kind of thing,' Warren grumbled, nodding to the floral tributes. 'I *hate* it. I'm forever having to remove dead flowers from a bench or one of the fences. It seems to me a very *American* thing to do. Ghoulish and sentimental.'

'I suppose it helps people feel a wee bit better.'

He screwed up his face and gave a theatrical shudder.

'And what about the gun? You still haven't found it?'

Lola shook her head.

'Do you think it's still here in the park somewhere? I wouldn't like to think of visitors stumbling across it. What if a child got hold of it?'

'We've searched the immediate area, sir,' Lola said, soothingly. 'The strong likelihood is that the killer — or killers — took it away. Guns are still surprisingly hard to come by, and can be traced.'

'I don't like it,' he said. 'Why here? Why not drive them out to the country?'

'We may find out in due course,' she said mildly.

He had to go, he muttered now. Lola, who'd only alerted him to her visit as a courtesy, was happy to see the back of him.

'From the family,' Kirstie told Lola when they were alone, holding up her phone and thumbing through a series of photos she'd taken of the messages written on the little cards. One read:

To my baby in Heaven.
Love Mum
xxx

Walking back to the car, Lola asked, 'And how are you doing, Kirstie? After everything.'

'I'm fine, thanks.' Her tone was impassive, her face unreadable.

'How are you feeling being back on a team with DS Pierce?'

A momentary pause, then: 'I'm okay. He . . . he's being different. Better, I think.'

'Is he?'

'For now,' Kirstie said. 'And if something happens, I think I can handle it. But thanks for checking, boss.'

Lola nodded and they walked on in silence. Pierce had made Kirstie's life hell during the summer, first breaking a personal confidence, then using it to bully her. His behaviour had led to an explosive confrontation between him and Lola, but one that had led to this apparent armistice. She wasn't convinced peace would last, and intended to keep a watchful eye on Pierce and a protective one on Kirstie. But for now she was content to wait and see.

'Someone moved those stones ahead of time, didn't they?' she said to Kirstie now. 'Someone knew about this spot and prepared the ground. Can't have been long before or Mr Warren would have noticed. It wasn't a spur-of-the-moment choice of location. It was thought out.'

She gazed at the woods around them, at the tussocky fields opposite, where Highland cattle stood about looking laconic and hairy.

'Why here?' she asked. 'Right by a road?'

'Easy access?'

'Could be. But . . . well, you'd almost think they wanted the body to be found, wouldn't you? And sooner rather than later.'

CHAPTER TWENTY-TWO

4.34 p.m.

The press conference was better attended than she'd anticipated. Corporate comms had alerted media contacts that it would be an update on the investigation into the murder of Sean Rennie, with some further information about the weapon used and key timings — hardly earth-shattering. Yet the room was packed.

Waiting to start, she checked her phone. No text from Joe, but there was a message from Graeme Izatt. Pierce had apologised to him for the incident the day before — to Marcus, too.

Wonders will never cease, she thought to herself, pleased — but not without a creeping suspicion, based on experience, that Pierce was up to something.

'Good turnout,' Kirstie murmured, eyes ahead.

'Maybe they know something we don't,' Lola whispered back.

Lola read out the facts as they knew them, including about the firearm — a nine-millimetre pistol that had still to be located. She gave an update about Rennie's fiancée, leaving out Fiona Balfour's name, but knowing full well that they'd use it in any reporting. Then she referred to Sean Rennie's business dealings, and watched as several satirical eyebrows raised around the room. Everyone here knew Rennie had been a criminal, from a criminal family. "Business" was an almost comical euphemism, and no one was fooled. She finished with a call for information about any aspect of the murder: the timings, the location, the weapon used or motive. Then she called for questions.

Hands went up. She chose the nearest, belonging to a reporter from STV news. He asked if there was any truth in rumours that Rennie's fiancée had been tied to his body. Lola said she couldn't confirm that.

Pens scribbled.

'Yes, please.' She pointed to a woman in the second row.

'Amanda Wray, *Online News Now*,' the woman said. 'Can you confirm whether a link is being made between this incident and a similar one in Liverpool in 2017, where a couple were found dead in a city park?'

An excited murmur travelled quickly round the room. Lola let it settle, taking the opportunity to swig some water from a glass on the table before her.

'I can't confirm that,' she said, and glanced at Kirstie beside her.

Kirstie gave an infinitesimally small nod, indicating she'd already made a note.

'Next question.' She nodded across the room at a familiar face. 'Yes?'

'Shuna Frain, *Daily Chronicle*,' the woman said, a self-satisfied smirk on her face that made Lola groan inwardly in grim anticipation. 'Rita Rennie believes you're not doing enough to bring her son's killer to justice. Are you aware that Mrs Rennie is planning to hold a press conference of her own on Sunday evening where she will reveal evidence of the identity of her son's killer?'

The audience loved that. Necks craned and faces peered to get a look at Shuna Frain. Lola tried to remain expressionless and quell her rising panic.

She waited for the crowd to quieten. 'We are in constant touch with the Rennie family. We are as keen as they are to find Sean Rennie's killer.'

With that, trying not to let her irritation show, she closed the conference and made quickly for the door.

CHAPTER TWENTY-THREE

Saturday 29 October
2.02 p.m.

'The Rennie family have requested that I should chair this meeting,' Alex Beedie said, once introductions were out of the way.

They were in the boardroom of the solicitor's Bath Street office. Beedie was a tall stick of a man, resembling someone from another era in his tailored pinstripe suit with a pink triangle of hanky protruding from a breast pocket. He had thinning, slicked-back hair and a pale bony face with lips so lusciously red that Lola wondered if he was wearing lipstick.

The entire Rennie clan was in attendance. Rita sat at the head of the table, her hair pinned up in a bun and wrapped in a black shawl like Queen Victoria in mourning. Gerry sat at her side, and next to him were his sisters, Therese and Bernadette. The sisters wore black suits and scowled at Lola as if she was something to be reviled.

Lola had acted swiftly after yesterday's press conference, going direct to Rita's house with Kirstie. She'd told the woman and her son that she knew they were planning to publicly divulge information, and that it must not happen. If the evidence they had was genuine, then to ignore the proper legal processes could risk justice never being done. Rita had risen from her seat in a rage and treated them to a tirade of foul language. Gerry calmed her down, then told Lola and Kirstie to go. They did.

It was an hour later that Alex Beedie phoned and invited Lola and her colleagues to this special "summit". Lola had rallied her team, and they flanked her now: Pierce, Marcus and Jonno. Kirstie was away at Ladymere Farm. After some consideration, Lola had asked Elaine Walsh if she could attend, and Elaine had abandoned family plans to be here.

'Rita's a dangerous woman, Lola,' Elaine had told her. 'I've been asking about. Word is she was the brains behind Mickey Rennie's whole operation. When he was killed she promoted the two boys. She has millions in offshore accounts, and her name's been linked to at least three executions in the past twenty years.'

'Is that right?' Lola had replied grimly. 'Well, at least we know who we're dealing with.'

'Mrs Rennie will speak first,' the solicitor said now, adding sourly, 'then I shall invite Miss Harris to make her case.'

Lola folded her hands in her lap patiently. She despised being managed like this, especially by a supercilious prick like Alex Beedie.

'Mrs Rennie,' Beedie intoned obsequiously.

A hush fell over the room.

'My darling Sean,' Rita began in her rough smoker's voice, 'has been dead for six days. Tonight is the one-week anniversary of his murder, and yet you—' she jabbed a hooked finger at Lola — 'have failed to come up with so much as a suspect.'

'That's not strictly—'

'Please, Miss Harris!' Beedie cut in. 'Do my client the courtesy of listening to what she has to say.'

Lola sat back and breathed deeply. She sensed Elaine shifting beside her and risked a glance. Elaine's face was studiously blank.

'And yet, in that time,' Rita Rennie went on, 'my family and I — mere amateurs in the study of crime — have uncovered evidence pointing directly to one person. Then you have the *gall* to come and demand it from us, as if it was your *right* to take it and claim the credit.'

Lola opened her mouth, but Beedie silenced her with a sharp look.

Rita barked on, spewing insults at Lola and essentially accusing her and her colleagues of conniving in her son's murder — even, perhaps, of welcoming it.

At last she fell silent.

Lola turned to Elaine. The super raised an eyebrow, to which Lola responded with a little nod. Earlier they'd discussed the possibility that Elaine might take the lead.

'Miss Harris?' Alex Beedie said, turning to Lola.

'Detective Superintendent Walsh will speak,' Lola said politely.

'Is that so?'

'Mrs Rennie,' Elaine began in a stentorian voice, 'my officers operate to the highest standards at all times. I have seen no evidence of any inappropriate conduct. You, however, have apparently chosen to withhold evidence of murder. That is an offence.'

Rita Rennie started to speak.

'I understand that you are grieving,' Elaine carried on, raising her voice, 'so I propose we draw a line under what has gone before. And I ask you now to share with me and my colleagues any evidence you are holding, and to explain how you came by it.'

Lola managed not to smile. She stole glances at her colleagues, who were doing equally well at remaining inscrutable.

At the far end of the table, Rita fell into whispered conference with her son, then the two of them turned to confer with Beedie. The discussion went on for some minutes, after which Beedie nodded, then sat up and cleared his throat, saying in a reedy voice, 'My clients have a proposition to make.'

'Oh?' said Elaine.

'They are prepared to share with you the evidence that they have . . . obtained, on condition that you will cease all investigation into Sean Rennie's business dealings, including any examination of his personal or business finances. I shall draw up a document which—'

'Absolutely not!' Lola cut in, sitting up. 'Mr Beedie, we are investigating a serious crime here. We are not negotiating a deal, or anything else for that matter. Frankly, I am appalled that a man of the law would propose such a thing.'

'Miss Harris—'

'It's Detective Chief Inspector Harris, Mr Beedie.'

'All my clients want is for a speedy resolution so that they can get on with their lives, and mourn their much-loved son.'

'Listen to me, Mrs Rennie,' Lola said, leaning forward, looking the seething woman directly in the eye. 'We will be investigating your son's murder with every resource we can. We will be examining every business contact, every deal, every company and every bank account — here and abroad, if we can — to look for reasons why someone might have wanted him dead. We will be overlooking *not one single thing*. You and your family have admitted that you are knowingly withholding evidence relating to a murder. Are you going to release that evidence to us now, or are we to arrest the lot of you?'

Lola nodded to Pierce and the DCs, then stood, calmly ready to come round the table to take the Rennies into custody.

'You can have it!' Rita Rennie shrieked. 'You can have all of it! Though we know what you'll do with it, don't we? Jack shit, that's what!'

Then she drew her lips into a tight pucker and spat a gob of saliva that sprayed across the beautiful smooth leather of Alex Beedie's board table.

CHAPTER TWENTY-FOUR

6.47 p.m.

'She was here most of the morning,' Fi said when Cat asked her about the time she'd spent with the detective constable. 'She was very nice to me really. Didn't bully me or ask me if I'd murdered anyone, anyway.'

They were in the kitchen at the little cottage, Cat busying herself peeling the cellophane off an M&S pizza, while Fi sat at the wee table, picking absently at her fingernails.

'I've given her three names,' Fi said now.

'Three?' Cat stared. 'Alistair Howe being one?'

'Yes.'

'So who are the other two?'

'When we got talking, I remembered there'd been this other guy. I don't think I ever told you about him. He was called Roddy. I don't even know his surname. He was in my halls. Bit of a geek. You'd think he was harmless, but he had an anger problem. He asked me out once. Asked all the girls out. He was a bit of a laughing stock. I remembered he thought some girls were laughing at him in the common room and he lobbed a milkshake at them. He got a warning.'

Cat bent to study the display on the oven. It was old and taking an age to warm up. 'Wine?'

'Yeah, go on. There are glasses on the draining board. They were dusty so I gave them a rinse.'

'Do you have any reason to think it might be him?' Cat asked, bringing the glasses to the table.

'No, not really. But she kept pushing me, and I remembered he had no boundaries. That, together with his anger problem, and she seemed to think he was worth considering.'

'The university will have his details, won't they?' she said, pouring red wine into Fi's glass.

'I guess so.'

'So who was the third guy?'

'It wasn't a guy.'

She stalled in the middle of pouring her own wine. 'Oh?'

'It was a girl called Aoife Norris. No — it's not what you think. *She* didn't ask me out. She accused me of stealing her boyfriend . . . which I suppose I kind of did.'

Cat sat down. 'What happened?'

'He was called Gregg. I snogged him at the Garage nightclub one night. Aoife was back home in Edinburgh because her gran was dying or something. Anyway, Gregg was off his face and so was I. I didn't *mean* it to happen, but it did. It was really late. Throwing-out time. We went and got chips and . . . I sort of ended up back at his place. This was several weeks before I started seeing Ali Howe, by the way.'

'I see.'

'Don't look like that!'

'How did she find out?'

'Another girl who'd been at the Garage — she spilled the beans. Aoife came back to Glasgow the next day and caught us together at Gregg's place. It was really bad.'

'Fifi . . .'

'I know. I thought I really liked him.'

The oven's light clicked off to signal it was at temperature. Cat rose and put the pizza in and set a timer on her phone.

'So, what happened?' she said, returning to sit at the table.

'Aoife went mental at him. Started hitting him. Then she went for me, tearing at my hair. He told her to get the fuck out, but she wasn't having it. He said he'd have to call the police. She went after that.'

'I don't remember hearing about any of this,' Cat said, trying to hide the alarm she felt.

'Yeah, well, I wasn't very proud of myself. Honestly, he was lovely looking. Really hot. Played rugby and was going to get a good job in IT. But you know how these things go — something didn't click between us so I said I wasn't really that interested. He'd dumped Aoife by then, so I think he maybe regretted that. She was so angry with me. I said I was sorry, but . . . well, we weren't friends after that.'

'And do you seriously think it could be her?'

'No, but DC Campbell seemed to think it was worth considering. Aoife attacked me once, so she might again.'

'Right.'

Fi was looking at her strangely.

'You think it's nonsense, don't you?'

'It's not that. I—'

'You don't believe me anymore, do you?' she said, her voice rising. 'You think I imagined all of it. Or that I'm lying. Maybe you think I killed Sean too. You're like DCI Harris. You're like Rita Rennie.'

'What? Fi, no! Where's this come from?'

Fi began to cry.

Catriona came to her side of the table and leaned down to embrace her.

'Of course I believe you,' she said.

'I'm sorry.' Fiona cried in big heaving sobs. 'It's just so horrible feeling hunted, and no one believing you.'

'I do believe you. I'm pretty sure the police do too. Honestly, if they didn't they wouldn't be spending time looking into it.'

Fi seemed mollified by the logic.

'I remembered some other things today too,' she said, wiping her face with a paper towel, and fixing Cat with a level gaze, as if to signal that what she said next would be a test. A test of allegiance. Or of faith, at least. 'Do you remember the "save the date" cards Sean and I sent out? It was in February.'

'Yes, but . . . what about them?'

'Do you remember I ordered samples from a few companies?'

'Yes. I . . . well, I can't really remember.'

This was difficult territory for Cat. Early on, Cat had made it clear she had misgivings about Sean. The sisters had had a falling out, after which they'd come to an agreement that Fi wouldn't involve Cat in the wedding planning.

'I got samples from three or four different places, but then another sample arrived in a plain envelope.'

Cat waited.

'They weren't "save the date" cards. Cat, they were funeral cards.'

'*Funeral* cards?'

'You send them when someone dies. They're blank so you can write your own message, but they're edged in black.'

Cat stared. 'Could have been a mistake, maybe, or . . .'

'Or maybe not. Anyway, I decided just to ignore them. I threw them away. Then I remembered two other things.'

'Oh?'

Cat's skin was crawling. She steeled herself.

'Someone had spilled confetti in the close. At the bottom of the stairs and outside on the pavement. Cat, it was *black*. It was *black confetti*.'

'Black confetti?' She managed a little laugh. 'Can you even get black confetti?'

'You must be able to. I don't know, maybe goths like it.'

'When was this?'

'It was after the funeral cards arrived. The thing is, I didn't really think about it at the time. I just saw all these tiny bits of black paper all over the place.'

'You said you'd remembered three things. What was the third?'

'Someone tied black roses to the railings by the railway track, opposite the flat. I don't remember when it was. I thought maybe there'd been an accident there, on the road or on the railway. You know the way people tie flowers to railings and lampposts. I thought the roses had maybe been red and had died and gone black, but . . . they don't, do they? If anything they go a sort of horrible brown.'

'Did you tell DC Campbell about these things?'

Fi nodded.

'What did she say?'

'Nothing much. She just wrote it down.'

Fi was waiting for her to say something, she could tell. To say she believed her, perhaps. But she was saved by the timer on her phone. The pizza was ready.

CHAPTER TWENTY-FIVE

8.35 p.m.

'Ah, good, you're still here,' Lola said when she spotted Kirstie at her desk. 'How did you get on with Fiona Balfour today?'

'She gave me three names to follow up,' Kirstie said. 'People who might have reason to attack her. And then . . . well, she started remembering things.'

Lola listened as Kirstie recounted what Fiona Balfour had told her.

'Black confetti? Black roses? And you don't believe her, do you?'

'No, boss. I don't think I do.'

Lola nodded. 'Do you think she did it?'

'She could have done it. She could have paid for it, and had the attacker tie her up so she appeared to be a victim too. It's the ultimate alibi.'

'So, she had the means and opportunity. What about the motive?'

'I don't know.'

'And what about disposition, Kirstie?' she asked now. 'Does she strike you as someone who could commit murder?'

'Maybe.' She frowned at Lola. 'Did you want me for something, boss?'

'Follow me,' Lola said, and led the way to one of the bigger meeting rooms. She unlocked the door, then went in, turning on the lights.

On the table were three transparent evidence bags containing items that Pierce and Jonno had collected from Rita Rennie's house earlier in the day.

'Rita's evidence,' Lola said.

Kirstie stared, taking it in.

'Take a good look, and tell me what you make of it,' Lola urged.

The constable studied the items on the table, and Lola followed her gaze.

First was an A4 page showing a grid of smartphone screenshots depicting a conversation in text messages. Each screenshot was headed "FB". The conversation was between FB and whoever owned the phone. It detailed an agreement for the owner of the phone to carry out something referred to as "the task", in return for "the agreed payment". The job would be carried out "at the weekend as discussed" and the payment would be delivered "according to the method agreed".

'"FB",' Kirstie murmured grimly, and stepped to the right, leaning in to study the next item.

It was a black and white photograph, apparently taken at night. Judging by what the woman pictured was wearing — what looked like linen trousers and a light jacket — it was summertime. The image clearly showed Fiona Balfour glancing in the direction of the photographer, a furtive expression on her face, apparently about to pass a thick envelope, folded over and secured with string or rubber bands, in through the window of an expensive-looking car. The photo didn't show the registration plate.

'Looks like a Mercedes, boss. Fiona Balfour says it could have been a Mercedes that drove at her.'

'Or a BMW or an Audi,' Lola pointed out. 'She wasn't sure.'

The next item was a USB memory drive inside a square, transparent plastic wallet, sitting beside a short, typed transcript.

'It's a voice recording,' Lola said. 'In it you can hear a young woman telling a man that "Sean's left the flat now". The man confirms that everything's in hand. It sounds like Fiona Balfour speaking. We need to get a recording of her voice to make a comparison, but . . .'

'Where did they get all this from?' Kirstie asked, eyes alive.

'It arrived in an envelope at Rita Rennie's house on Thursday evening, delivered by hand. Taken together, it's astonishing,' she said. 'But it's *so* indicative that I'm almost inclined to believe it's a clever fake.'

'What do we do, boss?'

Lola sighed. 'There's only one thing we can do, isn't there?'

CHAPTER TWENTY-SIX

10.02 p.m.

They'd eaten in the living room, watching *Ocean's Eight*.

Cat hadn't finished her food. Her stomach felt knotted and uncomfortable. She sat in the half-light, letting the movie wash over her. Fi, who'd eaten her half of the pizza, was now working her way happily through a bowl of cheesy Doritos. She was rapt by the film, giggling and making admiring remarks about the outfits during the heist scenes at the Met Gala.

Cat had defended Fi's personal vendetta theory to the inspector, highlighting her conviction that she had an unknown enemy. The incident at university had been real enough — she herself had helped pick up the pieces the night it happened. She believed the business about the car too. Sean had certainly believed it. But when it came to the series of suddenly recalled sinister incidents — the black confetti, the roses, the funeral cards — to believe Fi about these required a suspension of disbelief. She'd recounted the incidents in such a frenzy that Cat's gut instinct was that they were delusions, if not deliberate fictions.

Then there were the three names. For years there'd been just one person with a question mark over his name — Ali Howe. Now there were two more.

Then, of course, there was the photograph that had come through Cat's door.

The film had finished and Fi was all smiles, reaching for the wine to top up her glass. Then she saw Cat's face.

'Didn't you enjoy it?' she said.

'Yeah. Yeah, it was great.'

'What's wrong, then?' That watchful, suspicious look was on her face again, as if she had a sixth sense of what Cat was about to say.

'You told me you were leaving Sean because you found out he'd had someone attacked,' Cat said, and swallowed, hearing it click in her throat.

'What about it?'

'It wasn't true, was it?'

'Yes, it was. I heard him ordering it. A guy called Billy Raymond did it for him. Sean was going to pay him five thousand pounds.'

'He might have done,' Cat said, feeling as if every muscle in her body was tensed, 'but that's not why you decided to leave him, was it?'

'Yes it was.' Fi made a perplexed face.

'You were going to leave him because you were seeing someone else.'

'Someone . . . ? *What*? What are you *talking* about?'

'You've been seeing Gerry, haven't you?'

'Gerry? Gerry Rennie? Sean's *brother*?' Her voice rose, not in anger but in a kind of wild amusement. 'You're saying I was leaving Sean for *him*?'

'Yes.' She heard an unwelcome tremor in her voice now. 'That's exactly what I'm suggesting.'

'But . . . but that's *mad*. It's not true, Cat!'

'Isn't it?'

'Why do you — I mean, why would you even say such a thing? Has somebody said I've been seeing Gerry, or—' her voice rose in querulous rage — 'or is it just that you have such a *low fucking opinion* of me — your *own sister* — that you think that's the kind of shitty thing I'd do?'

Cat sat quietly, endeavouring to centre herself, to repress the welling emotions.

Fi was up now, pacing the room like a trapped animal.

'Someone sent me a photograph,' Cat said quietly.

'A photograph? Of what? Me and Gerry Rennie holding hands? Me and Gerry *snogging*?'

'Pretty much,' Cat said.

Leaving Fi staring open-mouthed, she got up and went to the kitchen for her satchel. Back in the living room, Fi's face was twisted in anger.

Cat went calmly into her bag for the envelope and slid the photograph out of it. She glanced at it once, to check she hadn't, in some mental storm, imagined what it showed. She hadn't. She passed it to her sister.

Fi looked at it and her face changed, from one of disgust to one of disbelieving horror. She looked at Cat, lips parted to speak, but then looked down again, back at the photograph in her hand.

Cat sat again, ready to wait for whatever explanation might come.

'Where did you get this?' Fi said, still on her feet, her voice shaking. 'Where?'

'It came through the door.' She managed to keep her voice low and level. 'On Thursday.'

Fi was staring at the image again, shaking her head in disbelief.

'It's not me,' she said after a minute. 'It's not.'

'Fi, don't. Please. Of course it's you.'

'But it's not!' Her voice rose to a scream. 'It's not, it's *not*! I've never even been *alone* with Gerry Rennie. It's . . . Someone's made this. It's a fake. A joke. It's . . .' Her expression changed suddenly. 'You did this, didn't you? You've always been so desperate to control me — to *save me* — only you couldn't save me from Sean. You've had this made using

116

some kind of software, so you can take control properly. Why? Do you want to blackmail me or something?'

'Fi, no! Oh, God, of course not. Why would you think that?'

Fi was crying now. Standing, hugging herself with both arms and sobbing with abandon. She swayed.

Cat jumped up and took her by the arm. 'Sit down. Come on. Sit here.' She led her to the settee.

'Do you remember when Mum died and we realised it was just us two left, and we got the flat together?' Cat said gently. 'We said we'd always be there for one another. We said we'd never lie to each other. We said—'

'I'm not lying! I'm *not*! Oh, God, this is insane . . .'

'Okay,' Cat said, and pulled her sister into an embrace. 'Okay.' She rubbed Fi's back until she was calm again.

'What's happening to me?' Fi said at last. 'I'm going mad . . .'

'You're not going mad. And I'm here, I promise. Let me make us some coffee, eh? We can talk about what to do.'

Fi nodded.

Cat knew something wasn't right the minute she entered the kitchen. There was too much light outside. She peered through the little square of window in the door. Spotlights moved on the ground, low down, like the light from hand-held torches. There were people outside.

Then came the knocking at the door, and a woman's voice, raised and commanding: 'It's the police. Open up, please.'

CHAPTER TWENTY-SEVEN

10.25 p.m.

'I can't believe you're doing this,' Cat cried, back against the doorjamb, as the three of them — DCI Harris, the female constable and a man she didn't recognise piled past her into the living room, where Fi stood, trembling hands to her mouth, terrified. 'I can't believe you'd treat her like this. She's a victim, for God's sake!'

Diana Croy was there now, in pyjamas and dressing gown, wellington boots on her feet. She was closely followed by Tom, who looked as if he'd been asleep. His mop of blond hair was all over the place. Diana came up to Cat and put a hand on her arm. Her face was stricken.

'Ms Balfour,' the DCI said. 'We've come into possession of evidence that appears to indicate you commissioned the death of Sean Rennie.'

'*What*?' Cat said. 'Fi, say nothing until we get you a solicitor.'

DCI Harris told Fi she was under arrest and that the evidence leading to the arrest would be shared with her in due course. She asked her to confirm her name and date of birth. Then told her she was being taken into custody.

'What evidence?' Cat demanded now, her whole body wracked with stress but feeling utterly helpless.

The DCI turned to her. 'Do you have a solicitor you can call?'

'Yes. But I've no signal here. I'll need to call from the house.' She turned to Diana. 'Is that all right?'

'Yes, of course.'

'Did you really need to do this tonight?' Diana snapped at the DCI. 'We have young children! They're in bed.'

'Call the solicitor,' DCI Harris said to Cat. 'Tell them to go to Govan police office at Helen Street.'

She nodded, unable to think what else to do or say.

'You stay with her, Cat,' Tom said, eyes blazing over Diana's shoulder. 'Tell me who to call and I'll go do it now.'

'Thanks, Tom.'

'Cat?' Fi sobbed. 'What's happening to me?'

'Please come with us,' the DCI said to Fi, standing back so that the constable could take her gently but firmly by the arm and lead her from the cottage.

CHAPTER TWENTY-EIGHT

Sunday 30 October
9.04 a.m.

'She's doing okay,' Robyn McArthur told Cat. 'Surprisingly well, in fact.'

They were in the solicitor's Mini Cooper, sitting on the main road by Bellahouston Park, five minutes' walk from the police office at Helen Street in Govan. Robyn, acting as Fi's solicitor at Cat's request, was just back from a meeting with her client ahead of the morning's planned round of questioning. 'I'd say she's an extraordinarily resilient young woman.'

Cat nodded, too choked to speak.

Robyn had arrived at Helen Street a few minutes before midnight, where she'd met Fi before allowing the police to question her. Then she'd attended the questioning until a little after one a.m., at which point DCI Harris had said she would be holding Fi for further questioning in the morning. Fi had been taken to a cell.

Robyn had explained the rules of arrest to Cat.

'Basically, a suspect can be arrested and held for an initial period of twelve hours while the police make enquiries. That includes questioning the suspect.'

'But why arrest her so late at night?' Cat had asked. 'Why not wait till Sunday morning?'

'From what I can piece together,' Robyn told her, 'it seems they think there's a chance they think Fi's in danger of retribution.'

'*Retribution*?'

'I'd say they think the Rennies might come for her. They've taken her into custody partly for her own safety.'

'My God . . . This is *insane* . . . Tom and Diana's farm is in the middle of nowhere. Surely to God, they couldn't find her there!'

'Try to stay calm. Let things unfold. I'll look after Fi. You look after yourself so you're ready for when she's released.'

'She didn't do it, Robyn,' Cat pleaded. 'Honestly. I can't believe my sister is a cold-blooded murderer. I need to get her out of there. I need to get her out and take her somewhere and keep her safe. I—'

'You need to calm down — *that's* what you need to do.'

She stared at Robyn, her friend — and ex-girlfriend — in dismay.

'I know you feel responsible,' Robyn said, matter of fact. 'But you're not.'

Cat watched her doubtfully.

'You're *not*, Cat. You can support Fi. You might well be able to make things right, but it's not your job to fix this. You can't carry everything on your shoulders.'

Cat stared at her, then sat back and studied her clenched hands in her lap. This was old ground. It had long been Robyn's belief that Cat needed to save people, to step in and parent them to safety, and it had been a point of contention all through their relationship. There was a good reason behind it — they both acknowledged that — one that went back more than a decade, to a time when Cat had failed to help a friend in desperate need. It wasn't healthy.

Acknowledging that was one thing, though; acting on it — or *resisting* the desire to act — was something else.

'She's my sister, Robbie,' she said in a small voice.

'I know. Which is why you need to let me step in and sort things out. The evidence they have—'

'Is fake! Of course it is!'

'But we have to prove that.'

'And how long will that take?'

'Dr Fischer can do it today — if we get the police to cooperate.'

Robyn had taken Fi at her word that the evidence was cleverly faked. A set of *deepfakes*, in fact, constructed using software to create an alternative reality that could convince the most sceptical person. Robyn had obtained a contact through a friend for Dr Anya Fischer, a digital forensic analyst based in Dundee. Robyn had received a reply from Dr Fischer at six a.m.

'What are the chances the police will let her look at the evidence?' Cat said now.

'I think they will. If they wait for their own analysts to get to it, it could take days. We're offering a solution that should make everyone's lives a lot easier.' She paused, seeing the expression on Cat's face. 'Why are you looking at me like that?'

'It's just . . . There's something I need to show you,' Cat said, quietly, hating herself for having kept this to herself.

'What exactly?' Seeing Cat's expression, Robyn groaned. 'What have you done . . . ?'

'Something came through the door,' Cat said. 'It's . . . a photo of Fi, with Sean Rennie's brother, Gerry.'

'*What?*'

'I'm sorry. I should have told you before.' She went into her satchel, withdrew an envelope and passed it to Robyn, eyes down. 'I challenged Fi about it last night. She denied it absolutely.'

'My God. And it came through the door?'

'The other night. You can see it's just got my name on it. No address.' She looked Robyn in the eye.

'You're sure it's this Gerry guy?'

'I met him once, at Fi's place. What . . . ? What is it?'

Robyn was peering closely at the photograph.

'The shadows aren't right,' she said after a moment. 'Look. See where the light's coming from? See how it lands on Gerry Rennie's face? Now look at the light on Fi's face.'

'You mean . . . ?'

'I think it's another fake.'

She was momentarily speechless. 'Oh! Oh, thank God. But what can we . . . Do you think Dr Fischer will confirm it?'

'There might be a quicker way,' Robyn said, thoughtfully. She paused, narrowing her eyes. 'How would you like a wee job?'

'You know I'll do anything.'

'Fi denied it was her in the photograph. Would Gerry Rennie?'

'Of course he would, if it's fake! But—'

'I think we should ask him. Rather, I think *you* should ask him.'

'Are you serious?'

'Go and see him. I take it you know where he stays.'

'With his mum, I think. I know where that is.'

'Go there. Get him on his own, then hand it to him and see what he says. Actually, don't. Take a snap of it on your phone and show him that. I'll keep the original.'

'But what if he—'

'If he admits it? Well, then we'll deal with that. But it would be pretty remarkable if he was shagging his brother's fiancée. It'd add a whole new dimension — one we could potentially exploit. But what I'm hoping is that he's shocked and denies it outright. That way, we might have a chance to demonstrate to the Rennies that someone is trying to fit Fi up — and then they might leave her alone.'

Cat busied herself with her phone, taking multiple snaps, including close-ups, of the photo of Fi and Gerry Rennie. Then she handed the original back to Robyn.

'Who's doing this, Robyn?' she said now. 'Who would want to implicate Fi in murder?'

'God knows,' Robyn said. 'Let's focus on proving the evidence to be faked. If we can do that, we can get Fi released. But first things first—' she looked at the clock on the Mini's dashboard — 'I need to get back in there. They're starting the interviews at half past.'

CHAPTER TWENTY-NINE

9.34 a.m.

After bringing her in the night before, Lola and Kirstie had questioned Fiona Balfour for an hour, during which time the young woman argued, coolly and unwaveringly, that she was the victim of a setup, and that none of the evidence put to her was real.

'That's an extraordinary claim,' Lola had said.

'It's an extraordinary amount of evidence,' her solicitor Robyn McArthur had chipped in. 'It must have crossed your minds that you're being played.'

It had, but Lola didn't say so.

Ms McArthur was a lithe and alert woman in her forties, smartly dressed in linen trousers and a knitted sweater, with sharply styled short black hair and an almost intimidating air of competence that put Lola on her guard.

'We would like to commission a digital forensics expert to examine the evidence for authenticity, with a view to assessing whether they might be deepfakes,' Ms McArthur had said.

Lola had pointed out that any digital forensic evaluation would need to be done by Police Scotland's own analysts — and that it could take days.

'We can't wait,' the solicitor had said. 'What if I found someone to do it? We're happy to foot the bill and you could ensure the evidence was protected.'

'I'll consider it,' Lola had said.

They were back in the interview room this morning: Lola and Kirstie on one side of the table, Fiona Balfour and Robyn McArthur on the other. The solicitor wanted to talk about the digital forensic assessment, but Lola stalled her, asking Fiona a series of questions relating to motive, seeking anything that might indicate that the young woman had considered herself trapped in her relationship with Sean Rennie, or that she desired revenge on him.

But the questions uncovered nothing.

'I would like you to let my client go,' the solicitor said, forty-five minutes in. 'We are of the strong belief that the evidence will turn out to be fraudulent, and we have proposed a way to prove that, which we're asking you to allow us to pursue. When we get the proof we need, my client will give all her assistance in tracking down who is responsible, and who killed Mr Rennie. She cannot help you while she remains under arrest.'

Rather than respond, Lola called a break.

'What do you think?' she said to Kirstie, back in the office.

'I think we need to allow them to test the evidence, boss.'

Lola nodded, troubled. 'If they turn out to be fake then they're incredibly well done. I'm going to call the super.' She saw Kirstie's expression. 'What? Why are you looking at me like that?'

'It *could* be a very clever double bluff.'

'Meaning what?'

'Fiona Balfour could have arranged the murder, hiring a killer and planting "evidence" against herself that she knew we'd prove to be false. Then we'd believe she was innocent after all — and she'd have got away with the perfect murder.'

Lola thought about it. She was tired and her brain wasn't functioning as well as she'd like.

'I'm fairly sure the digital forensics expert will find the evidence is faked,' she said with a sigh. 'We could put it to

Ms Balfour that she faked the evidence in a clever double bluff, like you suggest — just so we have a record of having asked. But then . . . well . . .'

'Boss . . . ?'

'Then we'll have to let her go.'

CHAPTER THIRTY

10.10 a.m.

Cat found the house no problem: the mauve-painted monstrosity stood out in the otherwise plain suburban street.

She parked right outside, hoping they'd see her through one of their CCTV cameras, then got out and rang the intercom fixed to the black metal gates.

She got a response of crackling static, but no voice came.

'It's Catriona Balfour,' she said into it, nice and loudly. 'I'm Fiona Balfour's sister. I want to talk to Gerry Rennie. It's important. Is he there?'

No response. She pressed the buzzer again.

'I want to speak to Gerry!' she said as loud as she could. Loud enough for neighbours to hear.

The gate clicked and sprang marginally open.

'Finally,' she grumbled to herself.

She squeezed between a black BMW and a low-slung MG with a soft top, before arriving at the front door. This, too, stood slightly ajar. She reached for the knocker, just as the door was drawn abruptly open.

A sharp-faced woman in her thirties stood there, slender and tanned, with long hair that looked as if it had been ironed. She was wearing brown leather trousers and a red shirt. 'What do you want?' she said unpleasantly.

'To talk to Gerry,' Cat said, smiling. 'Is he there?'

'What d'you want him for?'

'I've got something he'll want to see,' she said, raising her voice again, in case — as she suspected — Gerry was inside the hallway, hiding and listening. 'Something important that concerns him.'

The woman screwed up her face, and might have been about to tell her where to go, when a hand appeared and pulled the door wider. Gerry Rennie stood there, wearing jeans and a dark jumper and jacket. His green eyes were bright and furious.

'It's you, is it?' he spat, then turned to the woman. 'Thanks, Terri. I'll deal with her. Go sit with Ma.'

The woman grimaced at Cat, then turned and vanished into the bowels of the house.

Gerry stepped out of the house and pulled the door closed behind him, so it was just the two of them in the driveway. 'What d'you want?'

'I've got a photograph to show you.'

'Oh?'

'You're in it.'

He pulled a face. 'So?'

She went into her satchel and pulled out her phone. She found the photo and turned the phone so it filled the screen in landscape. Then she handed it to him and folded her arms, setting her expression to one of unfriendly, slow-blinking patience, all the time feeling her heart racing in her chest, while her fingers tingled.

He stared at it, face blank, for at least a minute.

'See who it is?' she said, her voice husky from her dry mouth.

At last he looked at her, eyes wary. No — frightened.

'Where was it taken, Gerry?' she said, pushing him.

He was breathing hard. 'It isn't real.'

'What makes you say that?'

'Because it isn't!'

He was frightened. *Good.*

'Where did you get this?'

'Never mind,' she said, taking the phone back and dropping it into her bag. 'You realise what this means, don't you?'

He stared, apparently speechless.

'Someone faked a photo of you and my sister.'

'Who?'

'I've no idea. Convincing, though, isn't it?'

'Who else has seen it?' He was nervous now. More than that, she realised. He was near to panic.

'A few people. Fi. Her solicitor.'

'Police?'

'Not yet.'

He swallowed, and she could see him thinking fast. She caught the half-glance he made back at the house behind him.

'See how easy it is?' she said. 'All you need is photos of the individual people and some software.'

'Where's the original?' Furtive now.

'Safe. What I want to know is: what are you going to do about it?'

'What do you mean?'

'All that evidence you've given to the police — all of that's fake too.'

His eyes grew large.

'And we're going to prove it. One of the best cyber brains in Scotland is going to analyse it today. You leave my sister alone from now on. I'm warning you.'

He stared and said nothing. What else could he do?

Driving back to Govan to tell Robyn the news, she felt almost sorry for him.

CHAPTER THIRTY-ONE

11.44 a.m.

Elaine Walsh had given Lola permission to make a deal.

Fiona Balfour would be released from custody while the tests on the photograph and audio recording took place. Those tests would be carried out today, at Helen Street, by the digital forensics expert, Dr Anya Fischer, with DC Kirstie Campbell in attendance. Dr Fischer's costs would be covered by Robyn McArthur. The outcome of the tests would have to be verified by Police Scotland's own digital forensics experts in due course, but Lola would take Dr Fischer's findings as "indicative".

'You're free to go,' Lola told Fiona, trying to ignore the light of triumph in Robyn McArthur's eyes.

'You mean it?' Fiona said.

'Yes. DC Campbell here will see you get your belongings back.'

The young woman stood, hands on her face as she wept with relief.

'There's something we need to talk about first,' Lola said. 'It won't take five minutes, but it's about your safety.'

'My *safety*?'

'She means the Rennies,' Robyn McArthur said.

'They'll know about your arrest,' Lola said. 'And they'll be keeping an ear to the ground. When they hear you've been released, they might . . . try to take action. I strongly advise you not to return to Ladymere Farm.'

'I like it there!' She turned panicked eyes on her solicitor. 'I feel safe there.'

'*Feeling* safe and *being* safe are not the same thing,' Lola said.

'The Rennies might know where you were arrested,' Ms McArthur explained gently.

'But I like it there,' Fiona said again, her voice rising. 'I like the cottage. I like the children.' She turned to Lola, chin up. 'If I'm free, then I can go where I like, can't I?'

'You can,' Lola said, turning helplessly to the solicitor.

'Let's get out of here, Fi,' Ms McArthur said gently. 'We can go to my place. Cat can join us, and we can talk about what's best.'

CHAPTER THIRTY-TWO

2.27 p.m.

Lola sat at her desk, chewing at the corner of a greyish sand-
wich bought from the vending machine and gazing miserably
at her phone. It was now three days since Joe's message telling
her not to contact him. And she hadn't.

'I need to know he's all right,' she'd sobbed to her sister Frankie on the phone last night, wine in hand. 'Surely I
deserve that much. Surely Marie can allow me that.'

'Not how she'll see it,' Frankie had warned.

'I need to *know*,' was all Lola could say.

'Text him again. I mean, the proverbial's already hit the
fan, hasn't it? What harm can it do?'

So she'd taken another mouthful of wine, and sat at her
kitchen table and composed a message. One she thought was
pragmatic, fair and from the heart:

> *I need to know you're okay Joe. It's not fair to cut me out,*
> *whatever Marie says. Please just keep in touch. For the sake*
> *of everything we had.*

She'd sent it just after nine p.m.

Now, more than eighteen hours later, he still hadn't replied, and a new emotion had crept in to join the pain and fear: a kind of shocked anger.

Was this really how it was going to end? In cold rejection?

Footsteps behind her.

'Dr Fischer's finished, boss,' Kirstie said, an inscrutable expression on her face. 'She'll explain what she's found.'

Lola had met Anya Fischer briefly when she'd first arrived, then left her in Kirstie's hands while she heard what Pierce and Jonno had to tell her about Sean Rennie's business dealings. Dr Fischer was petite, almost childlike, under five feet tall and stick thin. Her hair was striking: vinyl-glossy and gathered up on top of her head with what looked like steel chopsticks. Her face was painted geisha white, and her lips were a blood-red bow.

She was standing in the centre of the room, waiting for them.

'You've finished already?' Lola said.

'Yes,' Dr Fischer said with a single nod.

'And?' She was surprised at how anxious she felt. Her mouth was dry and her fingers tingled.

'The photograph and audio recording are clear fakes. Convincing to the human eye and ear, but simple analyses prove otherwise.' She gave a beam of pleasure, revealing beautifully white and even teeth.

'How sure can you be?' Lola said.

'One hundred per cent. The background is an adapted stock image. I can show you the original in three stock image libraries. An image of Fiona Balfour's head and face has been manipulated and introduced into the stock image. A differential in the pixel density confirms this.'

'My God.'

Another beam of delight, accompanied this time by a tinkle of laughter.

'What about the audio?'

'A sophisticated voice simulator was used, no doubt using an authentic sample of Ms Balfour's own voice, but the result cannot evade the detection of digital manipulation in the frequencies in the voice.'

'Thank you,' Lola said, feeling somewhat stunned. She turned to Kirstie and said quietly, 'I'll leave you to wrap things up with Dr Fischer,' she said. 'Would you contact Ms Balfour's solicitor and tell her the news? Then I think we'll need a meeting to decide what we do next.'

CHAPTER THIRTY-THREE

3.17 p.m.

Lola was in full flow, explaining to the room of attentive faces how the Rennies' "evidence" had been proven to be fake, when DC Marcus McVittie came in late, looking harassed and excited.

'Sorry, boss,' he muttered.

She gave him a moment to find a seat, taking the opportunity to study Anna Vaughan a little more closely. The new DS had come in a day earlier than she was expected, to attend this briefing and get up to speed on the investigation. She'd taken a prime spot at the front of the room and had listened to Lola with respectful attention, nodding along. She was a very attractive thirty-something blonde, willowy in a tailored grey suit, and sleekly groomed with perfect hair and nails. She'd already caught the attention of a few of the men in the room. Lola had seen Pierce muttering a sly aside to Jonno, then narrowing his eyes and tilting his head to appraise her; he'd all but licked his lips.

Once Marcus was settled, Lola went on.

'To date we have been considering three scenarios, which are as follows:

first, that this was a gangland killing, perhaps committed in revenge for a perceived "business" slight. We are actively pursuing this line of enquiry and we have a lead relating to a demolition contract. But there's a complicating factor: the callous and carefully planned involvement of Sean Rennie's partner, Fiona Balfour, in the crime. Rennie and his partner Ms Balfour were not together when he was killed, so she wasn't "taken along for the ride", so to speak. We can't explain why she was tied to his corpse but left unharmed.

'The second scenario was proposed by Ms Balfour herself. She believes — and has done for a number of years — that an unknown individual is pursuing a vendetta against her. She identifies key incidents, separated by a number of years, that confirm this belief for her. We have begun to consider her claim, but haven't prioritised it. Yesterday, DC Campbell spent time with Ms Balfour and managed to elicit the names of three people of interest. If the attack that resulted in Sean Rennie's death *was* part of this vendetta, then we cannot explain why he was harmed and she was not. We cannot say why he was involved at all, unless it was to psychologically traumatise her — a theory that seems overblown.

'The third scenario is the one proposed by Rita Rennie: that Fiona Balfour arranged the murder of her partner with some unknown third party. That she paid this third party to drug her and tie her to his murdered corpse, to give her an alibi. The photographic and audio evidence Mrs Rennie provided to back up her claim has, as I explained, been shown to be fake.

'Somebody created that so-called evidence and, if we're to believe what they've told us, fed it to the Rennies. The question now is, why? Who would want to implicate Fiona Balfour in the murder of Sean Rennie? If this was all about Ms Balfour, why not kill her? Is this a plan to make her suffer a false conviction for murder?

'There is, of course, the possibility that this is a double bluff.' She nodded to Kirstie to acknowledge this had been her suggestion. 'That Fiona Balfour has implicated herself, but with evidence we'd be bound to reject, thus proving — falsely — her innocence. We will examine this possibility, but it is, in my current view, remote.'

She took a deep breath, feeling some of the burden lifting, now she had shared it.

'Colleagues, we face a genuine puzzle here, but for now I'm focusing all of our efforts on two areas: Rennie's business dealings and people who might wish harm to Ms Balfour. Of course, another line of enquiry might emerge—'

Marcus's hand shot in the air. 'Boss!'

Heads turned.

'DC McVittie,' Lola said.

'Something you asked me to look into after the press conference on Friday,' he said. 'A reporter for one of the online news channels asked about similarities between this crime and the death of a couple in a park in Liverpool in 2017. I got the report through just a few minutes ago.'

A murmur of interest travelled round the room.

'Go on,' Lola said.

'A couple were found dead, under bushes alongside a footpath in Sefton Park in Liverpool,' Marcus read, his eyes tracking a document. 'Discovery was made at six fifteen a.m. on the twelfth of March that year by a dog walker. Victims were a thirty-year-old male, shot in the chest, and a twenty-nine-year-old female. She died from exposure — the temperature had dropped to minus five overnight. The female had no other injuries, though she'd been drugged heavily with ketamine, as had the male.' Marcus paused and glanced up at Lola, then around at his colleagues, whose expressions were rapt.

Her own heart racing at the development, Lola nodded to him to continue.

'He was a bar owner, she was his girlfriend, an interior designer. No motive established, despite extensive enquiries. No arrests made. Case remains open.'

'Let me see the report,' she said to Marcus. 'I assume you've got the name of a contact in Merseyside CID?'

Marcus nodded.

'Let's talk to them. Set something up for later today or first thing tomorrow.'

'Boss.'

With that, and a sense of renewed — and unexpected — optimism, Lola closed the meeting.

CHAPTER THIRTY-FOUR

4.29 p.m.

'There's a guy getting out of a black Beemer,' Robyn said, peering down from the bay window of the second-floor flat. 'Six-foot-ish. Dark. Good-looking.'

Cat got up and peered over her shoulder, down into the street. 'That's him.'

'Oh, God,' Fi whimpered quietly. She was curled up in one corner of the big L-shaped settee.

'It'll be fine,' Cat told her, coming away from the window. 'The ball's in our court now. He needs us.'

The buzzer sounded out in the hall.

Fi jumped up. 'I can't face him.'

'We're presenting a united front,' Cat said, taking her sister's forearms gently. 'We're not scared of him or his family. If you're not here, he'll think you're hiding.'

Fi nodded and sniffed away tears.

'Good girl.'

Robyn was already out in the hall, answering the buzzer, then unlatching the front door. This wasn't Robyn's flat — to have met a potentially dangerous individual there would have been madness. It belonged to a pal of hers who now lived overseas and who rented it out on short lets. She'd made it clear to Gerry Rennie that she was borrowing this place and wouldn't be back here after their meeting.

'You and me sit here,' Cat said, leading Fi back to the settee. 'Sit up and stay calm. You don't need to speak to him, but try to look him in the eye. That's how you show him that he has no power. Robyn will deal with him.' She smiled. 'And don't forget, she's a black belt, third dan in judo, so . . .'

Fi managed a laugh and Cat felt reassured.

Voices in the hallway: Robyn's friendly but firm, the visitor's low and diffident.

The living-room door opened and Robyn marched smartly in, a businesslike expression on her face. She dropped them a secret wink, a signal that she remained confident things would go to plan.

'Mr Rennie,' she said, stepping aside, 'you know Fiona Balfour, and I believe you met her sister Catriona only this morning.'

To Cat, Gerry Rennie looked like a man possessed by warring demons. Where this morning he'd been panicked and frightened, he now looked beaten down, upset and anxious — as if he wanted to be anywhere else but here. He came slowly into the room, hunched a little, eyes peering at Cat and her sister from under a furrowed brow.

Cat got up, hooking her thumbs into her jeans pockets, and gave him a nod of greeting. He returned it, but his eyes were, warily, on Fiona.

'Have a seat,' Robyn said to him, indicating a low armchair opposite the settee. She nodded to Cat to retake her seat, then she sat on an upright dining chair brought through from the kitchen.

'As I explained on the phone,' Robyn began, 'a digital forensics specialist has proved that the photograph and audio recording your family submitted to the police are sophisticated fakes. The specialist has not tested the photograph that appears to depict yourself, Mr Rennie, with my client Ms Fiona Balfour, but we intend to have it analysed too.'

'There's no need,' Rennie said gruffly. 'It's a fake. It's obvious!'

'Nevertheless, for our own purposes we are submitting it for analysis. We will share the findings with you once they're ready.'

He nodded, eyes down, cowed.

'The tests today were paid for by my client. The police will carry out their own in due course. I expect that at that point they'll communicate the findings to your family.'

'No one needs to see the photo,' Rennie said. ''Specially Ma. She won't believe it isn't real. It'd break her heart. The idea that I . . . that I'd . . .' He made a pathetic half gesture in Fi's direction.

'That you'd be seen dead with my sister?' Cat cut in, receiving a warning look from Robyn. She sensed Fi stiffening at her side, and regretted speaking.

'You mean,' Robyn said, 'that your mother would dismiss scientific proof?'

'I don't . . . Look, Ma, she's . . .' He was really struggling, Cat realised. She found herself feeling sorry for him. He had, after all, just lost his younger brother. 'Once Ma's set on something, it's hard to . . . to go against that.'

'You're saying,' Robyn said, leaning forward and eyeballing him, 'that there's likely nothing we can do to persuade your mother that my client is not responsible for Sean's death? That no evidence would convince her?'

He sat for a minute, staring miserably into space. Then nodded.

Robyn took papers from a folder beside her chair and leafed through them, giving Gerry Rennie time to process the reality in which he found himself. He drooped in the low chair and waited.

'I am concerned for my client's safety,' Robyn said now, remaining quite impassive.

Cat snuck a look at Fi. Robyn had explained the line she was going to take, and why, and that Fi's presence in the room would be powerful — intimidating, she hoped.

'I believe that your mother would like my client harmed. Dead, even.'

Gerry Rennie was staring at her. He didn't deny it.

'Based on what you've just confirmed to us,' Robyn pushed on, 'that threat will remain.'

'I . . . What do you want me to say?'

From her papers Robyn took out an A4-size copy of the photograph of Gerry Rennie with Fi. She put it on the coffee table in front of him, facing his way.

'It's a copy,' she told him. 'The original is locked away.'

'You're going to blackmail me?' Rennie barked.

'The police don't know about this photograph,' Robyn said. 'It'd be between you and us — and, of course, whoever made it and sent it to Catriona.'

'What do you want?'

'Your help.' Robyn smiled, a reasonable and practical dealmaker now. 'That's all.'

'What kind of help?'

'When the police come and tell your family the news that the evidence against my client is phony, we want you to ensure they accept it. We want you to persuade your mother that my client is innocent of any wrongdoing, and is in fact a victim.'

He gazed dismally at her, waiting for the inevitable. 'Or else?'

'Or else we take this photograph to the police and let things take their course.'

His face darkened. He looked again at the photograph on the coffee table, then up and into Fi's eyes.

Cat took Fi's hand and was pleased, glancing at her, to see she was staring right back at Gerry Rennie.

'What if I try to persuade them and fail?' he asked.

'We'll know you tried,' she said. 'We may also find it helpful if you were public about your acceptance that the evidence was faked.'

'Public?'

'You know a number of reporters. They'll be asking for updates every day, I'm sure . . .'

He sat very still, his eyes on the photograph.

'I'll do it,' he said. Then he lifted his eyes to Fi again. 'I'm sorry,' he said. 'I'm really sorry.'

Cat looked at her sister's profile, saw her chin rise a little. 'Thanks, Gerry,' she murmured. 'Thank you — very much.'

CHAPTER THIRTY-FIVE

6.46 p.m.

'Managed to find it, then?' Gerry Rennie said, uselessly, when Lola and Kirstie arrived at the run-down industrial estate.

'The directions were perfectly clear,' Lola said, as Rennie set about unlocking a padlock on a gate in a tall metal fence topped with lethal-looking razor wire.

When Kirstie had called and said she and Lola were on their way to the Rennie home in King's Park, he'd responded with gruff alarm. 'Don't want to upset Ma any more than I have to,' he'd told her, and suggested they come to his office instead.

He went first, holding the gate then closing and padlocking it after them.

'Can't be too careful,' he muttered when he saw Lola's face.

She took in the ramshackle buildings that formed a U around a grubby yard. Business signs told her this was home to a specialist in removing scratches from cars, a locksmith and a supplier of unspecified "goods".

Five minutes later, and through two heavily secured doors, and they were in an untidy upstairs room under the glare of strip lights. The windows were barred.

Can't be too careful.

'Tea?' he said, looking about, as if trying to remember what he'd done with his kettle.

'We're fine,' Lola said.

She peered about. There were shelves and shelves of ring binders, and beneath them filing cabinets. 'What business are you in, Mr Rennie?'

He bridled a little. 'Any reason why I should tell you?'

'Not particularly.'

'I'm in property, as it happens. Buying, renovating, selling on. Some letting when there are council contracts. Asylum seekers, homeless families, that kind of thing. Shall we?'

He sat on a creaking office chair behind a cheap-looking desk and gestured for Lola and Kirstie to sit on a blue fabric bench against the wall. He looked more downbeat than Lola had seen him before. He said, 'This is about the evidence, isn't it?'

'The evidence?' Lola enquired.

'The photo and the voice recording.' He looked momentarily wrong-footed. 'I thought . . .'

'You thought what, Mr Rennie?' Kirstie enquired.

'I . . . Nothing.' He shut his mouth.

Lola watched his growing unease. Either he'd known all along that the evidence was dubious, and had anticipated its exposure . . . or he'd somehow — and quickly — got wind of what the cyber specialist had discovered that afternoon.

'We're not here about the evidence,' she told him, but made a mental note to come back to the topic before they were finished.

He watched them warily, relaxing and looking relieved when Lola asked about the night Fiona Balfour had been followed by a car.

'Aye, I remember that,' Rennie said, forehead creasing. 'What about it?'

'Do you remember when it was?' Kirstie asked. 'The date? The time?'

He shook his head. 'End of July. Early August. A Saturday, I think. It was dark, but only just. After ten, I'd say. I could probably tell you when Sean called me. Let me look at my call record.'

He took out his phone and began scrolling, peering hard at the screen, shaking his head and muttering now and then. 'Here,' he said, at last. 'Aye, this is it. He rang me at 10.24, evening of Saturday the twenty-seventh of July.'

'Can we see?' Lola said, leaning forward for the phone.

He drew back. 'Not without a warrant. I know my rights.'

Knowledge instilled in him from a young age by his criminally minded mother, no doubt.

'Tell us what Sean said to you,' she said.

Gerry took his time thinking about it. 'He said, "Some creep's tried to scare Fi." That someone had followed her home in a car and driven at her, just near the flat. He said the guy took off, but could I go over and drive about with him. See if we could find the prick.'

'And did you go over?'

He nodded. 'We drove about. Pretty fucking pointless, though. We stopped a couple of gangs of lads and asked them if they'd seen anything, but none of them had.'

'Did Fiona come with you?' Lola said.

'Nuh. Sean said she wouldn't come down. Whole thing had shit her up and she was all for barricading herself in the flat.'

'Did you believe her?'

'Did I . . . ?'

'Did you believe what she'd told Sean — that she'd been followed?'

He watched them carefully for a moment. 'Why wouldn't I? Sean believed her, so . . .'

'Sean have any idea who it might be?'

His expression changed and his eyes hardened. The shutters were down.

'So he did,' Lola said.

'I never said that.'

Lola put her notepad away and nodded to Kirstie. The two of them got up.

'That it?' Gerry said, looking relieved as he rose to escort them out.

'Earlier, you thought we were here about the evidence,' Lola said conversationally, hitching her bag onto her shoulder. 'You thought we'd come to tell you it was a pack of lies, didn't you?'

He watched her, his nostrils flaring.

Angry? Scared? Or both?

'You already knew it, didn't you, Gerry?'

He said nothing. She heard him swallow.

'The question I'm asking myself,' she went on, nicely, 'is whether you knew it was fake when you and your Ma handed it in to us . . . or whether you just found out today — around, or shortly after, the time we did.' She paused for effect. 'Which is it?'

Gerry Rennie's top lip curled back in a snarl.

'I'm not answering any more questions without a solicitor.'

'That's fine,' Lola said pleasantly, and looked to the door. 'This the way out, is it?'

* * *

7.29 p.m.

She checked her phone as Kirstie pulled away from the kerb. There was a text from Pierce, saying he'd fixed up a Teams call with two detectives from Merseyside Police for nine thirty the next morning.

Good, she typed back. *See that DS Vaughan is there, please.*

Next she listened to a voice message from Robyn McArthur. She and Catriona Balfour had arranged for Fiona to stay in a shared safe house linked to the women's refuge. There'd be other women staying there, and a volunteer warden present all night. Ms McArthur had the address, should the police need it, but she didn't want to share it over the phone, for obvious reasons. It would be fine to call her at any time.

Still nothing from Joe.

'Y'okay, boss?' Kirstie asked, as she pulled onto the motor-way, and Lola wondered if she'd sighed aloud.

'Aye, Kirstie,' Lola said, biting her lip, eyes out on the darkening city. 'Aye. I'm fine.'

CHAPTER THIRTY-SIX

9.55 p.m.

'I hate it.'

Fi stood in the middle of the pink carpet, gazing miserably around at the bright little bedroom.

'A *single bed*?' she cried. 'I haven't slept in a single bed since I was in halls at uni!'

'It's safe,' Cat said, trying not to sound as annoyed as she felt. 'And remember, for some of the women staying here, this is near luxury after the hell they've been through.'

If Fi got Cat's meaning, she didn't show it, but continued to pout sulkily at the room's basic furnishings.

She turned suddenly. 'The bathroom's not shared, is it?'

'There are two,' Cat said. 'You share one with one other person and her young son.'

'Oh, *what*?' Fi threw her bag down, like a child having a tantrum. 'No, Cat. I'm not staying here. If I can't go back to the farm, then take me to a hotel. This is ridiculous! Why would you even *think* of taking me to some halfway house *dump* like this?'

'I want you to be *safe*. There are other people here who can keep an eye on you. There's an overnight volunteer who sleeps downstairs. You can wake her up any—'

'I'm not doing it.' She grabbed her bag off the floor and made for the bedroom door, then stopped and whirled round to Cat. 'I know what this is really all about,' she said nastily. 'It's not about me at all.' She gave a little laugh. 'It's about Lynne. You couldn't save her. Christ, you didn't even try. And you've spent the rest of your life making up for it. Well, you're not going to make amends to her by controlling every aspect of *my life*. I won't have it!'

CHAPTER THIRTY-SEVEN

Monday 31 October
9.03 a.m.

Lola could tell the three people on the screen were unhappy before any of them spoke. They sat in a glum row in a bright room: a young man in a grey jumper; an older, thick-set chap with grey hair in a dark suit and tie; and a woman in her thirties in a green suit, with a sharp face and a severe blonde bob. The two men looked shifty, the woman ready for a fight.

'Can you hear us all right?' Lola called brightly, fixing an expectant smile.

'Yes, fine,' the older of the two men grunted.

'Good. Well, good morning, and thank you for agreeing to talk to us so quickly.'

She quickly introduced Pierce, Kirstie and Anna. The four of them occupied two sides of a table in one of the meeting rooms and faced the screen on the wall.

The older man said he was DCI Mark McCaffrey, then introduced the man at his side as a detective sergeant, and the woman on his right as a senior corporate communications manager with Merseyside Police.

Lola groaned. A corporate comms manager in a meeting was never a good sign.

'Before we begin, I want to flag that we have concerns,' DCI McCaffrey began.

'Oh?' Lola raised her eyebrows.

He cleared his throat. 'We are confident you'll find this is a dead-end line of enquiry.'

'I see . . .' Lola murmured, and stole a glance at Pierce beside her, studying his apparently unruffled profile. He'd set the call up. Had he said something to their colleagues in Merseyside to prompt this defensiveness? 'Would you care to explain?'

The DCI on the screen shared brief glances with the colleagues flanking him. The woman gave him a little nod. A rehearsed performance, then. 'We've looked at the information your colleague sent over and we don't believe the patterns match.'

Lola sat in perplexed silence. Anna Vaughan was looking at her now, a frown wrinkling that smooth, tanned forehead.

'You'll need to talk me through your thinking,' Lola said, pen poised on her pad, breathing slowly.

A muttered conference at the other end of the Teams call, during which time Lola's ire swelled in her chest. It was the sergeant's turn to speak.

'While there are surface similarities,' he said in a thick Scouse accent, eyes firmly on the notes on the desk before him, 'we are clear, having looked more closely at the details you sent over to us, that these are different crimes, committed by different perpetrators.'

'Meaning what, precisely?' Lola said, just about containing her anger. There was something going on here. The presence of the corporate comms manager, who now glared smugly out of the screen at her, suggested that 'something' was politics.

'The victim in our case, Mr Darren Flanagan, was a business owner,' the DS said, eyes still down. 'He owned two bars: one in Lark Lane, a trendy student area of the city, and another in the city centre.'

'And?' Lola said.

The gruff DCI cut in: 'His businesses were scrupulously run, and the accounts watertight. There was no question of any involvement in gang-related crime, nor that his murder was the result of a revenge attack. While the crime remains unsolved,' he rattled on, 'we believe his death to have been the result of mistaken identity. So as far as your crime is concerned—'

'Forget motive for a minute,' Lola cut in. 'The MOs are similar — going by the reports we've seen.'

The DCI pulled a pained face.

'Not only the MOs,' she went on, 'the whole setup. The male victim was shot dead, female left unharmed — though yours died of exposure. Also, the locations where the victims were found: only metres from a popular path through a park that would be busy with dog-walkers from dawn onwards. Then there's the time: victims likely left there after midnight. Come on — the similarities are clear as day!'

'The victims weren't tied together in our case,' the DS chipped in.

'So the killer's innovated,' Lola pointed out.

Another whispered conference. This time someone at the Liverpool end had the cheek to mute the microphone. Lola thought she could guess who, as she watched the comms manager lean in to issue unheard commands.

The mic was unmuted.

The comms manager took over now. 'We are concerned not to cause any further distress to either of the victims' families in this case. We won't be cooperating with your investigation for the reasons we've already provided.'

'I'm sorry?' Lola barked. 'And your victims' families — don't they have a say? Wouldn't they want you to follow up any lead that might result in a conviction?'

DCI McCaffrey said, 'Mr Flanagan's family are clear their son's murder was a case of mistaken identity—'

'And the young woman? Ms . . .' She consulted the report before her. 'Ms Wilson?'

The older man's eyes swivelled to the comms manager.

'We have provided you with our views,' the woman said. 'That's the extent of the help we're able to give.' She sat back.

'Let me make sure I understand your position correctly. Based on the fact that your man, Mr Flanagan, was not a known criminal,' Lola said icily, 'you believe, while our murder was gang-related, yours was a mere case of mistaken identity.' She leaned forward, clenching her fists as the desire to jab at the screen with a finger was so strong. 'What if I told you we don't believe Sean Rennie was killed because of his gang connections?'

More muttering.

'I'm sorry,' the DCI said, lifting his head from the whispered conversation. 'We can't help.'

They said their chilly goodbyes and cut the call.

* * *

9.35 a.m.

'Lola? Lola Harris?' Charlie Quigley said. 'Long time no hear! No doubt you're after something . . .'

'Quite possibly,' Lola said, smiling at her old colleague's acuity. 'Though I'm always happy to talk to you, you know that. Is now a good time, or . . . ?'

'Aye. Aye, it's fine. And I'm on my own too, in case you were wondering.'

She softened him up with brief questions about his wife and daughters, eyes on the grinding traffic of the M8 below the meeting-room window. She turned the topic back to work: 'How long you been with Merseyside Police now, Charlie?'

'Coming up on eight years. How? Don't tell me you're thinking of swapping the Clyde for the Mersey?'

'Not yet. Listen, Charlie, I'm after the inside line on something. I'm getting the corporate comms brush-off on a case I'm interested in.'

'Ah . . .'

And with that single syllable she gathered Charlie knew exactly what case she was talking about.

'The Flanagan–Wilson murder,' he said.

'I need help, Charlie.'

'You talk to Mark McCaffrey?'

'Aye. Him, a DS and a corp-comms control freak.'

'Defensive, were they?'

'Practically *off*ensive. What are they so afraid of?'

The 'they' was deliberate: a figurative tug on his sleeve, pulling him apart from his colleagues.

Silence. Then a whistling of air between teeth.

'What they're afraid of,' Quigley said, 'is the male victim's dad.'

'Oh? Why?'

'Kenny Flanagan's a *very* wealthy businessman with fingers in a lot of pies. And a lot of ears ready to indulge every gripe.'

'Is he dodgy?'

'Flanagan? Not in the slightest! A true "man of the people". Proper philanthropist. Been a city councillor for years. His son's murder occurred while he was campaigning to be elected Mayor of Liverpool. He lost out to another candidate and blamed our investigation for "tarnishing his reputation", because we started looking for gang links Darren might have had and . . . well, the newspapers got word.'

'And were there any? Gang links, I mean?'

'None that we found.'

'This was six years ago. Why the caution now?'

He chuckled darkly. 'Because Kenny Flanagan's only gone and put his hat in the ring for police commissioner of Merseyside, hasn't he? The election's in three months' time.'

'I see.' Lola nearly laughed.

'So you can understand where this leaves us. He might be the new boss.'

'His own son, though, Charlie,' Lola murmured, eyes on the traffic. 'Doesn't Flanagan care who killed him?'

'Oh, he cares. A very great deal. I'd say it's eaten him up. I'd even say it's the reason he's got his eyes on the commissioner's job — so he can sort out what he sees as our "deplorable incompetence", quote, unquote. He's spent thousands — and I mean tens, if not *hundreds*, of thousands — on private investigators.'

'Has he?'

'All under the radar. The best people from London. Plus a couple of ex-FBIers. McCaffrey meets him and members of his investigative team every two weeks.'

'Wow. And yet — nothing?'

'Not in five years.'

Lola took a deep breath.

'Does he really believe it was a case of mistaken identity?' she pressed.

'I'm not sure. Mistaken identity is the narrative and it's carved in stone. Folk here have their own suspicions, of course.'

'Oh?'

'This is all off the record, isn't it? I mean—'

'Absolutely,' she said, sensing what was coming.

'I think he's terrified it's something to do with him and his business dealings. That someone offed his boy in an act of revenge. He's trying to reassure himself that's not the case by finding the real culprit.'

'Thank you for talking to me, Charlie,' she said, coming away from the window and easing into a chair. 'I mean it. Thinking aloud, though, I'm wondering where this leaves my enquiry.'

'If I were you, I'd go to Flanagan direct.'

'Aye, and how's that going to go down with McCaffrey?'

'Did he tell you explicitly not to contact him?'

'Well, no . . .'

'Look, Lola, no way is McCaffrey going to sanction you talking to Flanagan. You're just going to have to brass-neck it. And you know the old saying — ask for forgiveness, not permission.'

'Aye, well . . .'

'Go to Kenny Flanagan. Ask for his help. See what he says.'

'What about the other victim? Darren's fiancée.'

'Amber Wilson? Her mum's great. The father died a year or so after the murders.'

'How do I get in touch with the mum?'

'Patricia Wilson's the headteacher at Mossley Hill Academy. She's sensible. And she has a theory or two of her own.'

'Oh?'

'Talk to her. See what you think.'

'Thanks.' She scribbled the name on her pad. 'She wasn't about to leave him, was she? Amber, I mean. She wasn't about to break off her engagement to Darren?'

He made ruminating noises. 'Not that I'm aware. I seem to think they were only a month away from getting married. I think everything was on track with the wedding.'

'A *month*?'

'Something like that. Why?'

Lola didn't answer, but her mind was now doing somersaults.

'Do you have a theory, Charlie?'

'About who did it? No, I don't,' he said. 'Honestly, it's the single most baffling case I've come across. You wouldn't believe the amount of trouble it's caused.'

She came off the phone to find Kirstie peering in at her through the wee window in the meeting-room door. She waved at her to come in.

'That was Jonno on the phone, boss. He's been to see Fiona Balfour's neighbours in Pollokshields. He reckons you might wanna head over there yourself. Something interesting's come up.'

CHAPTER THIRTY-EIGHT

10.02 a.m.

'I'm sorry for what I said,' Fi muttered, eyes down. She lay her spoon down beside her bowl of untouched muesli. 'About Lynne.'

'It's okay,' Cat said. 'It was hurtful, but I know you were upset.'

They fell silent, each of them gazing gloomily about the too-bright breakfast room. The hotel was linked to the airport, despite being at least two miles from the terminal building. Part of a chain, it was clean and anonymous. People spent one night here, two max, before moving on to other, more exciting destinations. There were a couple of families — one with a pair of obstreperous under-fives having a meltdown — but the rest were business people, looking weary in their grey suits.

The ideal place for a woman to hide from her enemies.

Cat had booked Fi in using a last-minute website. Fi had asked her to stay with her, suggesting they request a twin room, but Cat made excuses. Fi's words at the safe house had cut her deeply. They'd been spoken in anger, yes, but she needed to be apart from her. Returning this morning, Cat felt calmer. Sanguine, at least.

'You couldn't have helped her,' Fi said now, looking Cat in the eye. 'Lynne, I mean. I know you think you should have done more, but . . . honestly, she decided what she wanted and . . . well, it was a kind of death wish in the end, wasn't it?'

'Do you think?'

'Well, yeah . . . Don't you?'

'Talk about something else.'

''Kay. Do you want coffee? I mean, it's not very nice, but—'

'I'm fine. Listen, Fi. I've been thinking — and talking to Robyn. I don't think you can stay here for long. Hotels hold data, and data can be hacked. You're here under a false name, but they could trace my credit card. I think you need to be away from the city.'

'But that's what I've been saying! I want to go back to the farm. I felt safe there. I could—'

'I know.' Cat stalled her with a hand. 'But you know what the police think, and Robyn agrees with them. It's too risky.'

Fi started to cry. Tears streamed down her cheeks.

'That cottage is lovely but it's isolated,' Cat went on. 'It's a distance away from the main house. There's no internet connection or mobile signal. I'm not convinced Tom or Diana would hear you from the house if anything . . . if something . . .'

'Why can't I stay in the main house?'

Cat stared.

'I could, couldn't I? The place is huge! There are empty bedrooms in the attic. I've seen them. One was an old nursery. Why can't I stay up there?'

'Maybe,' Cat said, thinking it quickly through, trying to envisage scenarios. 'Maybe. I'll talk to Robyn. If she thinks it could work, I'll get on to Tom and Diana. But, Fi — no promises, okay?'

CHAPTER THIRTY-NINE

10.16 a.m.

'Two of you!' The stout white-haired woman narrowed her eyes, then pressed her lips together in disapproval or bewilderment. 'Well, you'd better come in.'

She stood back to let Lola and Kirstie pass into the vast square hallway of the ground-floor flat. Doors went off in every direction, and a passage led away towards the back of the flat, towards the kitchen, perhaps.

Lola knew the flats on Fotheringay Road were huge. Desirable too, flying off estate agents' listings in days, if not hours. She'd heard this was the most desirable street in Glasgow's Southside, though it was still looked down on by the denizens of the city's classy, academic West End.

Mrs Grant closed the door behind them and eyed them beadily. She wore a cashmere jumper and purple tweed skirt. She was about eighty, her white hair folded and pinned neatly to her scalp.

'Thank you for seeing us, Mrs Grant,' Lola said nicely. 'Is there somewhere we could sit, perhaps?'

'Kitchen,' the woman barked. 'Follow me.'

She led them down the passage, making a dog leg into a bright, high-ceilinged kitchen.

'The kettle's just boiled,' she said as they took their seats at an oak table.

'We're fine, thank you.'

'Very well.' A small, exasperated sigh.

'This is uncomfortable for you, I expect,' Lola said, when Mrs Grant had taken her own seat.

'Frankly, it is.'

Lola waited, knowing an explanation would come.

The woman rolled her eyes and sighed again. 'If you must know, the neighbours expected something like this. Mr Rennie and his "partner" were not . . . like the other residents.' She pursed her lips, tilted her head as if waiting for Lola to give some signal that she knew exactly what the older lady meant.

'You'll need to explain a wee bit,' Lola said, mildly.

Nostrils flared. 'He was of a *different class*. So was she, though at least she was pleasant. Yes. A nice girl, really. *Goodness* only knows what she saw in *him*.'

'What did *you* see in Sean Rennie, Mrs Grant?'

'An aggressive manner. Verging on brutish, I would say. A thug.'

'Would you care to expand?'

'Not particularly! Besides, I already provided your colleague with my assessment of Mr Rennie's character.' She narrowed her eyes in grim satisfaction.

'Indeed,' Lola said. 'You also told DC Gillies about some—' she glanced at her notebook for Jonno's wording — '"shredded black paper" on the stairs.'

'Yes, he seemed very interested in that. I can't begin to imagine—'

'Mrs Grant, would you tell me what you told him?'

After some huffing and puffing, the woman explained how she had come across broadly scattered fragments of black paper at the bottom of the stairs one morning, sometime after ten. That she'd nearly slipped on the stuff.

'Packing, I thought. You know the sort of thing they put in boxes. Decorative — so that when you open it, out come all these *bits*. Usually it's ribbon or straw. Anyway, it was *everywhere*. All the way from the doorway to the steps and up as far as the first landing.' She shook her head.

'Who else saw it, Mrs Grant?' Kirstie asked.

'She did — the girl. Rennie's girlfriend. Came hurrying down, late for her train, no doubt. "Have you seen this mess?" I said. "Oh, dear," she said. Not a care in the world, that one! Just sort of *frowned* at it, then went hurrying on out, kicking through the mess like leaves.'

'Can you describe the fragments? Were they of a particular shape?'

'I can't remember that!' A look of disgust.

'Can you recall when this was?'

'I—' She stopped and put a hand to her mouth. '*Spring*,' she said at last. 'Yes, because some of it had got outside and had sort of fluttered into the flowerbed out at the front and got caught in the petals of the snowdrops. I remember thinking it looked like black teeth in a beautiful mouth.'

'So, what — February?'

'Possibly. Or early March.'

'Who cleaned it up, the mess?' Lola asked now.

'Maura did it.'

'And she is . . . ?'

'Maura Franklin, across the close.' She nodded towards the wall.

'Thank you, Mrs Grant,' Lola said, rising, thoughts whirling.

* * *

10.42 a.m.

Kirstie knocked on the neighbour's door while Lola checked her phone and found a text from Charlie Quigley, with Kenny Flanagan's private mobile number. A second text read: *You didn't get this from me okay? As I said — best to start with Pat Wilson. Just contact the school.*

The door opened and a young woman in running gear beamed out at them.

'I was just about to make some work calls,' she said, 'but they can wait. Come in.'

The flat was bright and modern, expensively minimalist and completely spotless. Ms Franklin led them into a living room where a mid-century-style leather sofa and armchairs were grouped around a glass coffee table.

'Coffees? Teas?' she asked smartly. 'I've got oat milk and soya but no dairy, I'm afraid.'

'We're fine,' Lola assured her, perching on one of the very low settees.

'Is this about upstairs?' Ms Franklin said, taking one of the armchairs. 'I mean, of course it is. Why else would you be here?'

'Bits of black paper,' Lola said, interested to see her reaction. 'Spilled out in the close a few months back. Mrs Grant says you cleared them up.'

The young woman stared, lips parting in confusion. Then a memory appeared to dawn, only to be replaced by more confusion. 'Oh, yes! But . . . I don't understand. What do you . . . ?'

'Did you clear up the mess, Ms Franklin?'

'Yes, I did.' She shrugged, then began to look irritated. 'I'm sorry, but you'll need to explain what this is about. Are you saying I did something wrong, or . . . ?'

'Not at all. How did you clear it up?'

'Oh . . . erm . . . with the handheld vacuum thing. I . . . er . . .'

'Can you describe the bits of paper?'

She stared past them, then scanned the ceiling, her lips working as she sifted through her memory.

'Just tiny bits of paper. The size of pennies. Different shapes. Quite a lot of them. Like a kind of confetti. Do you think it has something to do with what happened to the people upstairs, or—'

'What shapes, Ms Franklin?'

She took a breath and began to look pissed off.

'They were all different, okay?' She shook her head, looking mystified. 'I don't remember any more than that.'

'And did you empty the vacuum cleaner at some point afterwards?'

The woman was staring at her now in something like stunned realisation.

'Ms Franklin?'

'It broke!' she said, then clamped a hand over her mouth like a child who's said a naughty word. She took it away again and laughed. 'Oh, yes — it *broke*!'

'You're saying—'

'A day or two after I cleaned up the mess. I bought a new one but I didn't throw the old one away. I thought I'd take it to one of those repair places.' She rose — almost jumped — from the armchair. 'I've still got it. And . . . I don't think I bothered to empty it.'

They followed her into the hallway, where she was already rooting around in a beautifully kept walk-in cupboard.

Within a couple of minutes they were in the immaculate kitchen, Lola holding the broken machine in gloved hands, while Maura lay lengths of kitchen roll on her worktop.

'You press the red button down hard and it pops open. Do you want me to . . . ?'

'I know how it works,' Lola said, positioning the plastic cylinder low over the kitchen paper.

She pressed the button and the trap came stiffly open, releasing a quantity of dusty detritus. Among the mess were hundreds of tiny black paper shapes.

'That's it, isn't it?' Maura asked. 'That's what you were talking about.'

Kirstie's phone was going. 'Catriona Balfour,' she said quietly to Lola. Lola nodded and Kirstie ducked out into the hallway to take the call.

'Do you want a bag or something?' Maura said now.

'I've got one,' Lola said, going into her bag for gloves. 'I'm sorry, Ms Franklin, but would you mind leaving me for a few minutes?'

A thrilled look in her eyes, the young woman backed out of the room.

Lola used tweezers to lift a number of the paper cut-outs in turn, examining them under one of the downlights beneath the kitchen cupboards. The first was a tiny bat, wings outstretched. The second, a grinning Halloween pumpkin. The third a skull and crossbones.

'I'll be damned,' she murmured to herself, as the door behind her opened and Kirstie reappeared, phone in hand.

'Halloween confetti,' Lola said, holding out a hand so Kirstie could see the skull and crossbones pinned by the tweezers. Then she saw Kirstie's face. 'What's wrong?'

'Catriona Balfour's taking her sister back to Ladymere Farm.'

'*What?*' She lay the tweezers carefully down on the kitchen roll.

'She didn't want to stay at the safe house, and she hated the hotel. Cat says she has no choice.'

'It's not safe for her.'

'I know that. Apparently she's going to stay with the family in the main house. What can we do?'

'Find out when she'll be there, then you go see her. Try and get the community safety people over to check on the accommodation, advise them on locks, that kind of thing. Then at least they'll have a local contact.'

She checked the time on her phone.

'I'm seeing Rita Rennie with DS Vaughan at eleven thirty,' she said. 'Let's get this lot bagged and away to IB for a fingerprint check, not that I'm holding out much hope.'

'So, she telling the truth?' Kirstie said, eyeing the black confetti.

'God knows. She could have scattered it herself, couldn't she?'

Before leaving she asked Maura Franklin if she'd ever seen dead flowers — specifically blackened roses — tied to the railings across the road from the flat's main entrance.

'Dead flowers? Why would . . . ? Oh. Oh, God. Something horrible's going on, isn't it?' She bit her lip, all good cheer gone. She put her hands to her mouth. 'That poor kid. You know, we were chatting once. She mentioned — almost in passing — that she had this *enemy* from her past. That's what she said: an enemy. Someone who was out to get her. She was right, wasn't she?'

CHAPTER FORTY

11.26 a.m.

She and Anna Vaughan were just streets away from the Rennie house, waiting at lights, when Lola found her eyes resting on several bouquets of flowers tied to railings by the side of the road — no doubt marking the site of a fatal accident. She'd been thinking about Fiona Balfour and the confetti, and wondering if the dead flowers on the railings opposite her and Sean's flat had been real too. And suddenly she remembered another bouquet of dead flowers tied to a fence, one she'd seen with her own eyes, only days before. Heard, too, words spoken in a hectoring, upper-class voice.

She asked Anna to try Jeremy Warren's number and to put her phone on loud speaker. Anna did so, but the park manager's phone was off and not taking messages.

There was nothing for it. They'd have to go to Pollok Park and see for themselves, straight after their meeting with the bereaved mother.

* * *

'How are you, Rita?' Lola asked when Gerry Rennie led her and Anna into the smoky conservatory.

Rita Rennie, installed at the head of the marble-topped table, a pink cigarette propped between her fingers, peered at Lola and said nothing.

'Want me to stay, Ma?' Gerry asked.

She nodded. 'Get me a glass of water, son.'

Lola eased herself into the same seat she'd occupied last Thursday, determinedly adopting an unruffled air. Inside she felt anything but.

'You want to know how I am?' Rita Rennie said now, eyeing her steadily. She lifted the gold filter of her cigarette to her lips, and drew long and hard before releasing a white plume. 'My boy's still dead. I feel exactly the same as I did last week, and will for the rest of my days.'

'I'm sorry.'

'Who's she?' Rita asked Lola, nodding to Anna.

'Detective Sergeant Anna Vaughan,' Anna said smartly, before Lola could introduce her. 'I'm sorry for your loss, Mrs Rennie.'

Rita all but rolled her eyes.

Gerry was back with a glass of water, stepping round the back of his mother's chair and placing it solicitously on a gold coaster before giving her shoulder a squeeze. Rita put a hand over his, then nodded to the chair alongside her. Gerry took it.

'Go on, then.' Rita's eyes were back on Lola, gold filter moving back to her pink-painted lips. 'Say what you've got to say to me.'

Then get out? Unspoken, but surely what she was thinking. *Fine.* She wanted nothing more than to get away. To drive as fast as she could to Pollok Park.

'The evidence you provided had been faked,' Lola said. 'Cleverly but not expertly. It would have fooled most people.'

Rita smoked and watched her through angry, narrowed eyes, while Lola explained what Robyn McArthur's expert had found. While she spoke, Lola observed Gerry's demeanour. He was unhappy and uncomfortable. Not just in their presence but in the presence of his mother. Why? Had there been some falling out? Was it about the faked evidence or something else?

Anna sat at Lola's side, cool and collected, slender legs crossed, manicured hands folded in her lap. She was wearing a scent Lola couldn't place. Or was it skin cream? Shampoo, even? Whatever it was, it smelled expensive.

'We'll commission our own digital forensic analysis,' she said in conclusion, 'but it might take some days. We expect similar results, but it's what any court would expect.'

Rita said nothing. She finished her cigarette and slid another from the flat white packet. This one was peacock blue. Lola caught Gerry's eye. He looked sharply away.

Rita flicked her lighter, a heavy-looking malachite thing, and lit up.

'How did you receive the photographs, Rita?' Lola asked.

'Came through the letterbox,' Rita said, through a cloud of freshly exhaled smoke.

'Stamped?'

'Hand-delivered. My name on the envelope. No address. No return address, either.'

'When was this?'

'Don't remember.'

'Do you still have the envelope?'

Rita shook her head.

Lola watched her, trying to work out what the woman was thinking. What she really *wanted*.

'Did you know, Rita?' Lola asked her. 'Did you know they were fakes when you gave them to us?'

'How dare you?' Her expression changed from one of contempt to one of disgust. Her chin went up and her nostrils flared. 'It's her, isn't it? I'm not bloody stupid.'

Lola waited for Rita to go on.

'Bloody little bitch. Making it look like she's been set up. Then she's in the clear, isn't she?'

'Is that *really* what you think?' Lola asked, leaning in.

'Ma, it's not her.'

The three women's eyes turned sharply on him and Gerry Rennie seemed to shrink.

'*What?*' Rita snapped.

'It's not! I know you want it to be her, but it's not. It's . . . something to do with our Sean. Someone came for him, and . . . I don't know.'

Gerry's mother was regarding him as if all she felt was disappointment.

'He's right, Rita,' Lola said, as gently as she could. 'It's not Fiona. The girl's terrified.'

'Terrified of being found out.'

'No.'

'Get out.'

'Rita, listen—'

'I said, *get out*! Gerry, show them out this instant. Before I *puke*.' She turned her head, eyes on the bare yard outside the conservatory.

Lola glanced at Anna, and the two of them got up.

'I'm sorry,' Gerry Rennie muttered when they reached the front door.

'We'll talk again, Gerry,' Lola said, kindly, and meaning the kindness. 'Take care of yourself. And try and talk some sense into your ma, okay?'

* * *

12.17 p.m.

Lola stopped the car in the lane that ran between the fields and the wood, only metres from where she'd found Sean Rennie's body.

'Shit.'

'Is this where it was?' Anna said.

'Right over there. I'm sure of it.'

The bunch of dead flowers she'd spotted tied to the fence, and thought nothing of, was no longer there.

171

CHAPTER FORTY-ONE

12.37 p.m.

'Oh, yes . . .' Mr Warren nodded slowly, eyes away in the distance. 'I did, as a matter of fact. As I think I said to you on Friday, it's one of the several shocking liberties that people seem to feel entitled to take! Tying flowers here, there and everywhere, bits of cellophane coming loose. Forcing the rest of us to partake in their sentimental little gestures. I've even known them tie the things to trees!'

They were in Warren's tidy office in a converted stable block along a lane from Pollok House. Warren sat haughtily at his desk, while Lola and Anna perched on low antique chairs pulled out from one of the whitewashed walls.

'Sorry, Mr Warren,' Lola said. 'Just to be clear, you saw a bunch of flowers tied to the railings near the crime scene, and you removed them?'

'That's right.'

'When did you do this, sir?'

'The next day. Fresh bouquets had arrived, obviously for the dead man. I disposed of those too, then I spotted the dead flowers. I can't believe I missed them before that, but if you say they were there on Sunday, then you must be correct!

I chucked the lot in the back of my Jeep then threw the lot on the compost at the allotments down there.' He nodded through the wall, as if it was invisible and they might see the allotments through it. 'I took the plastic off, and put that in the appropriate bin. Look, what is all this *about*? Has somebody complained, or . . . ?'

'What kind of flowers were the dead ones? Do you remember?'

'What *kind* . . . ? No, I . . . Oh, roses, I think. I remember being careful of the thorns. I don't know *why* anyone would think to . . .'

And on he droned.

* * *

12.48 p.m.

'You're thinking Fiona Balfour was right all along, aren't you?' Anna asked, as the two of them made their way in front of the imposing edifice of Pollok House towards the car park.

'No,' Lola said wearily. 'I'm not thinking anything of the kind, if I'm honest. We have evidence the confetti she described was real. We have an indication that the dead flowers she described may not have been a figment of her imagination. But that's all. We have no evidence as to who put the confetti out in the close, nor that it was scattered there maliciously. And we have no evidence that Fiona Balfour didn't put it, *or* the flowers, there herself. In exactly the same way that we have no evidence that Fiona Balfour didn't commission those faked photographs herself. In fact—' she turned to the DS — 'all we have is yet more complication.'

Lola looked at her watch. 'I'm hungry. There's a café at the Burrell if you fancy a bite? My treat.'

CHAPTER FORTY-TWO

12.50 p.m.

'See? It's beautiful!' Fi cried, twirling in the centre of the attic bedroom.

Sunshine poured in through the south-facing dormer windows overlooking the fields behind the farmhouse, making dust motes sparkle and the many cobwebs gleam.

'Needs a clean,' Cat said.

'It's cleaner than that dump you took me to last night,' Fi said, and her mood was broken. She sat sulkily on the low double bed.

'I was only saying . . .' Cat said. 'All it needs is a feather duster. Look — so long as you're happy.'

'I am now.' A grudging smile.

'Here we are,' Diana Croy called as she came bustling into the room, bearing a tray with a teapot and cups, together with a plate of cake slices. She looked around for a place to lay it, and chose a chest of drawers.

'Thank you, Diana,' Cat said.

'I forgot to say, you'll be sharing a bathroom with the two eldest.' Diana gave her a rueful smile. 'I'm sorry, but all three bathrooms are already taken.'

'That's quite all right,' Fi said, beaming.

Cat recalled her reaction at the safe house the night before when she'd learned she'd be sharing facilities with another woman and her son.

'Is the bed all right?' Diana asked, pulling a face. 'It was Tom's great-aunt's. The bedding's clean, but the mattress is a little old. Tom says, if it sags, we can maybe put a door underneath it.'

'Everything's perfect,' Fi said, sweetly. 'Honestly, I'm so happy to be here.'

The sound of a car drew their attention, bumping into the yard below.

Diana peered out of one of the north-facing windows. 'I think it's the police detective,' she said. 'The young girl.'

'Oh, God . . .' Fi muttered.

'Be nice,' Cat warned her. 'They're doing their best to help you.'

'What, like arresting me and putting me in a cell?'

'Fi . . .'

'I'll go down and let her in,' Diana said. 'Do you want me to send her up here, or . . . ?'

'I think we'll come down,' Cat said. 'I'll bring the tray and the tea things.'

She picked it up, then turned to check Fi was following. But she wasn't. She was standing at the window overlooking the yard, unaware she was being observed, a look of sheer malice on her face.

CHAPTER FORTY-THREE

1.04 p.m.

'This place is incredible!' Anna Vaughan said, when they were at their table in the noisy cafeteria, relieving their trays of plates, cups and cutlery. 'Sort of hidden away right in the heart of the city.'

'Oh, the Burrell's a Glasgow institution,' Lola said. 'I first came here on a school trip in the eighties.'

'I'm amazed I haven't heard about it!'

'It's been shut the past few years while they fixed the roof and stuff.'

'I'll need to bring Nick. He loves the Impressionists. And that Islamic art! So *gorgeous*. Nick lived in Paris when he was a boy and his father used to take him to the Musée D'Orsay all the time. That's why we honeymooned there — well, for a week. Then we took a train to the Riviera. Bliss. That's what I really missed during the pandemic, you know? The chance to travel. Do you like travelling?'

'Me? Oh, not really. I mean, I enjoy a holiday, but . . . well, it's different when it's just you. I went on a walking holiday in Spain once with other people who were on their own. I didn't enjoy it.'

'That's so sad,' Anna said, tossing her blonde hair, tilting her head and frowning in pity.

'Not really. Horses for courses.'

'I'm never sure about coronation chicken,' the DS said now, eyeing Lola's baked potato, piled high with yellow chunks. 'I mean, what is it?'

'It's — well, it's curried chicken, I suppose. A sort of mayo with curry powder and chutney.'

'I know that,' Anna said, picking at her salad. 'It's . . . it's just always seemed to me a bit, well . . . *twee*.'

'Tastes all right,' Lola said. She smiled nicely. 'But tell me, how are you finding things in Glasgow? Bit of a change from London?'

'Oh, it's . . . lovely. It's . . . such a culturally rich place. And you get *so* much house for your money! We bought a place outright, did I say? A four-bed villa in Dumbreck. I mean it needs *work*. Of course it does. And I want to extend out the back.' She beamed, showing a lot of white teeth that Lola suspected were capped.

'And how was the conversion course?'

'Oh, fascinating! I mean, it was a trek going to the college every day. Lovely people, though. So many interesting life stories.' She smiled and ate some salad.

'And any first impressions of the team?' Lola tried not to sound pointed.

'Seem a *really* great bunch. Aidan's a dish, isn't he? Oh, maybe I shouldn't say that. I'm sorry. Me and my big mouth.' She giggled.

Lola said nothing. It *was* quite a big mouth, she thought. It had to be, to contain that many teeth.

'I mean, lovely dress sense and he's so funny.'

Is he?

As if she'd spotted something in Lola's expression, she amended her tone. 'And he seems so *committed*. I mean *genuinely*. He cares about the job and his career.'

Lola nodded.

'I think we're going to be great pals.'

Lola ate her coronation chicken.

CHAPTER FORTY-FOUR

2.25 p.m.

Alistair — Ali — Howe took them to a poky room on the third floor of one of the many buildings that made up the Queen Elizabeth University Hospital in Govan. His office, he'd called it, but it turned out he shared it with two other anaesthetic registrars. It was fusty, with dirty walls, holes in the ceiling and vertical blinds that hung, broken and sad, at a filthy window looking out across the hospital campus.

'Sit down,' he said to her and Anna. 'Sorry, not that chair. The back's broken.'

Lola picked hairs off the brown fabric back of another chair and sat gingerly.

Anna said she preferred to stand. Howe, dressed head to foot in blue scrubs, perched on the edge of a desk and put on an airy look, but Lola could tell he was terrified. His breathing was quick and shallow and he was sweating and kept swallowing drily — as if they'd come to arrest him, or to expose and humiliate him in some way. He struck Lola as a man with things to hide — but what, exactly?

'How can I help?' he said, licking his dry lips.

He was a big guy, tall, broad and dark, with a day's growth of stubble on his face. The rugby-playing type. Handsome in a solid and reliable sort of way. No ring on his left hand, she noticed.

'We want to talk to you about someone we believe you knew while you were at university,' Lola began steadily, watching him for signs he'd been expecting this.

'Oh?' Almost trembling with nerves.

'Her name is Fiona Balfour.'

A swallow. 'Fiona . . . ? I can't . . . I mean, I don't remember everyone I—'

'We believe you were in a relationship with her for a short time,' Lola said. 'You might have heard her name in the news this week. Her fiancé was shot dead.'

'Yes . . .' he said, in a hoarse whisper. 'I remember now.'

Lola nodded.

'When did you see her last, Mr Howe?' Anna asked smoothly.

He glanced at her, then back to Lola. 'I don't remember.'

'Don't you?' Lola said gently.

'Look, I don't know anything about this!' he broke out, high-pitched and panicked.

Behind them the door handle turned. 'Stay out, please!' Howe yelled. 'I'm busy.'

Grumbling from the other side of the door as it was pulled shut.

'I know who you're talking about,' he said, eyes down. 'I'm sorry. It was so long ago and I thought — I *hoped* — it had all gone away.'

He burst into tears, sobbing loudly, pressing the heels of his hands into his eye sockets. 'Oh, God . . .'

'Would you like some water?' Lola asked, though unsure where they'd get some if he did.

'I'm fine.' He gasped and sniffed, swiping at his tears with an expression of acute self-loathing. 'I'm . . . I'm sorry.'

'When did you last see Fiona?' Anna asked again.

He swallowed, eyes still on the floor. 'At uni. When it . . . Look, you obviously know what happened. You know what she accused me of. That's why you're here, isn't it? Well, that wasn't me. It *wasn't!* She had no grounds to accuse me then. You don't think I was involved in what happened to her and that Rennie guy, do you? Oh, God!' He started crying again, big heaving sobs that wracked his body, while he hugged himself. 'I can't believe this is happening again.' He looked up suddenly, his expression changed to one of antagonism. 'I want a solicitor,' he said. 'That's my right, isn't it? You can't question me like this.'

'You're entitled to talk to a solicitor at any time, Mr Howe,' Lola said mildly. 'But you're not under arrest. We're making enquiries, that's all. Following up the leads we have.'

He scowled at them, his face nasty now, his lip curled back. 'What's she told you about me? What *lies* has that bloody bi—' He stopped himself.

'Mr Howe?' Lola asked.

'I'm sorry.' He shut his eyes, calmed himself, taking deep breaths, and hung his head, a picture of misery.

'Where were you on the evening of Saturday the twenty-second of October until the morning of the Sunday?' she asked.

He blinked at her. 'I . . . I can't think. Give me a minute. A week last Saturday?'

'That's right.'

He went into his phone, jabbing and scrolling, shaking his head and muttering to himself.

'Saturday, *Saturday* . . . Yeah, I'd been on nights,' he said at last. 'Friday was my last night here. Got home at eight thirty in the morning and went straight to bed. I went for a run when I woke up and . . . and then I went back home. I got a delivery of food at some point. It'll be on the app, but . . . but I was alone the rest of the evening. I didn't see anyone till the Sunday night when I went for a few beers with a mate.'

'Do you live alone?'

'Yeah.'

'Where, Mr Howe?'

She saw his nostrils contract and his eyes widen as he tried to think of a way not to answer.

'Mr Howe . . . ?'

'An upper conversion on Newark Drive,' he said, swallowing so hard she heard the click.

'Newark Drive . . . in Pollokshields?'

He nodded, eyes averted.

'Not half a mile from Fotheringay Road, in fact. Less.'

Another miserable nod.

She watched him thoughtfully.

'What kind of car do you drive, Mr Howe?'

'What? Why?'

'What kind is it?'

'It's, erm . . . an Audi.'

'Series? Colour?'

His eyes got wider. The man was terrified of something.

'It's an A4. It's blue. Dark blue.'

She nodded.

'The evening of Saturday the twenty-seventh of July.'

'What about it?' He frowned, looking genuinely mystified.

'Remember where you were about ten o'clock?'

'No! Why would I?' He pulled a face.

'Maybe you could check your phone again.'

He breathed, controlling his panic, and began stabbing at his screen again.

'Mr Howe?' Lola prompted after a minute, peering at his face and noting the perspiration on his forehead and upper lip.

'I don't know,' he said at last, looking up at her with stricken eyes. 'I can't remember. If you tell me why you're asking, maybe I can help you?'

Lola levelled her gaze at him. 'You're not planning to leave Glasgow at any point in the next week or so, are you?'

She felt Anna's eyes on her as she spoke.

'Leave . . . ? No, but . . . Look, what's this about?'

She could see he was about to cry again.

'If you remember, you will let us know, won't you?' she said, handing him a contact card. 'Fast?'

* * *

2.51 p.m.

'You think I was too hard on him, don't you?' she said, as they made their way through drizzle towards the car park.

'Maybe a bit,' Anna said. 'He seems like a nice guy.'

'He was about to call Fiona Balfour a bitch. I know he was angry, but it's the ease with which he almost came out with it. It was there in his mouth.'

She glanced at Anna's frowning profile.

'He's a misogynist,' Lola said. 'I can always tell. The kind who's quick to whinge and play the victim.'

'That doesn't mean he's a murderer, though, does it?'

'Not at all.' She pressed her key fob and the car responded with a flash and a bleep. 'In fact,' she said, opening the driver's door, 'my gut feeling is he's most probably innocent.'

CHAPTER FORTY-FIVE

4.13 p.m.

'I've got fifteen minutes,' Patricia Wilson said briskly when she came to the phone. She was breathing heavily, as if she'd been running. Lola suspected it was nerves. 'I've a meeting with some angry parents at half past. Could we get quickly to the point? I . . . I take it this is about Amber.'

'Yes, Mrs Wilson,' Lola said, hunching over her desk, preparing herself for a tricky call. 'And I regret bringing up painful memories for you.'

'Thank you. But you're not "bringing up" anything. I live with bad memories every second of every day.' A cacophony at the other end of the line. 'Let me close this door.'

Lola waited, hearing the bang of a door followed by footsteps. She had the website of Mossley Hill Academy open on the screen in front of her, on the page with the head-teacher's welcome. In her photograph Patricia Wilson was mid-fifties, thin, her fair hair cut short. She looked tired, her smile a little strained.

'That's better.' Another sigh. 'You're calling from Scotland, I understand?'

Her accent was soft, northern English, only mildly Liverpudlian.

'That's right.'

Lola introduced herself, and said she was investigating a case that had some similarities to the one involving Amber Wilson.

'Similarities?' The woman hesitated. 'But the young woman in your case — she's alive?'

'Yes.'

'Thank God . . .'

Lola heard her murmuring to herself. It sounded like a prayer.

'And you've spoken to Chief Inspector McCaffrey about this?' the woman said now.

'I have.'

'Any joy?'

'No.'

'Well! That's Kenny Flanagan's influence, I'm afraid. He's got the lot of them terrified for their jobs. All the energy they *might* be expending on finding the killer of my daughter and Kenny's son, Merseyside Police seem to spending on damage limitation and PR. Not that I blame Kenny. He's in pain.'

'I was advised to come direct to you.'

'By McCaffrey?' She sounded surprised and sceptical.

'No, Mrs Wilson. By . . . a wise colleague. Mrs Wilson—'

'Patricia. Please.'

'Patricia. Who do you think killed Amber?'

Another hesitation. A longer one. Lola looked at the time. It was nearly half past the hour, and time for Patricia's next meeting.

'What makes you think I could even hazard a guess?'

'You must have theories.' She took a risk: 'I think I would, in your shoes.'

She listened to the woman's breathing. 'I'll help you if I can. But I need to know that you'll believe what I tell you. That you won't write me off, like the police here seem to have done.'

'I'll listen to whatever you tell me,' Lola said.

'It wasn't about him,' Patricia said.

'What do you mean?' Lola's body tensed.

'The attack. I don't believe it was about Darren Flanagan. The police do. His father does. But I don't.'

'I see.'

'You think I'm mad as well, don't you? I shouldn't have told you. Maybe I—'

'I don't think you're mad, Patricia.'

Silence. Then: 'Don't you?'

'Why do you think the attack was aimed at Amber and not at Darren? Nothing in the case files suggest that she was the target.'

'Because of what came before.'

'What do you mean?'

Sudden noise at the other end of the line: knocking on a door, then a voice. She heard Patricia Wilson cover the receiver, then her muffled voice speaking.

'I'm sorry. The parents are here. I'll need to go shortly.'

'You mentioned "what came before". What did you mean?'

'Well, McCaffrey dismissed it out of hand, of course. Look, I really have to—'

'Patricia?'

'I've kept it all. I could show it to you, if you came here.'

Lola thought fast, her skin tingling. Tried to picture tomorrow's diary. But what did it matter? This could be . . . everything.

'I can come tomorrow,' she said. 'What time do you finish work?'

More knocking at the door.

'*One minute*,' she heard Patricia snap at whoever it was.

She said to Lola, 'I can see you after four. Come here, to the school. Then we'll go to the house together. I'll take you there too, if you like,' she said, her voice darkening. 'To the park. To the place where they were found.'

CHAPTER FORTY-SIX

5.35 p.m.

'Why don't you stay for dinner?' Fi said, for about the third time. 'Diana says there's plenty of food, and the children would love you to see their Halloween costumes.'

'I've got work to do,' Cat said. 'I'm getting behind and people are relying on me.' She stood in the middle of the attic bedroom, hands in jacket pockets, her right palm folded reassuringly round her car keys.

It was true that she had work to do, but she could have stayed. In truth, she needed time alone. To sit in a darkened room, the TV on, to let her muscles relax and her thoughts achieve some sort of peace.

'You'll be fine here,' she said.

Fi nodded, but her eyes were down. She looked unconvinced.

DC Kirstie Campbell had come earlier and stayed an hour, waiting until two local community safety officers had arrived and taken a look around the property. They'd checked the doors and the downstairs windows and seemed satisfied that the house was secure, if isolated. They'd talked to Diana about the need to keep the doors locked at all times

— even for quick trips outside — and left phone numbers, saying help could be here within twenty minutes, any time of day or night.

Diana had seemed jangled by the visit, as if for the first time realising the danger her family, and not just her guest, might be in. But she pulled herself together and launched into a flurry of baking — one that warmed the atmosphere, quite literally, and filled the house with smells of bread, spiced buns and cinder toffee.

All afternoon, Fi was in her element, playing with the two youngest children until the three older ones returned from school, bouncing with Halloween glee, two of them wearing spider web face paint. Fi played mother hen to the younger ones, leading them on imagined "spooky" adventures around the rickety old house, and reading stories with them sitting in a circle on the living-room floor. Cat didn't do kids. One she could handle, preferably under the age of twelve months — or when they were older teens, and you could at least have a conversation.

'I'll get frightened when you're not here.'

Irritation swelled in Cat's mind. *No. I won't let you do this.*

'Diana's here,' she said. 'And Tom. And the kids. Anyway, you wanted to come here. You said you'd feel safe here.'

Indistinct muttering.

'I'll come and see you tomorrow,' Cat said, and turned to go.

Before she'd even got to the door, Fi was up, her arms encircling Cat's neck, fastening her in a hard embrace.

Cat turned.

'You're going to be just fine,' she said, pulling her arms down and away from her throat. 'Nothing's going to happen to you.'

CHAPTER FORTY-SEVEN

7.20 p.m.

'I managed to speak to McCaffrey's senior,' Elaine Walsh explained when Lola rang her at home. There were TV sounds in the background, and the sound of a teenager or two kicking off. 'A Superintendent Yvonne Miles.'

'And?' Lola steeled herself for a no, together with one of Elaine's terse warnings not to rock any boats. To behave herself, for once.

'Reasonable enough woman. A *lot* of respect for McCaffrey, and she made a strong plea for understanding the situation they're in. The England and Wales forces are becoming ever more politicised. We've got to recognise that.'

'But, boss—'

'As I say, she was very reasonable. I explained our interest in their case and said that we wished to interview the families of the two victims. That we'd do so with sensitivity and discretion. There'd be no mention of the visit in any media. Here or in Merseyside.'

'And?' Lola held her breath.

'She said that was okay. But she asked for particular sensitivity where Mr Flanagan is concerned.'

'Meaning?'

'He'd be likely to bring lawyers and PR people to any interview. Any refusal to accept his terms, and he'll walk away.'

'Jeezo.'

'Lola, there's a risk he'll use anything that crops up in an interview as a stick to bash Merseyside with. It could get rough.'

'I'll be discretion itself, boss.'

'Flanagan always wants twenty-four hours' notice, so you should try to get hold of him tonight. I've got a phone number for you. It's a personal one and he doesn't give it out to anyone.'

'I've already got it, boss.'

'Oh? How? Actually — don't answer that.'

Lola didn't.

'Who's doing this, Lola? Do you have any idea?'

Lola shifted her phone to her other ear. 'I reckon it's someone in each of the women's pasts. *Possibly* one of the three people Fiona Balfour named, or someone else she's forgotten to tell us about, but . . . honestly? I don't know. Ask me again when I'm back from Liverpool.'

Elaine was silent for several seconds. Lola could hear the sound of TV adverts coming from another room.

'If he's done this twice, there's a chance he's done it a third — even a fourth — time,' Elaine said.

'I've got two of my DCs searching the Police National Computer for any matching features,' Lola said. 'Including any indication the couples were about to get married.'

'And Fiona Balfour's three named individuals?'

'I spoke to the most likely of them today — the doctor. I'm not convinced he's a realistic suspect, but we're going to talk to him again and check his movements. We've found the other two and my sergeants are speaking to them tomorrow.'

'Have you requested a behavioural profile?' Elaine asked. These could be obtained, and fairly quickly, but at some expense.

'Not yet, boss. If you're happy for me to go ahead . . .'

'Might be an idea. DS Vaughan settling in okay, is she?'

189

'Seems to be, boss.'

Lola suppressed a twinge at the mention of Anna's name. A twinge of what? Doubt?

Plain distaste, more like.

'I take it Fiona Balfour is no longer a suspect in relation to the attack?'

'That's right, boss. Rita Rennie is still convinced she's behind it, though.'

'Tough. Where are we looking into Sean Rennie's so-called business activities?'

'There's nothing jumping out at me. Nothing to suggest he'd done the dirty on any likely individuals. We'll keep looking, but right now I'm almost certain this is nothing to do with Rennie at all.'

More TV noises as Elaine chewed things over. 'You're not wanting to go public on this, are you, Lola?'

'No, boss,' she said. 'Quite frankly, at this stage I think that would be the most damaging thing we could do.'

CHAPTER FORTY-EIGHT

11.37 p.m.

Lola spent the evening at her sister Frankie's in East Kilbride.

Frankie was deputy head of a tough secondary school in South Lanarkshire, and had heard — and seen — it all. If anyone could buck Lola up, it was her.

'The spineless shit,' she said when Lola showed her Joe's last text. She handed the phone back across the kitchen table and gazed at Lola with a mix of pity and angry disbelief. 'How many years of your life have you wasted on him now?'

'Too many, Frankie,' she said choked.

'Prick. Do you want a glass?' she lifted a bottle of red she'd already made a start on. 'It's not bad. Spanish.'

'No.'

'Not even a wee taste?'

'Okay. A mouthful, but then I'm onto Coke.'

Frankie retrieved a glass from a cupboard.

'Maybe you need hypnotherapy. You know it worked on me with the smokes.'

'Joe's not a packet of cigarettes.'

'But what you need is a kind of replacement therapy.'

Lola stared.

'A new fella! Something casual. Safe, obviously, but casual. A bit of fun.'

Lola said nothing. She wanted nothing of the kind. What she *needed* was to delete Joe's very existence — his face, his voice, his *smell* — from her mental hard drive. Once and for all. Maybe hypnotherapy wasn't such a bad idea.

'How's the personal training?'

'Stalled,' she said glumly.

'Well, that's bad.'

'I'm too busy.'

'Rubbish. Exercise is good for your mental well-being.' Frankie topped up her own glass, almost to the rim. 'Though, Christ, I wish I'd known that sooner. At school it was all, *Compete! Thrash the other side! And don't come last, whatever you do!* It's all changed now, thank God. Well, it has in our school. Well-being first. Nothing like a run to reduce stress.'

'Can we talk about something else?' she'd said. 'How's work?'

There'd been no more talk of Joe, but she'd thought of little else throughout their meal. Driving home, it was as if her car was taking her to his house. She could — *should* — have taken the fast orbital road that traversed the hills to join the M77 southwest of East Kilbride, but instead had found herself driving through Busby, then Clarkston, then Newlands and — *oh, God* — into Muirend.

Muirend, where Joe was kept prisoner in that little house.

She breathed hard, her heart racing, as she came along the main road. She felt hot, as if flushed with shame, and wound her window down when she came to a set of lights.

Waiting for green, she groaned.

What's wrong with you?

She put Radio 2 on. They were playing Simple Minds, "Don't You Forget about Me".

She turned it off, swallowing. The lights changed and she drove on.

The streets were empty. Dark but for amber pools every hundred metres or so. Closed shopfronts on one side. Four-storey tenements on the other.

The turn-off was coming up on the left. Then it was half a mile before another left turn, onto the narrow, sloping street where Marie's house was.

A shiver crept over the skin of her arms. She felt helpless, as if a force had entered her and taken over.

Don't do it.

But she'd already pressed the indicator and was slowing for the turn.

No, Lola!

But too late. She was turning the wheel.

She slowed, as if to make the misery last, passing house after house, until she reached the end of the Marie's street.

She stopped, taking deep breaths. So close, but still so far away. She calculated he was only three hundred metres from her now. No doubt in bed already, beside *her*. Maybe he was lying awake, thinking of Lola, while Marie slept the sleep of the self-righteous. Or was he sitting up, watching a film in semi-darkness, alone?

If she drove past, she'd know by the lights. If the house was dark, then they were in bed. But if lights played on the inside of the living-room blinds, then she'd know he was there.

Then what? Get out of the car, climb the steps and tap on the window?

No. But at least she could picture him. Know he was okay. Have a mental image to hold on to.

She turned the wheel and began to creep up the steep street, between the twin lines of parked cars, climbing higher and higher.

And there it was. The house. Tall, narrow, the third in a red sandstone terrace, atop a sloping rocky garden.

She stopped the car and peered up, holding her breath.

And yes, there were lights on. A single lamp, she thought, shining on the blind, and the flickering light from the TV.

Oh, Joe . . .

And what now? Sit here in misery, gazing up?

Her stomach churned and her heart hurt. She felt a sob swell in her like a giant bubble of misery. If she let it grow it might consume her.

Enough.

This was wrong. Toxic.

Stupid. A stupid, dangerous thing to do.

She shouldn't have come here, and needed to get away. Fast.

She drove a little further up the street, then remembered it was a dead end. She spotted a gap between the back of a Toyota and a van, and angled the Audi into it, inching forward, then stopped and reversed, keeping her revs low and quiet. God forbid Joe hear her and peer through the blinds. See her there. Realise she'd ignored his request and come here to, what — *stalk* him?

The turn was tighter than she'd anticipated. The Audi's parking sensors, front and back, bleeped almost continuously.

Her arms wrestled the steering wheel and she began to flush.

Thank God it was late and the street silent. The idea of anyone seeing her struggling like this . . .

She was into the gap now, at ninety degrees, and ready to ease herself out of the turn so she was pointing back the other way.

She put the gear lever into reverse again, eased off the brake and pressed the accelerator, turning, turning—

Kerr-unch, and the sick tinkle of shattered plastic.

'Oh, *Christ* . . .'

She pulled forward, heart racing, got out of the car and hurried, head down, to the back.

She'd collided neatly with the rear corner of the Toyota, shattering its brake light and gouging the paintwork in the process.

'Shit. Shit-shit-shit.'

She looked guiltily up and about.

No one. Only darkness and silence. She scanned the windows.

But no, she hadn't been seen or overheard.

She glanced back at her car and saw she was almost out of the turn, so she climbed quickly back in and manoeuvred out of the squeeze, then drove back to the end of the road, where, breathless and sweating, she pulled in.

What now? She couldn't *leave*. All it would take would be a security camera that had caught her reg. And what then for a police officer who'd caused damage and done a runner? The sack?

No, she had no choice.

She turned on the car's interior light and took a notebook and pen from the glove compartment, then wrote:

Sincere apologies for the accidental damage. I didn't know which house to knock at. Will pay all costs. Please contact me.

She needed a name. Any name. She thought quickly and wrote:

Susan Brown.

She wrote her mobile number, then tore the page from the notebook, got out of the car and scurried back up the hill to plant the note.

Task done, and with one last miserable, shame-ridden glance up at that TV-lit blind, she crept quickly away from the scene of her crime.

CHAPTER FORTY-NINE

Tuesday 1 November
1.34 p.m.

'DS Vaughan says she's just finding a room,' Kirstie said, returning to the table at the motorway service station. 'They'll be ready for us in ten minutes.'

'Best drink up, then,' Lola said, pointing at Kirstie's as-yet-untouched flat white.

Lola went on checking her emails, finding one from DCI Mark McCaffrey, grudgingly agreeing to meet her early evening, once she'd finished with Patricia Wilson and Kenny Flanagan.

For the fiftieth time that day, she checked her mobile. Still nothing from the owner of the Toyota. Another flush of burning shame at the memory of what she'd done — and at how reckless she'd been to go to Muirend at all. What if Joe had seen her down there? What if Marie had? What *then*?

'You okay, boss?'

'Aye. All good.'

They hurried to the car through the drizzle, then Kirstie set up her laptop and tethered it to her phone for internet. Rain spattered the window, blurring any view, and wind rocked the car.

'Can you hear me okay?' Anna's middle-class voice came brightly out of the screen.

'Fine, Anna,' Lola said.

Anna's image became visible. She was in one of the smaller meeting rooms, Aidan Pierce beside her. Lola felt Kirstie tense ever so slightly beside her. DS Pierce's impact on the constable remained tangible and toxic.

She adjusted the volume so they'd be able to hear over the strengthening rain.

'We saw Roddy Jackson first,' Anna began. Lola reminded herself that Jackson's was one the three names Fiona Balfour had given them. 'He's a teacher at St Rufus's Primary School in Renton. Quiet chap — or seemed so at first. Looked frightened to death, but then became quite angry. Turned quite nasty, didn't he, Aidan?' she said to Pierce. Pierce blinked and glowered into the camera. 'Anyway, he said he had no memory of Fiona Balfour at university. Denied hearing anything about the attack on the news. Said he'd sue us if his name ever got mentioned in public. Got *very* heated on the topic of slander. Lots of talk about his "good character".'

'Enough to make anyone suspicious,' Lola commented.

'Turns out he's got an injunction against him, in relation to a Zoe Beaumont of Kirkintilloch. They taught together at a different school. She accused him of stalking. Police involved, lawyers.'

'Jeezo . . . He told you that, did he?'

'No, boss. Aidan found it online.' She turned and gave him a little smile. Pierce accepted it with a self-satisfied smirk.

Lola had the distinct sense there was something going on between the two of them. Had he told her about their poor relationship? That he'd taken a grievance out against her? What else had he said? And how much had the new DS believed?

'Alibis?' she asked, itching with irritation.

'For both dates, boss. He was at his sister's wedding in Angus on the twenty-second of October. Says he was with people from ten in the morning till one or one thirty the next morning. We'll check, of course, though he got very twitchy about the idea — and we were back to the subject of slander and lawsuits all over again.'

'What about the July date?'

'In Menorca with his mother and aunt, from the Friday before until the Friday after.'

'Right.'

Not a very likely suspect, then.

'What about Aoife Norris?'

'She remembers Fiona Balfour very well!' Anna said. 'Seems rather pleased to hear she nearly died.'

'Nice.'

'She's a wedding planner. Seems very busy and pleased with herself. Said over and over that she had no time for this. Dismissive and pretty rude about the suggestion she might have had it in for Fiona Balfour all this time. Said she "gave the little cow what for at the time". Then became all philosophical, saying Fiona had done her a favour. That she'd shown her the boyfriend was a useless piece of you-know-what, and that her life now was pretty damned perfect, and so on and so on.'

'Believe her?'

'I think so. One of those mouthy types who gets it out of her system and moves on.'

Pierce was smirking away. He appeared to speak under his breath, making Anna dart a scandalised glance at him.

'DS Vaughan?' Lola said coldly.

'Sorry, boss.' An ill-concealed smirk from Anna now.

Lola considered calling them out, but thought better of it.

'Alibis for Ms Norris?'

'She had a meeting with two clients early evening on the twenty-second of October. Says she spoke to her mum on Zoom in the evening. Couldn't say when, but she'll check the app. As for July, she was at a friend's house near Falkirk till late on.'

'What happened to her boyfriend? What was his name?'

'Gregg Chadwick, boss. She "doesn't know and doesn't care" — her words. A pretty good indication that she is still angry, whatever she says. Oh, and Alistair Howe called in and spoke to Jonno. He now claims he has an alibi for the twenty-seventh of July. Says a friend came over with beers and they watched films. Want us to follow it up?'

'Yes,' Lola said, feeling oddly deflated. She'd had little hope that any of the names provided by Fiona Balfour would come to anything, but to see the leads dissolve into nothing was still dispiriting. 'Go see him. Look at his car. See if it has tinted windows. Take photos of it — and let him see you doing it. See how he reacts.'

'With pleasure. Oh, one more thing — Aidan's made an appointment with the forensic profiler this afternoon. Hopefully she'll be able to come up with something.'

'Good, but make it plain we've got more info coming in by the hour.'

'Of course.'

Anna blinked and gave a tiny jerk, as if — and Lola realised this with a sick, sinking feeling — for all the world as if she'd received an unseen nudge, or prod, from the person beside her.

'Everything all right, DS Vaughan?' she asked sharply.

'Yes, boss.' A sunny smile now.

Lola pretended to look at her notes, while she got a grip. Vaughan and Pierce flirting? It was a horrible idea.

'Anything else come up on the PNC?' she asked.

'Not yet, boss.'

'Well, keep trying. Focus on any victims who were due to get married in the coming weeks or months.'

She finished the call and she and Kirstie sat listening to the rain for a few moments. Lola didn't ask for Kirstie's reaction, but suspected she probably felt as sick as she did.

CHAPTER FIFTY

4.27 p.m.

Lola sat in the passenger seat of Patricia Wilson's VW Golf, Kirstie in the back, as the headteacher drove them to Sefton Park.

'It's not all that far from the school,' Patricia told them, pulling out of the school car park. She said it in a matter-of-fact way, as if she was talking about something ordinary — a new supermarket maybe. 'I tend to avoid it if I can.'

'I can understand that,' Lola said.

They'd got the preliminaries — the thanks and expressions of regret — out of the way in her office at the school.

'Look, I'm happy to help,' Patricia had said. 'Especially if it might help find out who murdered my daughter. Please have no doubt about that.'

Her pragmatism was a relief. Lola liked her. Her height and slenderness were emphasised by a practical dark trouser suit. Everything about her spoke of sharp efficiency.

They passed along curving boulevards, taking so many minor turns that Lola quickly lost her bearings. Here and there, residential tower blocks appeared between the tops of trees — potential way markers that quickly vanished again.

Lola had been to Liverpool only once before, for a hen party in her twenties. They'd stayed at a hotel by the water, a stone's throw from the Albert Dock, home of the nation's at-the-time favourite morning TV programme. She'd found the city strikingly beautiful, and the people oddly familiar: like Glaswegians with a different accent.

'Sefton Park is known as "Liverpool's lung",' the head-teacher said. 'An oasis for Victorians who lived their lives in a permanent smog from all the new industry.'

The trees had given way to vast swathes of green, stretching out on both sides of the road. Tree-edged path-ways bisected the green, creating expansive triangles of park-land. The place was vast, and had an openness that the more densely wooded Pollok Park lacked.

'The Palm House,' Patricia said, pointing ahead to where a grand, bulbous glass structure showed above the trees.

Lola said nothing. Amber Wilson's body, along with that of her fiancé, had been found only metres from the building. They were nearly at their destination.

Patricia turned into a small car park and pulled on her handbrake. She turned to Lola and her face was drawn and pale. 'Shall we?'

She showed them the way, walking a little ahead, but taking her time, eyes everywhere, as if needing to take it all in — or to check for danger. She led them towards the Palm House, a glass palace that appeared to have an upmarket café inside, then down a side path towards a stream. She stopped beside a giant rhododendron, stepping slightly aside to allow a woman and her dog to pass.

'Amber and Darren were here,' she said quietly, when they were alone again. She had her hands in her jacket pock-ets, her shoulders up as if she had only just felt the cold.

Lola came alongside her, while Kirstie hung back.

'I didn't see her here, of course. A very kind family liai-son officer brought me a few days later. I . . . I needed to see where it happened. Where she was found, at least.'

'I understand,' Lola said.

'This place is always busy. From dawn, there are dog-walkers, joggers, you know? Whoever did this to them wanted them to be found quickly. Wouldn't you agree?'

Lola looked around. As if on cue, a jogger was barrelling along the path. He muttered a breathless, 'Cheers,' as they made room.

'I would,' she said.

'But why?' Patricia said. 'It's so odd, as if he was only paying lip service to the idea of concealing his crime. Was this how it was with your case?'

'It was,' Lola said. 'And I've asked myself that same question.'

'It's the same person, isn't it?' the woman said now, eyeballing Lola, one eyebrow lifted. 'I mean, surely . . .'

'I can't say,' Lola said. 'There are still . . . differences.'

'Because your girl lived? Amber died of exposure, Inspector. The weather was colder than it should have been that night. A beautifully clear night, and the whole city froze. *I* think he meant Amber to live. I think he wanted her to wake up in the morning light and find herself beside Darren's body. I think it was planned as an act of almost unthinkable cruelty. But, instead, she died. Who would do such a thing?'

Patricia's phone beeped. She pulled it from her inside jacket pocket and squinted at the screen. 'Kenny Flanagan,' she told them. 'He'll be at the house in twenty minutes. We should go.'

* * *

5.17 p.m.

Patricia Wilson's house was a large 1920s semi on a quiet road in a suburb to the south of the city. There was a car already in the driveway, and she pulled in behind it.

As they got out, two cars parked on the road — a black Land Rover Discovery and a dark blue BMW — began to disgorge occupants.

'Kenny and his . . . "associates",' Patricia told Lola quietly.

When Lola had phoned him the night before, he'd been expecting her call. Patricia had been in touch, it seemed, to explain that the Scottish police wanted help — and that, in her view, the two of them should give it.

Lola moved forward and extended a hand. 'Mr Flanagan.'

'Good afternoon.' Gruffly courteous, but businesslike, as if setting the tone for difficult conversations to come.

He was short, stocky, handsome in a rough-hewn way, with a youthful thatch of sandy hair. Looked like a drinker. Like a boxer too, with his broad frame and slightly flattened nose.

Behind him came an older man, thin in a pinched, ill-looking way, with wisps of white hair trained across a mottled scalp.

'Mr Silkin,' Flanagan said. 'My legal adviser.'

Odd term, Lola thought, taking his bony hand. *Why not lawyer?*

Behind Mr Silkin came a young woman in a dark green suit, her dark hair piled on her head and pinned there.

'Miss Khan. Communications.'

'Miss Khan.'

Lola turned to Patricia. 'Shall we go inside?'

The house was dark and silent. Wood panelling clad the hallway and continued into the large dining room, where they took places around a mahogany table.

A faded older woman appeared in the room.

'My sister Carol,' Patricia told Lola. 'She offered to help with the teas. What would everyone like to drink?'

Amazed at Patricia's efficiency, and recognising that this gloomy party must have met like this on multiple occasions, Lola allowed herself to relax a little and let events unfold.

'Amber and Darren,' Patricia said, a few minutes later, passing Lola a silver-framed photograph. 'Taken the day they got engaged.'

Lola angled the frame so Kirstie could see too.

A vibrant, happy-looking couple, snuggled in an armchair, beamed out. Amber was slim, tanned, blonde and looked ecstatic. Darren, sandy like his father, grinned for the camera, while his arms encircled his fiancée beside him.

'I'm so sorry,' Lola said, handing back the frame and making eye contact in turn with Patricia and Kenny. 'When were they due to marry?'

'The third of April,' Patricia said. 'Three weeks after they died.'

Patricia held her gaze. Kenny Flanagan looked down at his interlaced fingers. Of the two of them, Lola could tell that Patricia had faced and come to terms with her grief. For Kenny, it was real and raw and he was suffering to this day.

Silkin, the wraith-like solicitor, broke the silence in a cracked, fluting voice. 'Mr Flanagan wishes to understand in detail your interest in his son's death, Ms Harris.'

DCI Harris, Lola nearly said, but let it pass.

She explained, taking her time, pausing only when the teas and coffees arrived on a trolley.

She could see, long before she finished, that Kenny Flanagan had grown agitated. He sniffed, pulled at his snub nose, cleared his throat, shuffled in his chair, darting looks between her, Kirstie and Patricia, and at his solicitor and his comms person.

'You were right, then, Pat,' he said when Lola had finished. 'All this time.' He looked fiercely about, seeking assurance he was right. 'It was never about Darren.' He turned to Patricia. 'You were right, *all along*.'

Patricia met his gaze but said nothing.

'They tried to say this was about our Darren,' he said to Lola now. 'That he was some kinda crook. That's what they think *I* am. They raked through *everything*.' He jabbed the table with a finger. 'Through *every fucking thing* in Darren's business. In mine. And we opened every door for them, didn't we?' This to Silkin. 'We gave them *everything* they asked for. But still they pushed and pushed. Interviewing me for hours and hours. Grilling Darren's poor mum — God rest her. But now this has happened up there, on your patch. It's the same evil bastard, isn't it? It was never about Darren.'

Lola let the silence settle.

'We can't say anything for sure, Mr Flanagan.'

'It's Kenny, please,' he said.

'Kenny, we need to meet with Merseyside Police and—'

'Oh, for fuck's sake . . .' He turned to Patricia. 'Well, that'll be a waste of fucking time, won't it?'

'We need to establish certain facts,' Lola said calmly. 'To get access to records and reports. Scene-of-crime photographs.'

An intake of breath from Patricia.

'Good luck with that,' Kenny growled.

Lola said nothing.

'Have you shown 'em the stuff the piece of shit sent Amber?' Kenny asked Patricia now.

'Not yet,' Patricia said, meeting Lola's eye. 'I'll go and get it.'

While they waited for her to come back, Kenny Flanagan enumerated what he perceived as the local force's multiple failings. These, it seemed, boiled down to their intense and — in his view — unwarranted scrutiny of his and his son's business dealings.

Patricia returned with a cardboard wallet. She retook her seat and lifted the flap, then drew out a number of A4 envelopes. Lola was conscious of Kenny's eyes on her, waiting to gauge her reaction.

'First came this,' she said, passing an envelope across the table.

Lola, who'd quickly snapped on latex gloves, took it and opened it.

Inside was an A5-sized card. Her skin prickled as she registered its black edges. A funeral notice.

In Memoriam, read curling silver script. Below this, inked in careful black handwriting: *Amber Wilson, 3 September 1991 to ?*

'When did this arrive?' she murmured.

'A month before she . . . before she and Darren died. It came here, to the house. Amber was living here.'

'Amber saw it?'

'Yes.'

'Did you tell anyone about it?'

'Amber didn't want to. I did. I spoke to the community constable who's attached to my school. She advised making an official report. But Amber dug her heels in.'

'Do you know why?'

'She said . . .' Patricia paused and appeared to be choosing the right words. 'She said that there were people in her past who were jealous of her.'

'Did she say who?'

'No. I got the impression this person, or people — that they were female. That the jealousy was because of Darren. Because of his looks. His wealth.'

Kenny watched Lola carefully from under his brows, as if checking she was understanding the import of what Patricia was telling her.

'And after the murders,' Lola said, 'did you show this to the police then?'

'She did,' Kenny cut in, eyes blazing. '*We* did, didn't we, Pat?'

'They examined it,' the headteacher said. 'They recorded it. It was taken into account at the inquest. And then it was . . . disregarded.'

'Dismissed,' Kenny corrected. 'Because they'd decided Darren was the target.'

Lola pushed the card back into the envelope.

'Next, this,' Patricia said, and handed her a flimsy pamphlet.

Ever Memories, read the front page. It was a catalogue of headstones. She leafed grimly through it, holding her breath, her skin crawling as she considered the bitter hatred of the mind that had sent this to a young woman.

'This came here too?' she asked.

Patricia nodded. 'About two weeks before Amber died.'

'And you showed this to the police as well?'

Patricia nodded. Kenny said nothing, but his mouth worked silently, angrily away.

'A week before Amber and Darren died, this was tied to the gatepost of the house,' Patricia said, and handed Lola a small plastic Ziplock bag.

She picked open the flap and took from it a length of black ribbon and a deflated bulb of black rubber.

'A single black balloon,' Patricia said, 'filled with helium so it floated.'

'Did Darren ever receive anything of the kind?' Lola asked Kenny.

He cleared his throat. 'Not that we know of.'

Lola sat quietly for some time, taking it in, and measuring the weight of what she now knew, firmly, horrifyingly, to be the case.

'Were there flowers at any point?' she asked quietly. 'Black roses, or dead flowers. A bouquet of the things?'

Patricia frowned and looked at Kenny.

'I don't . . .'

Kenny shrugged and shook his head.

'You don't seem very surprised by what I've shown you,' Patricia said.

'I'm not, entirely,' Lola admitted. 'You'll forgive me not saying any more just now. I hope to speak to DCI McCaffrey this evening. I will be talking to him about this.'

The bereaved parents sat very still. Patricia was a picture of calm, sad acceptance, while Kenny looked shaken. Bereft.

'Your crime's a copy of this one, isn't it?' Kenny asked Lola quietly. 'You think it's the same killer. The only difference is, your young lady lived to tell the tale.'

'It's a possibility,' Lola said.

'Then look after that girl,' Kenny said. 'Keep her safe. Promise us that, at least.'

She noticed that a change had come over the woman at her side. She seemed to sag in her chair, to wilt as if some controlling force had left her. A gasping sob escaped her and her eyes welled.

Lola very gently took the woman's hand in her own, and held it.

CHAPTER FIFTY-ONE

5.44 p.m.

'At least help me with the rocking chair before you go,' Fi implored, when it was clear her childish wheedling was only irritating Cat.

'Okay.'

It was a concession, but a small one, if it meant she could finally get away and be alone.

She'd meant to leave as soon as Diana returned from the station, where she'd gone to fetch Tom. The three older children were in their bedrooms, supposedly doing home-work, but no doubt on their phones or sleeping. The two youngest were in the dining room, hiding out in a den Fi had fashioned for them from the table, chairs and various cushions and blankets.

During the afternoon Cat had grown increasingly wrung out and bored. Bored of the kids, and of Fi's inane chatter about the kids. She was also disturbed at how seemingly *fine* Fi appeared to be, now she'd got her way and was reinstated at Ladymere Farm — and irritated at the way Fi seemed to remember her fear and vulnerability only when Cat wanted to leave her. Then she employed it like a weapon.

'We'll need the torches,' Cat said, tugging on her jacket. 'It's pitch black out there.'

They'd already been back and forth to the cottage for items Fi wanted with her in the attic room: two chairs from the kitchen, all of the bedding, including a threadbare antique throw, and even mugs. Cat had drawn the line at bringing pictures from the walls of the tiny living room. She thought they'd finished when Fi remembered the rocking chair. 'I think it would be lovely in the corner under the eaves,' she'd said. 'If I move the lamp, I could read there.'

Now, leaving the younger children to play in their den, they pulled on wellies and headed out across the muddy ground behind the farmhouse. It was freezing, the sky indigo and starry, the trees like black skeletons looming over the fields.

'This would have been easier in daylight,' Cat said, as they struggled back, carrying the heavy rocking chair between them, torches gripped awkwardly in hands that were already full.

They crossed the yard without slipping in the mud and reached the steps to the back door of the farmhouse. It stood ajar, showing a sliver of yellow light.

'Didn't you close it?' Cat asked.

Fi stared. 'I thought I did.'

Cat swallowed, trying not to let her mind run away.

They angled the chair and got it up the stones steps. Cat shouldered the door wider, peering into the back hallway. Nothing sinister.

They got the chair inside, and Fi closed the door behind them, turning the old-fashioned key.

Next they moved through an inner door and into the front hallway, to the foot of the stairs.

'Ready?' Cat said, breathless from the exertion.

Fi went first, bending to draw the chair up after her. Cat lifted from below, worrying about how they would negotiate the turn in the stairs.

One of the two younger children — Finn or Flynn, something like that — was watching them with wide eyes from the doorway of the dining room, resembling a ragdoll with his sticky-out blond hair and red dungarees. Cat gave him a smile that seemed to alarm him, and he withdrew into the room.

They got round the bend without a hitch, and up to the first-floor landing, where they manoeuvred the chair through a tight doorway to the bottom of the steeper flight of steps up to the attic rooms. She flicked a switch and a bulb came on at the top of the stairs.

'Okay?' Cat said.

'I think so,' Fi said, up ahead.

'Just take it easy.'

It took them several minutes, but they got to the little landing between the doors to the two attic rooms.

Fi pushed open the door, then recoiled and let out a cry.

Cat leaned in and stared, trying to make sense of what she was seeing.

The bed was black — draped with a cloth of some kind. And tied to the four bed knobs were the strings of black balloons, floating there.

'Downstairs,' Cat hissed. 'Now.'

Fi's face was deathly pale under the bare bulb. 'Do you believe me now?' she said.

Yes, she believed her. But she couldn't speak. Couldn't move, paralysed by the terrible realisation that whoever had done this might still be in the house — if not here in the attic, then downstairs now. Waiting for them.

The children . . .

'*Cat?*' Imploring. Terrified.

'We'll go together,' Cat whispered, and shifted the rocking chair so that it filled the doorway to Fi's room. It wouldn't stop someone getting out, but would slow them down.

She took Fi's arm and led her down to the first-floor landing, where she paused and held her breath, eyes on the nine or ten doors, some closed, others ajar, revealing blackness beyond. Which were the older children's rooms? She didn't know.

Keep going. Get Fi to safety, then come back up.

Down the next flight and round the turn.

The ragdoll — Finn or Flynn — waited for them in the doorway of the dining room, mouth open. Another child appeared behind him, sucking the corner of a towel.

'Go on in,' Cat urged, forcing brightness, pulling Fi after her.

The other of the two youngest, a girl called Maisie, was peering out of the den from under a blanket.

Cat closed the door and turned the key, then eased the key from the lock and stuck it in her pocket. There was another door into this room, leading, she thought, to the kitchen at the back of the farmhouse. No key in the lock. She tried the first key, but it didn't even fit.

'What matter?' Maisie asked.

'Nothing!' Cat sang merrily, grabbing a chair and wedging it under the handle. The floor was wooden and the chair's legs might slip, but it would have to do.

'The older ones,' Fi implored, hands to her mouth. 'They're still upstairs.'

'You stay here,' Cat said, pulling Fi's hands from her face and squeezing them. 'Get under the table with these two and stay there. I'll go upstairs and lock you in. I'll turn the light off too, okay?'

Fi was on the verge of tears. Cat gave her hands one last squeeze, then went to the door. She unlocked and opened it, then, with one last look to see that Fi was crawling under the table, she turned off the light and stepped into the hallway.

CHAPTER FIFTY-TWO

5.50 p.m.

Lola and Kirstie waited in DCI Mark McCaffrey's fourth-floor office while he sought out a colleague. The city stretched out below them in a net of lights. Lola calculated that the wide swathe of black to the southwest must be the River Mersey.

The office door opened. Lola rose.

'Sorry to keep you,' McCaffrey said, holding the door for a woman in a blue suit who strode determinedly in after him. 'My colleague, Carmel Adams, director of corporate communications.'

It was the woman who'd been on the Teams call.

Lola put out a hand but received only a baleful look in return.

The woman sat and peered at the Scottish visitors with a wrinkled nose, as if there was an unpleasant smell in the room.

'Right, what's the bad news?' McCaffrey said, when he'd eased his big frame into his chair.

Lola eyed him curiously.

'The *news*, Mark,' she began, avoiding any qualifier, 'is that I believe we're looking for the same perpetrator.'

McCaffrey shifted awkwardly, as if his joints were giving him pain.

She explained, and, to give him his due, McCaffrey listened, frowning, eyes away into a corner of the office. Carmel Adams scribbled away on a clipboard, stabbing out punctuation and apparently underlining parts of her notes.

At one point McCaffrey looked up sharply. 'And Kenny Flanagan thinks the theory's valid?'

'He does.'

McCaffrey stared at his comms director, eyebrows raised in amazement. She stared coolly back.

'This changes everything,' McCaffrey said.

'I think the "gifts" are the clincher,' Lola said. 'We have some of the black confetti back in Glasgow, but Patricia Wilson has kept hold of *everything*.'

She paused, giving McCaffrey a chance to see the point she was heading towards.

'Mrs Wilson showed you all of it, I believe,' Lola said.

McCaffrey breathed deeply in through his nose, before conceding with a sheepish nod.

'Mrs Wilson feels it was . . . disregarded.'

'Well . . . Well, I—'

'Her word. Not mine.'

McCaffrey swallowed. Carmel Adams was glaring at Lola with an almost violent contempt.

'And now he's killed again,' Lola said quietly.

The devil was in her. *Tough.*

'This is inappropriate,' Adams said, nastily. 'DCI McCaffrey, I strongly suggest—'

He held up a hand. 'It's okay, Carmel.'

'I'm doing you a favour,' Lola said now. 'There'll be a lot more of these questions, I expect. And from people a lot less nice than me. Kenny Flanagan for one. He was all for marching down here, but I asked him to hold off — for an hour or two.'

McCaffrey closed his eyes, while Adams looked as if she might swallow her own tongue.

'Now, will you lot help us?' Lola asked. 'Will you drop all this defensive nonsense and help us catch this evil bastard — or am I going to have to do it on my own?'

CHAPTER FIFTY-THREE

6.03 p.m.

Cat crept up the stairs on her toes, keeping close to the wall, neck craned to see round the bend. She'd realised she could have gone via the kitchen, and armed herself with a knife on the way.

Too late.

She reached the first-floor landing, heart hammering painfully.

'What's going on?' A girl's voice. Loud and demanding. Not a bit scared.

She was in the doorway of the room at the far end of the corridor, leaning against the jamb in a purple onesie.

Twelve or thirteen, Cat seemed to recall. Rachel? Rebecca?

'Is that your bedroom?' Cat hissed, coming towards her.

'Yeah. Why?' She made a mutinous, teenage face.

'Where are the others?'

The girl pulled a face. '*Why?*'

'The youngest two are downstairs with Fi. Where are the others?'

'Jamie and Max? In there.'

She pointed to the next door.

'They share a room?'

'Yeah? Why? What's wrong with you?'

Cat ignored her and rapped lightly on the boys' bedroom door. She turned the knob and pushed it open.

The beds made an L against two walls of the room. On each, a boy was propped up on pillows, each on his phone.

'What do you want?' one of them asked, lip curled in disgust at the adult intrusion.

'You need to come downstairs,' Cat said, attempting a smile. 'Everything's okay, but you need to come. Now.'

'What's your problem, anyway?' Rachel-or-Rebecca said behind her.

Cat turned on her. 'Just do as you're fucking told, okay?'

The girl's mouth dropped open in amazed delight.

'It's because of her, isn't it?' one of the boys said, on his feet now. He was the older of the two. 'Are the police here again?'

'Stop asking questions,' she hissed, 'and *get downstairs*!'

That worked. They were up and out of the room in a flash. The girl looked cowed and scared now.

Cat ushered them before her, down the stairs and into the dining room. Once inside the room, she turned and locked the door, then allowed herself to breathe.

Then they heard the explosion.

CHAPTER FIFTY-FOUR

6.12 p.m.

The roar of the explosion gave way to screaming. A woman's, from outside.

'My children! My *babies*!'

Diana.

'Mum!' the oldest girl cried. She shoved past Cat, scrambling at the key to open the dining room and get out into the hallway.

The front door stood open and Diana was there, scarf loose, coat flapping like wings. She fell on the girl, the wings folding round her. Then she saw Cat and cried, 'Where are the others?'

'They're all in here and they're okay,' Cat said. 'What was that noise?'

'I don't know! There was a bang and there are flames. I thought . . . I thought the house was on fire.'

Tom had appeared behind Diana, face white, eyes frantic.

'The children are here,' Cat told him. 'Everyone's okay.'

The children crowded round their parents. Tom pushed the front door closed behind him.

Fi was at Cat's side, her fingers digging into her upper arm. Cat wrenched herself free and made for Tom, saying, 'I need to talk to you.'

He gave her an uncomprehending look — one that contained something approaching disgust — then threw open the door to the living room. She went after him.

'No, Tom. You don't understand!'

He was through the living room and into the back hallway.

She caught up with him as he reached the back door and threw back the bolts. 'It's not safe!'

But he'd pulled the door wide, and they were bathed in the horrible reddish light of a raging fire that was consuming the little cottage. Flames had torn a gaping hole in the roof and smoke billowed from the shattered windows.

'Come back inside,' Cat urged him, hand on his arm. 'Please. Lock the door.'

He let her pull him, then stood in stunned paralysis as she turned the key in the lock.

'Somebody's been here,' she said, trying to control her breaths. 'He's been in the attic. He's done things to Fi's bed. I got the children in the dining room and then we heard the bang. We've got to get away from here.'

Tom was staring at her as if she was barking at him in a foreign language.

She took both his arms and gave him a shake. 'Do you understand me?'

'We only wanted to help you,' he managed, his voice choked, the bottom half of his face quivering. 'What have you done to us? What have you brought here?'

'I'm sorry. Tom, I'm so sorry. But listen to me. There's danger here. We've got to get away. *Now.*'

He turned, went into the kitchen. She followed.

'We'll drive somewhere,' she continued. 'We'll get the police.'

He was at the kitchen window now, staring out at the red dusk. At the flames licking at the branches of the trees growing behind the cottage.

'Okay,' he said, turning to her, eyes glittering. 'We'll go.'

CHAPTER FIFTY-FIVE

6.32 p.m.

Lola pulled in at Burtonwood Services, a few miles along the M62 out of Liverpool, so they could get fuel and coffees before embarking on the long journey back to Glasgow. While Kirstie filled up the car, Lola checked her phone and found five voicemail messages.

The first was from Anna Vaughan, letting her know Roddy Jackson — the school teacher who was one of Fiona Balfour's three names — had been in touch, demanding the number of the officer in charge. 'He sounds pretty rattled,' Anna's message went. 'Not happy about being questioned at his place of work. Says it's "tarnished his reputation" among colleagues and that he's seeking legal advice. Sounds like he's planning a complaint.'

'Let him,' Lola muttered, deleting the message. 'Prick.'

The second message was indeed from Roderick Jackson himself. Lola noted the use of his Sunday name and listened grimly to a high-pitched stream of vitriol, demanding apologies and compensation for distress. Shaking her head, she saved the message, in case it should be needed.

Next, a message from Elaine. She sounded oddly diffident, mentioning a complaint that had come across her desk that afternoon. One she would like a quiet word about. So, the hysterical Roddy Jackson had followed through on his threat. Elaine would be thrilled.

Next came a curt message from Shuna Frain, reporter at the *Daily Chronicle*. 'Give me a call, Lola. Sooner the better, for everyone's sake, including yours.'

'Cheeky cow,' Lola muttered, and deleted that one too.

Shuna was no idiot. She wouldn't waste her time on an aggrieved hysteric like Jackson, would she?

Elaine had left a second message just twenty minutes ago. She sounded gloomy to the point of grim. 'Lola, it's me again. The press have got wind of this . . . this issue. I know you're travelling but I need to talk to you — *urgently.*'

Seriously? What possible interest could the press have in a complaint from Roddy Jackson?

Kirstie was away into the service station to pay for the fuel. Lola called Elaine.

'Ah, Lola . . . Thanks for calling.' She sounded tired and pissed off.

'I only just got your messages, boss. It's been a worth-while trip, though—'

'I'll hear about it later. Right now I need to put a lid on a situation that's threatening to blow up.'

'Okay . . .'

'I'm going to say a name to you, Lola. I want you to tell me if it means anything to you.'

'Roderick Jackson, by any chance?'

'What? No. No it's not.'

'Oh. I thought you mentioned a complaint. Anna and Pierce interviewed him yesterday and he's threatening to—'

'Lola, it's not Roderick Jackson.'

'Okay . . .'

'Lola, who is Susan Brown?'

'"Susan Brown"? I . . .'

'She was in Muirend just before midnight last night . . . Lola, are you there?'

Lola closed her eyes as the earth tilted beneath her.

CHAPTER FIFTY-SIX

6.45 p.m.

Kirstie returned to the car with their coffees and began telling Lola about a call she'd just taken from Jonno. But then she stalled, eyeing Lola curiously. 'Are you all right, boss?'

'Oh. Um . . . No, not really.' She held her coffee in both hands, stared straight ahead and breathed, trying to get a grip on the panic that threatened to overwhelm her.

'Do you feel all right, or . . . ?'

'No. I've got a wee problem, that's all. Something I've done.'

Kirstie waited a few moments. 'Would it help to talk about it?'

'I've been so stupid, Kirstie . . .' Her throat felt dry. She swallowed and lifted the cup and sipped. The coffee was scalding and stung her mouth, but that helped in a way. She closed her eyes and felt the tears well up. 'I've been so bloody stupid. I hate myself. I really do.' She opened her eyes and peered, shamefaced, at Kirstie beside her. 'That man I told you about — the one I'd been seeing, only I'm not anymore — well, he's ill. He's got cancer. He's not replying to my texts, and I was worried. I went and drove past his house last night and — *oh, God . . .*'

She told Kirstie what she'd done. About the note she'd left. The fact she'd used a false name.

'Not because I wanted to evade responsibility. I put my actual phone number. I mean, I'm happy to pay the damages. I just thought, what if Marie saw the note, or heard about it? What if she knew I'd been there late at night?'

Getting the words out was a relief, but the kind of relief you got from vomiting after drinking too much. She still felt dreadful. *Wracked.*

'It turns out someone saw me. A man walking his dog. I didn't see him but he took a note of my registration and he reported it this morning.'

Kirstie was watching her with a look of grim anticipation of where the story was heading.

'It landed on the desk of a local officer. He checked the reg and saw who owned the car.' She paused, pondering the dark games the unfeeling universe could play. 'Kirstie, he *just happens* to be a pal of DS Pierce's — so he rang him and told him.'

Kirstie stared at her open-mouthed.

'And though the constable has talked to the Toyota's owner, and she's happy for me to pay for the damage without making *any* kind of official complaint . . . the story has *somehow* found its way to the desk of Shuna Frain of the *Daily Chronicle*. Three guesses how that transpired. Elaine Walsh wants me to go to her house tonight, no matter how late.'

'I'm so sorry, boss.'

'So am I, Kirstie.' She took another sip of scalding coffee. 'What was I *thinking*?'

'The super's very fair,' Kirstie told her quietly. 'And she likes you.'

'Aye, well . . . She might not after this. She'd be within her rights to suspend me.'

'Really?'

'It's possible. And what if Pierce goes to his uncle? You know he'd just *love* to stick the knife in — show Uncle Clive what I'm really like.'

They sat in silence for some moments, during which Lola tried to rationalise her way to a zen-like acceptance. What was done was done. What would happen would happen.

She groaned, noting the time on the dashboard. She stowed her coffee cup in the holder behind the gear lever. 'We'd best get back on the road.'

They'd gone a mile or two when Kirstie reminded her about the call from Jonno.

'He and Marcus have found another case,' the constable said. 'I mean, another case like ours — and like the Flanagan–Wilson murder.'

'Go on . . .'

'It was in Leeds. Three years ago, in the March. Not an exact copy of the other cases, but some similarities — the victims were due to get married the month after it happened. Marcus has spoken to West Yorkshire CID and they're eager to help. What's more, the woman in that case survived. And listen to this: she thinks she knows who was behind it.'

CHAPTER FIFTY-SEVEN

7.12 p.m.

'I've destroyed their beautiful home,' Fi said, speaking for the first time since they'd left Ladymere. 'That's what I've done. Their perfect, beautiful home.'

'You haven't,' Cat said. 'The cottage was old. It'll be insured. And, anyway, it's not your fault.'

'I wasn't talking about the cottage.'

Cat glanced at her sister, in the passenger seat of the Fiat beside her, and knew exactly what Fi meant. She took her hand.

They were parked behind the Mackenzie-Croys' people carrier, in a passing place in a lane beside a high hedge. They'd driven for ten minutes to get to this spot — the place Tom knew he could get a phone signal. He'd tried to call the emergency services from the house, only to find the lines were, apparently, down. The internet too. None of the adults spoke their fear aloud, but they all knew what that signified.

A few minutes after parking up, Tom got out of the car and made his way to Cat's window. She dropped it a few centimetres.

'Fire service is on its way. I gave them the exact Google coordinates, so they should find it okay. They're sending police to the house too, just in case whoever did this is still there. I said we'd go to the police station in Beith. The 999 operator's calling ahead to say we're on our way.'

They were in the little town twenty minutes later.

'This feels . . . surreal,' Fi said, as they climbed out of the car and headed for the doorway of the police station. 'Are you coming?' she said to Cat, seeing she was hanging behind and looking at her phone.

'Two minutes,' Cat told her. 'I'll phone DCI Harris.'

CHAPTER FIFTY-EIGHT

11.57 p.m.

Elaine Walsh returned from her kitchen with coffees just as Lola came off the phone.

'That was DC Campbell,' Lola told her. 'Fiona Balfour's safe. That's the main thing.'

'Where did they take her?'

'A flat in Strathblane. Kirstie's there now. Witness protection came through quickly. It's a two-bedroom place. Catriona Balfour is going to stay there for the next few nights.'

'Strathblane's not too far from here,' Elaine commented. 'Five miles west, I'd say. You don't take milk, do you?'

'No. Thanks.'

She passed her a mug. It was a chunky pottery one — homemade, by the look of it. Somehow, as well as parenting three teenagers, Elaine managed to maintain a number of hobbies, including painting, horse riding and pottery. Lola remembered she had a kiln in an outhouse of the former manse on the edge of Lennoxtown.

'Does Fiona know what you found out in Liverpool?' Elaine asked now, taking a seat beside Lola on the settee.

They were in her study at the back of the house. The rest of the family, including Elaine's husband Bob, were in bed.

'In outline only,' Lola said. 'We wanted to reassure her that we'd made progress, but . . . we didn't want to cause undue alarm. To know you're the victim of a serial offender who's acted before and got away with it . . . that's a lot to process.'

'I understand. What about the family who live at the farmhouse?'

'They've a friend with a sizeable rental property in Largs. It's empty the next three weeks, so they're going there for now.'

'Even with the Balfour woman having left?'

'The attack was so spiteful. They've got five children, including two infants . . .'

'God love 'em,' Elaine said. 'Anything from IB at the scene?' Identification Bureau officers had already begun scouring the site for forensic evidence.

'They think the perp got in through a utility room beside the kitchen. Lock neatly smashed.'

'Noisy?'

'Probably. But it's a big house. Thick walls. Solid interior doors. You wouldn't necessarily hear anything.'

'And there's no chance Fiona Balfour could have done any of this herself?'

Lola shifted as she thought about it.

'She *could* have done the stuff in the bedroom,' she said. 'But I can't see how she could have set the explosion.'

'Gas?'

'No supply to the cottage. Must have been fuel of some kind.'

'You think she's in the clear, don't you?'

'I do now, boss. In large part because of what I learned today. Then there's this case in Leeds. I need to talk to CID there, but based on the info Jonno and Marcus have collected already, it certainly could be. I'm doing a Teams call with West Yorkshire CID in the morning, then speaking to the young woman myself . . . That is,' she added carefully, eyes on her boss's face, 'if you're not about to suspend me . . .'

It was time to acknowledge the elephant in the room.

They watched each other, Lola shamefaced, Elaine unhappy and seemingly unsure how to say what she knew she needed to say.

Elaine sighed and put down her mug.

'I'm very sorry, boss.'

Elaine said nothing, no doubt sensing, in her empathetic way, that there was more to come.

'I was stupid. I panicked. When I bumped the car, I . . . well, I didn't want Marie to find out I'd been there. I . . .' She swallowed and breathed, aware that the reservoir of tears was perilously full. 'I didn't want Joe to know either. He told me not to contact him again. I've been so upset, you've no idea. This thing with Joe — it's been eating away at me.' She shut her eyes while she steadied her breathing and got hold of herself. She opened them again. Elaine was watching her, listening, thinking. 'I'm mortified.'

Elaine nodded.

'I don't know why I even wrote a name,' she went on. 'I didn't *need* to put a name at all, did I? I could have given my mobile number. And anyway, the damage wasn't even that bad!'

'The damage isn't the problem,' Elaine said quietly.

'I know.' She closed her eyes again.

It was the fact she'd used a false name. It reeked of dishonesty. Of lawbreaking.

They sat in unhappy silence. Which felt, at the same time, oddly comforting. Elaine wasn't about to bawl her out or dress her down. They were, she felt, in it together — to an extent, at least.

'Is there any proof Pierce went to Shuna Frain?' Lola asked quietly now.

'Proof? No.' Elaine watched her narrowly, taking her time. 'But there's plenty of talk.'

'What can we do, boss? I mean . . . what can *I* do to make things right?'

227

Elaine took her time before replying. 'Brass-neck it,' she said. 'Do your job, be breezy. And let me talk to Shuna.'

'You'll do that? You'll talk to her?'

'I can try.'

'But how could you possibly—'

'Talk her out of it? I don't know. I could offer her a titbit or two . . . if you thought it wise . . .' Elaine raised a meaningful eyebrow.

Lola's skin tingled. 'To go public on the other cases, you mean?'

'We could, couldn't we? Might it not be the right time to try and flush this creep out of the woodwork?'

She was momentarily speechless. Too stunned to form words.

'It might,' she managed at last. 'Thank you, boss.'

'What for?'

'For backing me up.'

'Is that what you think I'm doing?'

Lola shifted in her seat.

'I'm interested in discipline, Lola. I can't have leaky investigations. If there's a leak, I'll plug it. If I find the leaker, I'll plug him. You and your behaviour — that's another matter.'

'Boss.'

'You're heading for a verbal warning, Lola. I have to be honest with you. An improvement notice if you're *very lucky*. And get that woman's taillights fixed — pronto.'

'Yes, boss.'

'Oh, and one more thing, Lola.'

She sat up.

'Deal with Joe, once and for all. He's your Achilles' heel. Put it to bed, *please*. For all our sakes. Most of all *yours*.'

CHAPTER FIFTY-NINE

Wednesday 2 November
8.40 a.m.

'Good morning, Aidan,' Lola said brightly, beaming in his direction.

Pierce stalled in the middle of typing. She saw his shoulders tense inside the fine-weave Italian shirt. He peered coolly at her under his perfect eyebrows and said nothing, but there was malice in his gaze.

'Hello, Anna,' she chirped next, seeing DS Vaughan returning from the kitchenette with a mug in hand.

'Oh, hi!' Anna said, smiling awkwardly. She knew about Lola's misdemeanour, then. Did she also know that Pierce had ratted her out to the press? Had he perhaps told her?

Lola was faking her brightness. In truth she was knackered, but at least she'd slept — and thank God she'd remembered to cancel today's dawn session with Johnny, which gave her another hour of rest.

Lola walked Anna to her desk and said, loudly enough for Pierce to hear, 'Anna, I'm talking to West Yorkshire CID at nine fifteen, then to the victim of the Leeds attack at nine forty-five. I'd like you on those calls with me.'

'Sure.' Another strained smile.

Lola caught Pierce's eye on her way back to her own desk and shot him the blackest look she could muster. One that told him she knew exactly what he'd done. And that she might well destroy him for it.

CHAPTER SIXTY

9.16 a.m.

Lola got the preliminaries out of the way, then asked the two West Yorkshire detectives on the screen to tell her and Anna about the attack in the spring of 2019.

'We got a call from a dog walker,' the older of the two men, a DI, said. 'The eighth of June, a Saturday, a little after six a.m. Her German shepherd brought her attention to what she thought was a pair of corpses — one male, one female — under bushes beside one of the main paths through Horsforth Hall Park, in a western suburb of Leeds. Fright of her life. She had her phone with her and called 999. We were there, and an ambulance, within a quarter of an hour. Turned out only the male was deceased. The female was alive but unconscious. Drugged. Heavy dose of phenobarbital. According to the PM, the dead man had been drugged too — then shot twice in the back of the head. Male victim was a Kevin Stainthorpe. Manager of a warehouse in Pudsey — that's between here and Bradford. Age thirty-four. No criminal record. No suggestion of anything dodgy at all. Female victim was Claire Grainger, then age twenty-six, beauty therapist with her own mobile business.'

'Were they tied together? The report didn't say.'

'No. She was lying drugged beside his body.'

'And Ms Grainger wasn't injured at all?'

'She had bruises on her arms, possibly from when she was grabbed by the attacker. That's all.'

'Any suspects?'

The DI glanced briefly at the DS beside him, then said, slightly strained, 'None that we'd qualify as likely.'

'Meaning . . . ?'

'I believe you're aware that Claire Grainger has her own theory as to who attacked her and killed her fiancé.'

'Yes.'

'She is of the opinion it was a gentleman with whom she had been on a single date, some years previous. Name of William Cavendish. The date went well enough, but this Cavendish bloke turned weird pretty quickly. Monitoring her, she says. Stalking her. Sending her things.'

'Things? What sort of things?'

'Cards. Chocolates. That sort of thing.'

'What about flowers? Dead ones?'

'I . . . I don't recall.' The DI looked at the DS, who shook his head, at a loss. 'You'd have to ask Ms Grainger.'

'I will.'

'I take it dead flowers feature in your case?'

'They do. Did you interview this Mr Cavendish?'

'No. He vanished.'

'I see.'

'We did everything. We put out a call on TV, using the photofit Ms Grainger provided.'

'A photofit? Can I see it?'

'Of course. I'll send it over straight away. Not that anything came of it.'

'Nothing?'

'It was like the fella never even existed.'

* * *

'I'd been to a client's house a few miles away in Cookridge,' Claire Grainger told them, eyes away somewhere in the past. Occasionally she glanced at the woman detective sitting beside her, as if for reassurance. 'Her and her sister — they both wanted manicures. They were going to a cousin's wedding the next day. I was there till gone eight, then I drove home. I let myself into the house and saw Kevin wasn't back yet. He hadn't answered my text saying I was on my way home, so I started to wonder where he was. Then I went into the kitchen and saw a note on the counter. It said, "Surprise for you in the garage." All in capital letters. It didn't even occur to me Kevin hadn't written it. I thought, *What's he gone and bought me now?* And I was laughing. I went into the garage through the door from the kitchen. And there's this van parked in there. A white van. Kevin didn't have a van! The doors at the back were standing open so I went round and . . . and Kevin was in there, lying on the floor, on his side, and I could see he was tied up. Then . . . I'm sorry, even now it's difficult.' The woman on the screen took a moment to collect herself. 'Then he grabbed me from behind. One hand over my mouth, the other round my wrists. Next thing . . . I'm in the park and I'm frozen to the bone and there are people everywhere. And Kevin's there next to me on the ground.' She began to sob. 'He was dead.'

'I'm very sorry, Claire,' Lola said after a moment. 'We really do appreciate your time — and your willingness to help.'

She was very thin, in an unhealthy, underfed way. And, curiously for a former beauty therapist, she wore no make-up and wore her hair in a ponytail. Lola wondered if she'd made an effort — conscious or otherwise — to move away from her past career. Her past self. She worked in a bank now, she'd explained at the start of the call. Admin in a back office, away from the public.

She wiped her eyes with a tissue and nodded. 'I want you to catch him,' she said. 'You will, won't you? Because the police here have failed.'

She said it without any animosity — certainly none towards the woman at her side, a detective who'd been her point of contact for the past four years.

'We'll do our very best.'

Claire nodded and wiped her nose.

'I understand you believe you know who did this to you and Kevin,' Lola said.

'Yes. His name's William Cavendish. Will, he called himself. I met him on a dating app eighteen months before me and Kevin got together. We went out once. He seemed normal enough at the start of the evening, but I could see he . . . wasn't right. I thanked him for a nice night and he said he wanted to see me again. I made excuses, meaning to text him later . . . only I didn't get the chance, because he turned up at the house — literally, ten minutes after I got back. He must have got the next taxi and told it to follow me home. This was when I was living in Headingley. He knocked on the door, saying he couldn't let me go home without him, and could he come in? So I said, "No, you can't." Then he got nasty with me. Foot in the door. Called me a "frigid little bitch". Said he thought I was different, but I was "just like all the other frigid bitches". Then he said he'd make me sorry.'

Lola's blood was rushing in her veins, and she had so many questions. But she made herself wait.

'He pushed his way into the house, and I got my phone. He knocked it out of my hand. I ran into the kitchen and got the back door open and went into the yard. My next-door neighbour was in her kitchen and I started screaming at her to help. She got her husband to come out and he was halfway over the wall when Will saw him and did a runner.'

'Did you call the police?'

'Yeah. They were lovely.' She gave a little shrug, as if to acknowledge that "lovely" didn't quite cut it. 'They tried to find him, but the number he'd given me was for a . . . a "burner" phone, I think they call it. The place he said he worked — they'd never heard of him.'

'What about the dating app?'

'He'd deleted his account. The company's based in America, and they refused to give the police any information. Said it was to do with his privacy and blah, blah. What about my privacy, eh? What about my safety?'

'When did the date take place, Claire?' Lola asked.

'Second of October, 2016.'

'And did he ever try to contact you in the months after it?'

'Oh, yeah. He sent me things.'

'What kind of things, Claire?'

'Chocolates. Posh ones. From Fortnum's in London, the first time. All done up in a kind of hamper with tissues and things. I thought: these must be from a client. One of my richer ones. But there was a card inside. No name, but it said, *Where there's a Will there's a way.* Capital W — so I knew they were from him. I took them to the police, but they'd come straight from the shop. He'd paid for them in person, with cash, and asked the woman to write the message for him because he had "arthritis in his hands". They got a look at him on CCTV but he was in a hat and had the collar up on his coat. They showed me some stills. I'm sure it was him. Anyway, I didn't touch the chocolates. The police took them away.

'Then there were the cards. An "in sympathy" one with flowers on it. One word inside: *bitch.* Nice, eh? Then another one, a postcard from the Tower of London — postmarked London as well. It showed the block where they used to chop off people's heads. He'd put *you're next* on the back.'

'Did you ever receive flowers that could have been from him?'

'Flowers? No. I don't think so.'

'I understand you and the police made a photofit.'

'Yeah, but only after the attack, when Kevin was killed, which was two and a half years after the date. I did my best, but it wasn't easy. They put the photofit on *Crimestoppers* and on the police Facebook page, but no one came forward.'

Lola nodded. With luck the photofit would be waiting in her inbox when she came off the call.

'Why do you think Will Cavendish was behind what happened to you and Kevin, Claire?'

'Well, because of what he did, of course. Following me home like that. Pushing his way into the house. Threatening me. And all the stuff he sent.'

'*Could* there be someone else? Someone else from you your past, who—'

'No.' Sharp. Angry. 'Don't you think I've been over all this a million times? At the time and since. No, it was him, I'm sure of it.'

Lola nodded, believing her.

'You and Kevin were due to get married, I believe.'

Quietly, 'Yes.'

'When exactly?'

'In the July. A month later. Why? It is important?'

'It might be,' Lola allowed.

'I don't see why . . . unless . . .'

'Unless, what?'

'Unless he wanted to stop the wedding.' She frowned. 'Like he heard about it, and didn't want it to happen because he was so bitter and jealous.' She gazed at them out of the laptop screen, eyes widening as she came to a new realisation. 'Is that why he let me live, do you think? So I'd wake up next to Kevin's body, a month before we were due to get married? So that he'd traumatise me, and ruin my life forever?'

Lola didn't reply, but kept her expression blank. Because, as far as she could tell, the woman was bang on the money.

'One more question, if you don't mind.'

Claire nodded.

'Where was William Cavendish from, do you remember?'

'London, he said. Except, I didn't believe him.'

'Why not?'

'Well . . . he had a Scottish accent for a start.'

236

CHAPTER SIXTY-ONE

10.32 a.m.

Lola, Kirstie and Pierce crowded around Anna's desk to see the screen of her laptop.

'Can you make it bigger?' Lola said.

Anna tweaked the touchpad. 'That better?'

On the screen was the photofit image, created by computer from the description Claire Grainger had been able to give of the man she'd known as William Cavendish.

Lola saw a squarish face with thick and dark brows and regular features. He was handsome in a standard, nondescript way. His hair was dark but skinhead-short. He'd have looked thuggish, if it weren't for his big eyes and full lips.

The mouth — something twitched in the back of her memory. She covered the top half of the face with a hand to isolate the mouth and chin. But, no, nothing.

'Did she identify any distinguishing physical features?' Lola asked Anna, who had the description printed out on her desk.

'None, boss.'

'The hair would probably be different now,' Kirstie said.

'Aye,' Lola said, but studied the hairline nonetheless. It was low on his forehead and square. Grown longer, his hair would be thick and grow forward.

'We could put it out on social media for starters,' Kirstie said. 'No details. Just say we're keen to make contact with the man pictured, and that he was known to be living under the name Cavendish in the North of England in 2019 and that he has a Scottish accent.'

Lola thought about it. 'Not yet,' she said after a moment. 'Remember West Yorkshire CID got zero response, and their call went out on TV as well as online. I want to show it to Fiona Balfour first. Kirstie, we'll go see her now. You can come with me. That reminds me — Anna, can you send photos of Ali Howe and Roddy Jackson to Claire Grainger? I doubt there's much point, but we need to make sure.'

Pierce answered his mobile and ducked away, keeping his back to them as he talked. She followed Anna's eyes on his back. Anna jumped and, seeing she was caught, effected an innocent smile. Lola wasn't fooled.

Pierce came off the phone, eyes bright, excited. He looked at Anna, and seemed about to speak when he caught Lola's eye.

'Something important?' she asked him.

'The profiler,' he told her, begrudging the information.

'And?'

'She's produced a report. She's going to email it over.'

'To you?'

'Yes.'

'You'll send it on to me immediately, won't you?'

'Yes.'

'Good. Kirstie? Let's go.'

CHAPTER SIXTY-TWO

11.35 a.m.

'Fi's in the shower,' Cat told Robyn, closing and locking the door of the flat once the solicitor was inside. 'She was awake half the night. So was I, actually. She's been sleeping till now.'

'How are you doing?' Robyn said, shrugging off her coat.

'I'm okay.' She couldn't quite manage the smile that etiquette required, but she was grateful to be enquired about before Fi. 'Come through to the living room,' she said. 'The place is microscopic. It's not good for my claustrophobia at all.'

It was an austerely furnished two-bedroom flat, but half the size of Cat's own place — and barely a quarter of the size of the one Fi had shared with Sean. The windows were small, and the ceilings low, making it dark.

Robyn took a seat. 'You look tired,' she said bluntly. 'Exhausted, actually.'

'Thanks.'

'You need to look after yourself. I don't want you drained and ill. You need a break too.'

'I'd go for a run — a walk, at least. But I can't leave Fi. You know that. What if something happened? I'd never forgive myself. I just thank God I was there last night. Can you imagine if she'd been there on her own with the kids? A psychopath in the house . . .'

Robyn watched her in that calmly analytic way of hers. 'What about using a couple of the volunteers?'

'What do you mean?'

'You've got a bank of them, haven't you? The ones who staff the safe houses overnight. They're tough women. You could have them staying here in shifts.'

She thought about it, but quickly put it aside. 'Fi wouldn't like it. It has to be me.'

'Why?'

Cat looked at her, feeling herself stiffen defensively under her friend's cool, evaluative gaze.

'She . . . she needs me,' she said, resenting the catch in her voice. 'I'm her sister.'

Robyn eyed her sceptically, saying at last, 'So, this isn't about Lynne, then . . . ?'

Hearing the name spoken was like being doused in cold water. Cat nearly gasped, but managed instead a chilly reply: 'No. It isn't.'

'Bullshit, Cat.'

She sprang up, affronted and enraged. 'How dare you?'

Robyn, still sitting, shrugged. 'An observation,' she said. 'But I believe I'm right.'

Cat glared from the living-room window at the view of Dumgoyne, looming darkly over the roofs of the village.

'Why won't you ever talk about it?' Robyn pressed from the settee behind her. 'It's been so long. It might help.'

'There's nothing to talk about,' she said, forehead touching the window, reassured by its smooth, cold solidity. But still the face of her dead school friend swam before her eyes, smiling, taunting. The sob surprised her, escaping from her throat like a gasp.

'Hey, it's okay.' Robyn was up and behind her in a flash, arm around her shoulder, pulling her in for a hug.

Cat resisted, levering herself out of the embrace. They stood apart, facing one another across the bare little room like fighters — or opposing counsels.

'What happened to Lynne wasn't your fault, Cat,' Robyn said, opening for the defence.

'I could have stopped it.'

'Her boyfriend was violent, Cat. He'd attacked women before. Christ, he broke his own mother's jaw!'

'She came to me for help. I didn't answer.'

'Because you were ill! You had flu. It was bad timing. Very bad luck.'

'But I should have been ready. I should have been there.' Crying now. 'I should never have let her go back to him. I should have taken her away somewhere. I . . . I . . .' Hands to her face to try to stem the tears.

'You were *ill*. She was a twenty-three-year-old woman with her own mind. And yes, I agree, she shouldn't have gone anywhere near that animal after what he'd already done to her, but she *did* — and it wasn't your fault. And you *must* — for your own sanity — realise that at some point.'

Cat dropped her hands and sagged where she stood, head down, eyes closed. 'Don't you think I know all this?' she said quietly. 'Don't you think I've tried to rationalise it, to reason with myself?'

'Cat . . .'

'Don't you?'

'One man did this,' Robyn said. 'One man. Not you.'

She opened her eyes and looked about the little room, everywhere but at the woman opposite her.

'Will I put the kettle on?' Robyn said.

Cat nodded. 'It's through there.'

Her phone rang after Robyn left the room.

It was the DC, checking she was at the flat, saying she and DCI Harris were on their way. They had a photofit image of a man's face and they wanted to show it to her sister.

'I'll be here,' Cat told her. 'Robyn McArthur will be here too.'

Robyn came back from the kitchen a minute later. 'I spoke to Gerry Rennie this morning,' she told Cat, casual as anything. 'He asked after Fi. You too.'

241

'Did he?' Cat stared.

Seeing Cat's startled expression, she shrugged. 'I think he's okay, Cat. Genuinely. I know his family are dodgy, but he . . . he seems like a nice guy.'

'Right . . .'

'He's clear Fi had nothing to do with Sean's death. He knows someone's out to get her — to frame her. Said even his mum's coming round. She now accepts that the so-called evidence was faked.'

'You've been talking to Rita?' Fi said from the doorway to the hall, making them both jump. She was in a dressing gown, a towel wrapped round her head like a turban. 'Well?'

'To Gerry,' Robyn said, taking Fi's challenge in her stride. 'He was asking for you. The Rennies have accepted that the evidence was faked. They want to help.'

'To help *me*? Why?'

'They want to catch whoever murdered Sean. Why wouldn't they?'

'So, what — we're all going to team up in a happy band to find the killer?' she enquired nastily.

'I doubt it. But it's progress, isn't it?' Robyn looked to Cat, as if for backup.

'I'm not sure,' Cat said. 'I don't trust him. I certainly don't trust Rita.'

'He asked if we want him to talk to the press. He says he's happy to tell them Fi's a victim in all this.'

'Gerry said that?' Fi asked.

'And what did you say?' Cat said.

'I said, "Thanks, but no thanks".'

Cat saw Fi watching Robyn with a curious expression, eyes narrowed, watchful. Oddly calculating.

'What are you thinking, Fi?' she murmured.

Her sister turned her watchful gaze on Cat, an unpleasant smile now lifting the corners of her mouth. 'I'm thinking I might quite like that. I might quite like Rita telling the world she's sorry.'

In the kitchen the kettle was boiling. Robyn went to see to it.

'You'd better get dressed,' Cat said to Fi. 'The police'll be here in ten minutes. They've got something to show you.'

CHAPTER SIXTY-THREE

12.04 p.m.

Kirstie read out the forensic psychologist's description of the killer they were seeking, while Lola drove them north out of the city towards Milngavie, beyond which, nestled against the Campsies, was the village of Strathblane. The profile, based on crime scene evidence, witness testimony and statistics, was incomplete, given everything they'd discovered in the past two days. Lola had asked Anna to update the forensic psychologist — Dr Enid Burrows — with the new information they'd learned in Liverpool, and from West Yorkshire CID and Claire Grainger. An updated profile would follow soon.

'*Perpetrator is likely a white male in his late twenties or early thirties,*' Kirstie read, scanning the text of the initial report for key points. '*Likely not in a relationship. Heterosexual. Possible history of short-term, intense but highly dysfunctional relationships. Possibly physically attractive, superficially charming, but quick to anger. Becomes frustrated at his own inability to maintain meaningful relationships. Possible history of obsessive infatuations or stalking. Likely to have been in trouble with police and other authorities in his teens and early twenties, but less likely as he grew older and smarter.* Erm . . .' Kirstie's thumb moved on the screen of her phone. '*Likely*

*educated no higher than high school or further education — if the lat-
ter, likely vocational. Background probably unstable. Possibly brought
up in care or a degree of instability. Location: likely to be based in or
near Glasgow, probably renting and living alone. Unlikely to be living
close to the crime scene — suggest he lives within five to ten miles away.
Access to a vehicle — possibly a van. Most probably self-employed, having failed to hold down employed or traditional work. Manual skilled
labour is likely: examples include electrician, plumber, carpenter, also
possibly military, though he would be unlikely to have stuck at a job for
any length of time. Also has sophisticated digital technology skills, but
these are likely self-taught — or he has access to these skills through
an accomplice. Psychologically, he's highly organised, comfortable out
of doors, possibly with interests in sailing, hunting, fishing. Might be
a member of online communities that appeal to "incels" or men who
fantasize about sexual violence against women.'*

Lola thought it over in silence, letting the killer's possible characteristics settle in her brain, Tetris-style, some
landing and fitting together neatly, others jarring, leaving
gaps. They were beyond Milngavie now, clearing the top of
a wooded hill, and had a view of mountains going on forever,
some with snow on top.

'Doesn't sound a bit like Alistair Howe,' Lola murmured. 'But we can ask about hobbies, interests. We checked
if he had a criminal history, didn't we?'

'Nothing, boss.'

'Roddy Jackson . . . ?'

'He's not self-employed either. And remember he had
alibis — which we've now checked.'

'Gerry Rennie?'

'I don't know, boss. He hasn't been in the picture before
now.'

'And what about Tom Mackenzie? He's an old friend of
Cat Balfour's, isn't he? He's known Fiona a long time. Could
have formed an attachment. Torching part of his own property could have been a diversion. Especially if it's insured . . .'

'We haven't interviewed him as a possible suspect, but
we can,' Kirstie said.

'I'm thinking about the photofit,' Lola said. 'If the man who killed Sean Rennie is the same person who Claire Grainger believes she dated, then he isn't Gerry Rennie *or* Tom Mackenzie. The face is different.'

Descending into Strathblane, negotiating a hairpin bend, Lola experienced a brief flutter of panic in her chest.

The case was complex and baffling. Finding further cases in two English cities had enabled them to triangulate a lot, and to isolate patterns. It had also raised their hopes. Those hopes now depended on the possibility that Fiona Balfour, a traumatised young woman, would recognise a photofit of a man who might — or might not — have been involved in one of the other attacks.

And if she didn't recognise him? Then they were back to square one.

CHAPTER SIXTY-FOUR

12.44 p.m.

'Take your time,' Lola said.

She sat beside Fiona Balfour on the little settee, their backs to the window for maximum light, and held up the photofit. Robyn McArthur and Cat Balfour sat with Kirstie round the circular dining table in one corner of the sparse living room.

'You hold it,' Lola said, and let the young woman take the clipboard.

For a minute Fiona said nothing, during which time Lola practised patience . . . and waited. She glanced at Kirstie and the two women beside her and saw in their faces a tension that matched her own.

Lola had explained to Fiona, her sister and her solicitor where the photofit had come from. That they'd spoken to the surviving victim of a double attack in Leeds. She'd let on that there were some similarities in that case with what had happened to Fiona and Sean, but didn't give details.

'I don't recognise him,' Fiona said quietly at last, eyes still on the computer-generated image before her. 'I'm sorry, but I don't. I . . . I hoped I would.'

'Keep looking,' Lola urged her gently. 'Another few minutes. Try covering parts of the image with your hand. The eyes might seem familiar, if not the mouth. And his hair might have been different.'

The young woman studied it intently, scanning the features, frowning, almost wincing as she focused in on different details.

'I can't remember,' she said at last, meeting Lola's gaze with dismal eyes.

'That's okay.' Lola reached for the board.

'It's his eyes,' the woman said, and Lola immediately tensed. 'But I can't . . . I can't remember . . .'

'What about his eyes?' she asked carefully.

'I don't know, but . . .'

Lola held her breath.

'They seem familiar,' Fiona said.

'The colour, maybe? Or the shape?'

'The stare.'

Lola waited some more — until she realised Fiona had said what she was going to say. Then she asked, 'Does a name occur to you?'

Fiona took her time. 'No.'

'Alistair Howe?'

'No.' She screwed up her face. 'That's not Ali.'

'Roddy Jackson?'

She considered it, eyes on the face, then shook her head. 'No.' She turned sharply to Lola. 'You and your colleagues have seen both of them recently. It's been years since I knew them. If *you* didn't make a match with this picture then I'm not going to, am I?'

'Possibly not,' Lola said. 'But remember this image was produced from memory, based on a single meeting with a man over five years ago. People change. You might recognise him from the way he used to look.'

Fiona nodded, but looked doubtful.

'What about you?' Lola said to Catriona.

Catriona took the photofit from her sister, holding it gingerly with the tips of her fingers, and eyeing it with little enthusiasm. She looked at it for a minute, then handed it back with something like relief. 'I don't know him.'

'You sure?'

'Yes, why?'

'He might be known to the two of you, that's all. A family friend or acquaintance.'

'He isn't.'

Lola nodded. She turned back to Fiona Balfour, sitting awkwardly on the settee before the window.

'Does the name William, or Will, Cavendish mean anything to you?' she asked.

'No. Who is he?'

'It's the name this man—' she tapped the photofit — 'gave to the victim in Leeds.'

'Will Cavendish . . . ? No. I'm sorry.'

'You never knew anyone with that surname?'

She took a moment. 'No. I'd remember it. It sounds . . . upper class. Like an aristocrat.'

Lola nodded.

'Can I keep the picture?' Fiona asked.

'Yes,' Lola said. 'And if you remember anything — anything at all, no matter how trivial you think it might be — you must tell us immediately.'

She nodded.

'While we're here, I'm afraid we've got a few more questions,' Lola said.

'Do you feel up to it, Fi?' Robyn cut in, rising from the dining table.

'I don't mind.' Her gaze was away in the middle distance, in the past, Lola hoped, scanning her memories for a pair of eyes, a familiar stare.

'Should I stay?' Cat asked.

'Best not, I think,' Robyn said, with a smile that was firm but looked designed to reassure. 'I'll stay with her. You go for a walk — get some fresh air.'

'I'll be okay,' Fiona told her. 'You go.'

* * *

'Dates?' Fiona said, wrinkling her brow in confusion. 'Yes . . . a few. Well, quite a lot, actually. Especially in my early twenties. But I couldn't possibly remember them all.' Then she seemed to understand. 'You think he's someone I went on a date with? Someone I turned down? Is that how he . . . is that how he met the others?'

'We think it's possible.'

Fiona drew in a deep breath. 'I . . . I don't know where to start . . .'

'We need you to try. Categorise them, if it helps. Men you met when you were out with friends. Ones people introduced you to. And . . . ones you met online.'

The young woman had recognised something in Lola's tone. 'It's the online ones you're interested in, isn't it?'

'Yes. But the others too. Would you have used the same app, do you think?'

She thought about it. 'I used two.' She named them. Lola had heard of them, and knew they'd been around some time.

'Check if you can log back in,' Lola said. 'Check if you can see your own history. If you can't, contact the companies and ask them to give you your data. DC Campbell will help you, if you like.'

Robyn had listened carefully to this point. 'What sort of numbers are we talking?' she asked Fiona. 'Is it in the tens, or . . . ?'

'More,' Fiona said sharply. 'But don't judge me. If I want to go on dates, I can go on as many as I like. I—'

'No one's judging you,' Lola said. 'But we need the information.'

'I'm sorry. I understand.'

'And I'm afraid we're going to need it quickly.'

CHAPTER SIXTY-FIVE

1.27 p.m.

Outside, the air was cold, but the weak sunshine that found its way into the valley felt wonderful on Cat's back.

She walked along the main road into the village, barely taking in her surroundings, enjoying the freedom to move her limbs and the sensation of blood moving in her veins. For hours she'd felt trapped, cooped up in the tiny modern flat with its minuscule windows and the ceilings pressing ever downwards. Not just a physical entrapment either, but an emotional one too. Her feelings were secondary to Fi's. Fi could give vent to every fear, every anxiety. She must sit on hers. Be the rock, the one Fi could cling onto — or kick against.

She jumped as a truck thundered past, and she was back in the moment, becoming properly aware of her surroundings for the first time. The pretty cottages lining the road, the way the land climbed to the east, dotted with fir trees before becoming high and craggy; the way it fell away to the west into a dip clogged with firs.

The village was long and thin, clustered around a main road running north from Glasgow towards the Trossachs: a near-wilderness of wooded hills and nestled lochs. She'd give anything to return to her car and drive off into the mountains, to find a section of forest and lose herself there for a few hours. Maybe book into a B&B. Give a false name. Hide in her room, working her way through the second-hand paperbacks that would surely be available in the B&B's breakfast room. Trashy novels, thrillers, and those Highland time-travelling adventures that were so popular.

There were shops up ahead. What looked like an upmarket gift shop or interior design place. Beside it, a grocer's, then a café with chairs still — optimistically — set up outside. She'd get a coffee. Maybe a slice of cake. And then she'd go back.

Her phone started ringing as she settled at the wobbly table on the pavement, mug of coffee before her, a slice of Victoria sponge on its way. It was Fi.

She pressed the red 'reject' icon, then wrote a quick text:

Is it urgent? Just getting coffee. Back soon.

The three dots came and went while Fi typed her reply. Cat groaned, preparing herself for the worst.

No but don't be long. Police have gone and Robyn wants to see you before she goes.

For God's sake . . . Couldn't she even have twenty minutes to herself?

She typed:

I'm having a break. R can ring me later. You'll be fine for another 15 mins. X

Fi replied quickly:

Okay. Have a nice time.

'I will,' Cat grumbled. She put her phone on silent and tucked it away.

Beyond the little café the road dipped. Just over the ridge a man was bending beside a dark-coloured car, inspecting one of its tyres. She watched him as he prodded at the tread, then begin to beat the rubber in exasperation, and felt oddly cheered that someone else was having a difficult day.

He stood, eyes still on the tyre, wiping his palms on the sides of his jeans.

He was young. Nice looking, average height but well built, in a blue and white rugby top, with curly blond hair. He had his phone in his hands now and was jabbing away at it. He lifted it to his ear. Listening, his eyes fell on Cat. She nodded and gave him a rueful smile. He accepted it with a nod, then drew his phone from his ear, clearly having no luck.

'You can use mine if you're struggling to get a signal,' she called to him, waving her phone.

'Do you mind?' he called back. He gave the tyre a demonstrative kick. 'This thing's got glass in it and it's going down at a rate of knots. My repair kit's gone walkabout.'

She got up and walked his way, phone held out. 'Here you go.'

'Thanks so much,' he said, giving her an endearing wee-boy smile. 'Always happens when you're in a rush.'

Preoccupied, he'd barely looked her in the eye. No flirting. Just a pleasant guy having a bad day.

She hung back while the man used her phone, enjoying the afternoon, the way the sunlight tipped the tops of the firs so that they glowed greeny-gold against the cold blue sky.

'Signal's rotten on yours too,' he said.

'I'm sorry. I'm sure they'd let you call from the café. Do you want me to ask . . .'

His expression was torn. 'I feel like such an idiot.'

'Don't be daft.'

'It's such a small bit of glass. You can hardly see the hole. See if you can see it.'

He was crouching, head on one side, squinting and pointing.

Back along the road the café owner had brought out her cake and was looking around alarmed for her customer. She spotted her and waved before disappearing back inside.

'Look,' the man said.

'Where?' She crouched.

'Just there.' He'd opened the car's back door, as if that might make it easier for her to see the puncture.

The next second his hand was gripping the back of her neck. She tried to rise, to cry out, but he squeezed and she felt herself somehow being pulled and pushed downwards at the same time. Then—

Darkness.

CHAPTER SIXTY-SIX

2.55 p.m.

Robyn came off the phone to find Fiona maintaining her vigil from the living-room window, the one overlooking the main road through the village. It had been well over an hour since Cat had left.

'Let me guess,' Fi said, eyes still fixed on the view, 'she said not to worry.'

'Not exactly,' Robyn said, coming close and standing at Fi's shoulder, so that she, too, had a view of the village. 'She's sending two of her officers, and she's alerted the local police.'

'Where is she, Robyn?'

'I don't know.'

'He's taken her, hasn't he?'

Robyn didn't answer. She wasn't one to speak platitudes, nor to answer rhetorical questions.

'I think we should go out and look for her,' Fi said now.

'Absolutely not.'

'She's my sister,' Fi said, turning, her lip curled back in a snarl. 'Maybe you don't give a fuck about her, but I do!'

Robyn ignored her and went into the little kitchen to fill the kettle.

'I'm sorry!' Fi called after her.

She forced herself to reply: 'It's fine.'

It was possible, Robyn decided, that Cat had simply had enough. That Fi had finally pushed her too far, one minute frail and needy, the next accusing her of neglect, or at best an inability to empathise.

The kettle began to heat up and she busied herself rinsing mugs and fetching teabags and milk.

Silence from the living room. She'd be back there at her lookout, gazing along the road.

Robyn had come to terms with the fact that she didn't like Fi. And that was okay — it would be a saintly lawyer who liked all her clients, or a naïve one. People were people. Some got on your nerves. That didn't mean they were undeserving of legal representation, or protection from harm.

But this was nothing to worry about, Robyn tried to reassure herself. Cat would be back any time. Weary but calmer, ready to resume her role as carer-in-chief, and Robyn could get on her way. Could get back to her other clients, some of whom were becoming impatient.

A chill of anxiety coursed over her shoulders and down her spine.

Please God, let her be okay.

She made the tea, fished out the teabags, added milk and took the mugs into the living room.

Fi was no longer at the window, but perched on the edge of the little settee, hugging herself tightly as she frowned down at the photofit image the police had left behind.

Robyn set the mugs down on the coffee table beside the image.

'You all right?' she asked Fi.

Fi lifted her head. 'Yes,' she said quickly — and defensively, Robyn thought. 'I just . . . it's nothing. Thanks for the tea.'

'Fi, have you recognised him?'

'No. No . . . I . . .' She smiled unconvincingly. 'It's nothing.'

CHAPTER SIXTY-SEVEN

4.43 p.m.

'Are you here to meet Superintendent Walsh?' DS Anna Vaughan asked, jumping up as Lola hurried into the office.

'I am, but I'm running late.'

'Well, don't worry,' Anna said, coming round to Lola's desk, all willowy in a fine grey suit, a big fake smile plastered on her face. 'So is she.'

'Oh?'

'She's got someone in with her. A last-minute thing, I think.'

'Right.'

There was something in the way Anna was looking at her, the way she held her head on a slight tilt, that seemed off.

She looked cautiously around. The place was empty. Pierce, Marcus, Jonno and Kirstie were all in Strathblane, Kirstie staying with Fiona Balfour, while the others helped local officers with a door-to-door search for Cat, who'd now been missing for three hours.

'Who's she with, do you know?' Lola asked.

'I did hear the name. Oh, what was it again . . . ?' She effected a frown and bit her bottom lip as she pretended to try to recall the name. 'Shona somebody. Shona Frain?' Her eyes were sharp on Lola, anticipating a reaction.

'*Shuna* Frain.'

'Yes, that's it!' A wee smile. 'From one of the newspapers.'

'I see.' Lola beamed at her, determinedly unbothered. 'You met the psychologist?'

'Yes,' Anna said. 'She's a very pleasant woman, isn't she?'

'She is.'

Dr Burrows had agreed to meet Lola and Elaine at five to share her thoughts in light of the new evidence.

'Do you want me to come to the update meeting?' Anna asked sweetly.

'Oh, I don't think you need to.' She was smiling so much her cheeks ached.

'Oh. Right. Only, I thought—'

'Isn't that your phone?' Lola interrupted.

Anna returned to her desk and answered it, just as Elaine's door opened and Shuna Frain emerged, all tinkling laughter, as though she and the super had been having a gay old time. Head down, Lola watched as Elaine came out after her and led her towards the door to the stairs. They seemed very pally. If Shuna saw Lola, she didn't show it.

Anna, engrossed in her call, apparently saw none of this.

Lola checked her texts, finding one from Kirstie saying Fiona Balfour was panicky but coherent.

Lola replied with a thank you, acknowledging an earlier offer from Kirstie to stay at the Strathblane flat overnight with Ms Balfour if Catriona wasn't found.

Anna was coming off her call. 'That was Marcus,' she called across. 'He's talked to a woman who thinks she saw Catriona Balfour talking to a man. She runs a café on the main street and had just served her. The man seemed to be having trouble with his car and Catriona was talking to him. She didn't see her again, and when she went back outside, she saw she hadn't touched her coffee or cake.'

'Can she describe the man?'

'Curly blond hair, stocky. Rugby top. Car was dark. A BMW, she thinks. She didn't notice the registration.'

Curly blond hair. Stocky. She thought about the initial draft of the profile. An outdoors type. Attractive. Superficially charming . . .

'Lola,' Elaine called, reappearing from the stairwell. 'Ready?'

'Just one moment, boss. Anna? I want you to track down Tom Mackenzie.'

'From the farm?'

'Find out where he is now. And get a photo of him to Marcus ASAP. Ask him to show it to the woman from the café.'

'Boss.'

'Lola?' Elaine, getting tetchy.

'Coming.'

* * *

4.54 p.m.

'It was Pierce, wasn't it?' Lola asked, taking a seat.

'Shuna's not saying. Of course she won't! That's her code, and if we don't like it, tough.'

'So, what's she going to do?'

'Nothing.'

Lola stared, disbelieving. 'Really?'

'Really.'

'Right. But . . . how did you . . . ?'

'I promised her a scoop. I'm not happy about it, but it worked. I said once we find the killer, you'll talk to her about how you made the connection with two other cases in England — that made her sit up right away. She'd heard the rumours, but she didn't know it had been confirmed. I said, too, that you'd maybe be able to persuade Fiona Balfour to talk to her once all this was over.'

'I see.'

'Ms Balfour might prefer not to — that's up to her. Bottom line is, Shuna's off your back. Silly mix-up, I said. And I warned her to be careful whose gossip she listened to in future — some blokes are just out to ruin their female colleagues' reputations. She liked that. Shuna can be difficult, but she's also a hardened feminist.' Elaine smiled.

'Boss . . . I don't know what to say, apart from thanks for having my back.'

'I'm not doing you any favours,' Elaine said. 'The last thing I need is a scandal in the papers. What you did was wrong, and you know it.'

'Boss.' Her face burned.

'It's unlikely I can pin the leak on Pierce — not without a certain person agreeing to go on record, but I'll have him in here and I'll frighten the knickers off him. Let him know I'm watching him and that I've got a hotline to his uncle, should it come to that.'

'"A certain person", boss?'

'Yes.'

Elaine didn't move. They watched each other like chess players.

'Who?'

'What's said in this room *stays* in this room, Lola. Do you understand?'

'Yes.'

'It was Anna.'

Lola stared, mouth open, while Elaine's eyebrows rose and her lips pursed in amusement.

'My God . . .' Lola laughed. 'I got the impression she thought he was bloody wonderful.'

'Did you?'

Lola nodded.

'She's a clever woman,' Elaine said. 'Apparently Pierce bragged to her and another officer that he was planning to make your life "hell".'

'Nice . . .'

'She was *disgusted* — her word — at his behaviour. And she told him. She says she had her fill of "misogynistic wankers" in London, and she wasn't about to tolerate that kind of behaviour here. I rather think she ripped him a new arsehole.'

Lola realised her jaw was hanging open, and shut it. 'Did she tell Pierce she was coming to you?'

'Yes.'

'My God.'

'I know.'

Elaine's eyes stole to her watch. 'Oh, look at the time. We're late for Dr Burrows.'

CHAPTER SIXTY-EIGHT

5.01 p.m.

Cat came round in stages.

First, an awareness that she was in semi-darkness.

Second, that she was somewhere strange. Somewhere cold. A comfortless, alien place.

Third, that she was enclosed in a small space.

And fourth, that her head hurt. Not just her head. Her neck and shoulders felt horribly bruised.

Then it came back to her, in a cold drenching of horror: the man with the car. The pain of his vice-like grip on her neck. Him forcing her down and forward, head first into the back seat of his car — then blackness.

She'd been kidnapped. Panic rose, and she whimpered but managed to stem it. She got a grip and made herself take stock.

A man had abducted her. Had hurt her. Had brought her to this dark, horribly enclosed place. Her wrists were tied together, but she could flex them. Her ankles were not tied. That was something.

Keep very calm. Work out where you are and whether you're trapped, and if so, how.

She lifted her bound hands and pressed the tips of her trembling fingers on the close walls and ceiling. She was in a wooden box. A cupboard of some kind.

Keep calm. Do not panic.

She made herself take her time, feeling the surfaces for cracks or hinges that might reveal a door or hatch. No hinges, but a draught from one of the short edges between the wall at her feet and the lid.

She tried to sit up, bumping her head but managing not to cry out, and wriggled down the box, breathing steadily and purposefully, keeping a lid on her instinct to panic, to scream, to kick out . . .

Yes. A draught and a millimetre-wide gap. Her nails were short but she was able to run them along the gap. She worked at it, pulling, pushing, trying to shake the wood. But it wouldn't move.

Fuck.

She lay back, breathing, thinking. Trying to work out how she might possibly get free.

And then she heard footsteps. Rubber squeaking on a hard floor. Concrete, maybe. A heavy, purposeful tread, echoing within a big space.

She kept still, not breathing, and listened.

The footsteps stopped, as if he was listening. Then he was walking again, pacing about. She heard the sound of items being lifted, replaced. The sound of something being dragged.

'I can hear you!' Cat yelled. 'I know you're there. Let me out!'

The footsteps had ceased. He was listening.

'Come on, I'm half your size. Let me out and we'll talk!' It was important, she knew, to engage him. To let him air his grievances. To buy herself time. 'You can tell me what you're angry about. I'll listen!'

'Shut your mouth, stupid bitch.' A growling voice.

Fast running footsteps now and a deafening thud as he kicked against the box, making the whole thing shake. Again he kicked it, sending shock waves through Cat's body.

He fell silent and she held her breath, listening.

'Bitch,' she heard him mutter, then the footsteps retreated.

She breathed, tried to pin herself to the moment. Not to panic. To focus. To think of . . . *anything*.

CHAPTER SIXTY-NINE

5.08 p.m.

Elaine tapped quickly at the keyboard of her laptop while Lola brought a chair round so they could both face the screen.

While the Teams call loaded, Lola recovered her composure. Anna had defended her. More than that. She'd bawled Pierce out. It was . . . remarkable.

'Hello?' a high, disembodied voice said from the screen, then the picture loaded.

Dr Enid Burrows was in her office at the university, an austere and brightly lit chamber with whitewashed breeze-block walls. A single bookshelf behind her head held a number of gloomy-looking tomes and, unnervingly, what looked like a real human skull, ivy or something similar growing from its eye sockets.

Dr Burrows was as austere as her room. Dressed in black, she was gaunt and sallow-skinned with long grey hair working its way loose from an Alice band and making a frizzy halo round her face.

'I shan't beat about the bush,' she began. 'From the evidence you've now provided, I agree with you that he is exacting revenge on women he deems have slighted him in some way, following only minimal interaction. He keeps track of these women, over the course of several years, until they are due to marry. This, it seems, is his trigger. In the weeks before the wedding is due to take place, he kidnaps the couple and kills the male, with the idea that the female will awaken and find herself beside his corpse. He hopes this will traumatise the female very deeply — as well as deprive her of many years of happiness with the person she loves. A particularly brutal and spiteful revenge.'

Lola said, 'In the Liverpool case, the young woman died.'

'Yes, but of hypothermia,' Dr Burrows said. 'He got it right by the time of the Leeds attack.'

'He made a mistake with the weather in Liverpool,' Lola said. 'It seems as if he hadn't realised how cold it would be overnight.'

'Indeed.'

'The Leeds attack was at the beginning of June,' Lola said, talking more to herself than to Elaine and Dr Burrows. 'It would have been warmer. The attack here — that was the end of October. There could easily have been a frost overnight.'

'But there wasn't.'

They sat in silence.

'The places are important, aren't they?' Lola said. 'The places where he left the victims.'

'I think they are. I think that part of his plan was to put the bodies somewhere they would be found early in the mornings, probably by dog-walkers. He placed them beside paths, clearly visible in the undergrowth.'

'To maximise the chances of finding the women alive?'

'I think that's a key point. The women's survival is fundamental to his plan.'

'But it's such a risk,' Lola said. 'Fiona Balfour had signs of hypothermia. If I hadn't come along when I did, she might have deteriorated quickly. It was only luck I happened to pass by and see the car.'

Dr Burrows was silent for a time. 'Do you think?' she said at last. 'I wonder.'

And in that moment, Lola began to understand.

CHAPTER SEVENTY

5.37 p.m.

'Get up,' his voice snapped, and the box was flooded with light. Electric, not daylight.

She stared up at him, looming over her with a contemptuous snarl on his face.

Don't act frightened. Look calm. Comply.

She sat up and stretched her arms in front of her, as if she'd just woken up, and her wrists just happened to be tied together (with plastic straps, she saw now). She made her face insouciant, ignoring the pain in her head and shoulders, and slowly stood.

'Get out.'

She took her time and noted her surroundings. A large, high-ceilinged room. Rubberised floor, windows along two walls, but high up, darkness behind them. Stacked gym equipment, weights on pyramidal stands.

A gymnasium. And the box she'd been in was one of several lining one wall. Long boxes for storing gym and sports gear. They locked with padlocks, she saw.

'Fuck's sake, hurry up,' he snarled.

She stepped over the side of the box and her leg joints screamed with stiffness. She sublimated the pain, said meekly,

'Thank you for letting me out. Now maybe you could explain why I'm here. You owe me that, don't you?'

'Shut the fuck up.'

She saw a single chair in the middle of the room behind him. Coils of rope ready at its feet. And before it a tripod for his smartphone.

'Please don't tie me up,' she said. 'I won't run away. I just want to know why I'm here and what's troubling you.'

'I said shut up!' He swung at her. But she was fast, and threw up her tied fists to meet his arm, driving it sideways, while she shifted her weight at her hips and launched her right leg, straight at the knee, up in an arc and into the side of his ribs. He coughed out a yelp and staggered sideways.

'Bitch,' he managed, righting himself and coming at her again, this time with a fist lifted and swung in a backhand swipe towards her head.

She ducked, but he caught her ear, causing pain to flash through her skull and sending her off balance — something she used to her advantage, as she broke her fall, rolling and twisting so that she spun, and rose to face him.

'Nice try, bitch,' he spat, as they faced one another.

'You hit me first! I haven't done anything to you! What's *wrong* with you?'

'Nothing's wrong with me,' he said nastily, then rose.

He took a backpack off his shoulder and rooted in it. Then brought something out and showed it to her.

A gun.

CHAPTER SEVENTY-ONE

5.40 p.m.

'But what could he possibly want with Cat?' Robyn asked DC Campbell. The two of them were in the little kitchen of the Strathblane flat, Robyn making yet more tea.

'It's impossible to say.'

'Is it?' Robyn turned off the tap and took the kettle back to its base. 'Don't you think he means to use Cat as bait, to draw Fi out of hiding?'

The DC met her gaze. 'If it is, then it won't work. We won't let it.'

Robyn set the kettle to boil.

The constable said she had to nip to the loo, and Robyn carried the teas through to the living room.

In the living room Fi was on the phone, her laptop in front of her. 'That's right,' she said to someone on the other end, then jumped guiltily when she saw Robyn.

Robyn set the tray down, then looked expectantly at Fi.

Fi had moved from the laptop and was standing by the window, as if that gave her more privacy. 'And do you know where he is now?' she asked stiffly, casting another guilty glance in Robyn's direction.

Robyn moved to the settee and grabbed up the laptop to see what was on the screen. Fi saw her and looked alarmed then angry.

'What do you mean?' Fi said now into the phone, voice rising in irritation.

The laptop showed a Facebook page: an enlarged photo of five people in their early twenties. Three women, two men, on a night out somewhere. The Facebook timeline belonged to a woman called Aoife Norris. The photo was dated 3 October 2014. The caption under the photo read: *Another mad one at the Garage.* It was tagged with the names of the people in the photo: Aoife Norris, Gregg Chadwick, Mhairi McKay, Paul May, Freya Lanigan.

Robyn sensed that Fi's phone call related to the picture — or to the people in it.

'Well, will you?' Fi was saying now. 'Please, Aoife! It's very important. No, I can't tell you why . . . Because I can't!' She pulled the phone away from her ear. 'Oh, *God*!'

Aoife, it seemed, had cut the call.

'What's going on?' Robyn demanded.

They stood in tense stand-off, Fi looking mutinous.

'Have you remembered something?' She held up the laptop. 'Is it someone in this picture? If you know something, then you have to say!'

'What's going on?' the constable said, returning from the bathroom.

'I think I know who he is,' Fi said, sagging. She came round to the settee and sat, miserably. 'The man who's doing this.'

'Who?' Robyn said.

'His name's Gregg,' Fi said now. 'Gregg Chadwick. He was Aoife Norris's boyfriend.'

CHAPTER SEVENTY-TWO

5.45 p.m.

The women's survival is fundamental to his plan. Those words, spoken by Dr Burrows, had led Lola to her epiphany.

In Liverpool, Amber Wilson had died from exposure, following an unexpectedly cold night. Her body had been found early, but it was too late. In Leeds, the victims had been found early, but it was June and the risk of exposure minimal. The attack in Glasgow had occurred in late October, when a chilly night was all but guaranteed. It had been crucial the scene should be found early, and the killer had ensured it was — and by none other than a police detective, someone who'd act fast and see that the woman was okay.

Johnny had chosen their route. The finish line for her mile had been within metres of the place the bodies were found. He'd then kept a good distance from Fiona Balfour, using the excuse of feeling queasy around death. Lola hadn't suspected a thing. She'd even felt sorry for him.

But he'd planned it. And he'd used her.

Coming off the call, she'd gabbled out her theory to Elaine, who listened bewildered.

'But *you* booked the sessions with *him*,' Elaine pointed out. 'He didn't pick you.'

'He advertised on the website of the Glasgow Police Fitness Club. He even offered a discount. Someone would have booked in with him before long. It was just *my* bad luck to be the one he chose to discover the murder scene.'

They looked online, finding his details had been removed from the website. Lola googled "Johnny Blake" and "Feel the Fear with Johnny Blake" but failed to find him.

'Hang on one minute,' she told Elaine, remembering something.

She'd found his details on the website and, in a rush, taken a photo of the screen, capturing not just his name and phone number, but his grinning face too.

She went into her phone's photo app and scrolled back through several weeks of images, skin prickling when she found the one she was looking for — and enlarged it.

'Curly blond hair too,' she murmured to herself.

Adrenaline coursing through her, she called Kirstie. She told her she was about to send over an image, one she should show to Fiona Balfour.

'I'll call Anna in,' Elaine said. 'We need to plan, and fast.'

CHAPTER SEVENTY-THREE

5.52 p.m.

'That's him,' Fiona said, eyes fixed, horrified, on the constable's phone. 'He looks . . . I don't know. Different somehow. Maybe because he's older. But that's definitely him. That's Gregg Chadwick. He was Aoife's boyfriend. I went home with him one night at uni. Neither of us planned it. His girlfriend Aoife found out and came back to Glasgow. She flew at me. Gregg dumped her there and then. He said, why didn't we start seeing each other? And I said, yeah, okay. Only . . . it didn't work out. He was . . . controlling. He had this *nasty* streak. You'd never think it to look at him. He was so handsome. He started obsessing over who else I was talking to, where I'd been. Wanted to check my phone. Wanted to know all my plans. So I told him. I said, "It's not going to work out." I said, "Why don't you go back to Aoife?" Only by then I think she'd realised what he was really like.'

'How did he take it when you rejected him?' Robyn asked.

'He wasn't happy. He just sort of closed down, all cold.'

'Was that before the thing that happened in your room? When someone broke in?'

Fiona stared at Robyn for a moment. 'Yes. You think that was *him*?'

'Could have been,' Robyn said.

'So he's been following me all these years. Maybe he chased me that night in the car too. But to hold a grudge over a rejection that happened years ago . . . And he's done it to two other couples as well?'

'Two others that we know of,' DC Campbell pointed out.

'It is madness, isn't it?' Fiona asked, looking from Robyn to the constable. 'It's a kind of insanity.'

'Perhaps,' Robyn said quietly. 'But maybe that's letting him off too lightly. He's clearly driven by something. A kind of . . . *sadistic hatred*.'

'And now he's got Cat,' Fiona said. She stood up from the settee and moved to the window to look out at the night. 'We've got to stop him.' She wheeled round to the constable. 'We can, surely? Now we know who he is!'

'We will do everything we can,' DC Campbell said. 'We really will.'

CHAPTER SEVENTY-FOUR

5.56 p.m.

'What did Fi do to you?' Cat asked, when her captor was done tying her to the chair, arms and torso lashed to its strong back, her ankles strapped to the two front legs. 'Honestly, what did she do?'

He stood before her, gun safely away in a back pocket of his jeans now. He was fiddling with a phone. It looked like hers.

'Passcode?' he demanded.

'I can't remember.'

'*Fucking* tell me!'

'I can't!'

He ran at her, the gun out, but gripping the muzzle instead of the handle, and smashed it into the side of Cat's face, sending a bolt of black pain juddering through her skull.

The world tilted and spun. Flashing light filled her vision, and pain screamed in her head.

'Again?' he screamed in her face. 'Want me to smash your other cheekbone?'

'Can't . . .' she managed.

Her face felt wet. Bloody.

He bent close to her face. 'Tell me your fucking pass-code, dyke.'

She tried to speak, but nausea stopped her. She shut her eyes.

He roared with frustration and a second later the gun was smashing into the other side of her face, sending her head snapping over.

Cat's world was an explosion of pain. She coughed out vomit as her vision came and went.

He was stalking away from her, across the gym, out of the range of her vision, when darkness came over her like a wave and dragged her down.

CHAPTER SEVENTY-FIVE

6.41 p.m.

'What do we know about Chadwick?' Lola said.

She and her team, joined by Elaine, were huddled round a table in the meeting room of Milngavie's small police office. Pizza boxes ranged across the table, some empty, others with only the odd slice remaining.

'Age twenty-seven,' Anna read from her notes. 'Self-employed digital forensics specialist. Home's a flat in one of the modern blocks by the river in Partick. Registered direc-tor of an IT company. Parents deceased. There's an older brother, Colin, but he's had nothing to do with Gregg for a number of years. Something about a fight. Two convic-tions: one for driving under the influence, for which he got a six-month ban, another for theft of property from a former employer. We've been to the Partick address, but he's not at home. We've applied for a warrant to enter, but a neighbour says she hasn't seen him there for several months.'

'What about his Johnny Blake persona?' Lola asked.

Anna looked at her notes. 'No company registered, no taxes paid. Website's down, but its managed by a ser-vice provider in the Philippines. Last thing, boss: the call for information has gone out on Police Scotland's social media channels, and it's getting some traction, but nothing concrete. STV's *Ten O'Clock News* editor's on standby to run with a call, if we want it.'

Lola sat back and blinked, taking in the information.

'We're relying on leads from the public,' she said. 'I don't like it. There must be another angle we can pursue. What about money? I paid him with a bank card. I'll still have his bank details. I'll dig them out.'

'Did he work out of any fitness premises?' Jonno asked.

'He came to my house and we jogged together to the park, but I seem to remember him saying he used a gym for clients who were weight training. I've no idea where. Any ideas?' She looked at the weary faces around the table.

Marcus said, 'We've put it into the Facebook call. I'll check if there've been any responses.'

'How's Fiona Balfour doing?' Elaine asked now.

'Panicking about her sister,' Lola said. 'Robyn McArthur's taken her to her place in Anniesland. Kirstie's gone with them. Chadwick knew where to go to get his hands on Catriona Balfour. God knows how. It's not safe for her to be anywhere near Strathblane anymore.'

'Boss . . .' Anna said sharply, eyes on her phone. 'Gartcosh have got a trace on Catriona Balfour's mobile. It was turned back on four minutes ago.'

'And?' Lola said, trying not to get her hopes up.

'It's in the south of the city,' Anna said, moving her fingers on her phone's screen as if she was studying and expanding a map. 'Area around Moss End, West Pollokshields — Pollok Park, by the look of it.'

'The park,' Lola said, thoughts racing. 'He's taken her back to where he left Sean Rennie and Fiona Balfour?'

'Could be,' Anna said.

Marcus answered a phone call. 'Really?' he said after a moment, eyes on Lola. He listened some more, then pulled the phone from his ear. 'It's Kirstie, boss. Fiona Balfour's received a video on WhatsApp. It shows her sister, alive but badly injured, slurring her words. She's forwarding it to you now. Sounds like Fiona's near hysterical.'

* * *

7.01 p.m.

Marcus linked Lola's phone to the AV system in the meeting room, and everyone waited in grim silence for the video to appear on the wall monitor.

The screen showed Catriona Balfour in a brightly lit room, a whitewashed wall behind her. Her face was bloody, swollen on the left side, and her left eye was barely open. Her top lip had burst and blood and saliva were wet on her chin. She held her head very still, at a slight angle, as if dictated by pain. She was trying not to cry, was shaking — with fear or agony, it was hard to tell. A bubble of blood grew from one nostril then burst.

'He's got me, as you can see,' she began, voice reedy. 'He's going to kill me. He wants you, Fi.' Her voice broke and she coughed out an anguished sob. 'I told him he can't have you but he wants you.' She began shaking her head, as if to refute the dark reality she found herself in.

A voice off camera began to prompt her, too low to make out the words, but male and gruff.

Catriona closed her eyes, then opened them again, one eye remaining nearly closed due to the swelling. 'He says he'll do a swap. He'll hand me over if he can have you, but—' The voice cut and the film jumped, as if a rough edit had been made. She was talking again: 'He'll let me go if you come to him. He wants . . .' Struggling now, voice faint, head lolling a little, as if she was losing consciousness. 'He wants you to come to the place we used to go. Our special place. He . . . he made me tell him. You know where. But after dark. Alone. Nine p.m. tonight. Fi—' voice rising in panic — 'Fi, don't—'

279

The picture cut. On screen appeared white letters on black:

DO AS SHE SAYS OR SHE DIES
YOUR OLD PAL

Lola called Kirstie.

'We've just watched it,' she told her, conscious that all the eyes in the room were on her. 'Where's the "place" she's talking about?'

'Fiona won't say,' Kirstie replied. 'I've tried to reason with her. So has Robyn McArthur.'

'Christ . . . she knows where he's talking about, though, doesn't she?'

'I think so, boss.'

'Right. Give me Robyn McArthur's address.'

Kirstie read it out.

'I'll be there in twenty minutes,' Lola said, and hung up.

'There's a new comment on the Facebook post,' Marcus said, excitement in his voice. 'Guy's asking his pal if this is "that Johnny guy who does training out of Cowglen".'

'Cowglen's on the south side of Pollok Park,' Lola said. 'There's a golf club there.'

'And a new fitness centre,' Jonno pointed out. 'It was built last year, in the playing fields by the new housing scheme.'

'Anna, Aidan, go there now,' Lola said. 'Take Jonno and call for uniformed backup.'

'Boss,' Anna said, rising. She turned to Pierce. 'Aidan?'

He didn't even make eye contact with her. Merely grunted. Lola noted it, but put it quickly away. Right now, she had to focus everything on finding and saving Catriona Balfour from a killer.

CHAPTER SEVENTY-SIX

7.26 p.m.

Robyn caught the tail end of Fiona's phone call and froze outside the room, holding her breath and listening while Fiona said a quick goodbye.

Fi jumped guiltily when she saw Robyn.

'Was that Gerry Rennie?' Robyn asked.

Fi stared, perhaps toying with the idea of denial.

'Well?'

'What if it was?'

'Did you call him, or . . . ?'

Fi began to weep, hugging herself with one arm while covering her crumpled face with the other hand.

'Fi, talk to me!'

The constable appeared in the hallway, drawn from the living room by the raised voices.

'He's going to kill her,' Fi cried. 'He's going to murder Cat. He found out Sean and I were effectively finished and that his death didn't have the effect on me he wanted. God knows how he knew it. From his online stalking, probably. Now he's going to take my sister. A swap, he says. But that's not what it's about. He wants to murder Cat in front of me,

281

and there's *nothing* the police can do. They can't stop him! He's a psychopath. Look what he's already done to her poor face!'

'I know. Come here.'

But Fi repelled her attempt at an embrace.

'So Gerry's going to help,' she said.

'Help? How's he going to help?'

'Gerry Rennie?' DC Campbell demanded.

'He knows people,' Fi said, almost smiling as her tone darkened. 'He says not to talk to you lot. He'll go there with me. Him and his associates. They'll stop Gregg. Kill him, if they have to. And they'll save Cat.'

Robyn stared in amazed horror. 'No, Fi. No, no, no. You're playing with fire. *Worse* than fire. This is serious. This is *people's lives*!'

The constable was already on the phone.

Fi turned on Robyn a face of pure cold anger, her top lip curling, making her involuntarily recoil. She said, 'You won't stop me saving my sister.'

Just then the doorbell rang.

* * *

7.35 p.m.

'What "place"?' Lola asked again, following Fiona Balfour into Robyn McArthur's living room and trying to pin her with a stare. 'Where is it? Tell me. *Now*!'

The young woman kept her eyes averted and her face set.

'She won't say, because she thinks she can fix this herself,' Robyn McArthur said, standing at Lola's shoulder.

'You *promised*,' Fiona said, rounding on her nastily. 'You said—'

'I promised nothing,' Robyn snarled in return. 'Now, for God's sake, grow up. Tell us what place Cat's talking about.'

'No.' Eyes down, arms folded, mouth working silently away. Then she jumped up and stepped around Lola, heading for the door to the hallway.

'Where are you going?' Robyn snapped.

'Out! I'm a free person, aren't I?'

'Fiona, please listen to me,' Lola said, chasing her into the hallway, closely followed by Kirstie. 'You're at risk of making things worse. Do you understand? Gerry Rennie's acting outside the law. Everything could be at stake — including a conviction when we get our hands on this man.'

Fiona looked at her steadily, as if she was finally hearing. But then she turned, said a quick, 'Sorry,' and reached for the door.

CHAPTER SEVENTY-SEVEN

7.52 p.m.

Fiona walked quickly, but Lola and Robyn McArthur kept pace, crossing roads, zigzagging from block to block, all the time trying to reason with her.

Kirstie drove Lola's car, keeping her distance, but ready to give chase should the rendezvous Lola feared materialise.

'Fiona,' Lola said, breathless from several minutes' fast walking, 'I will arrest you if I have to.'

'What for?' the woman said, wheeling round, face aghast. 'For trying to do your job for you?'

And she was on her way again, stalking ahead, nearly at the Anniesland Cross. She had her phone out and jabbed at the screen before looking sharply about.

'Fiona, stop!' Lola commanded, just as a black BMW swerved quickly and soundlessly into the kerb. The passenger door came ajar. Fiona pulled it wider and got in.

'Fiona!'

But the door slammed shut and the car screeched quickly away.

* * *

Kirstie pulled over and Lola jumped into the passenger seat of the car. 'Get in,' she ordered Robyn, who obeyed, clambering into the back seat.

Kirstie drove fast along Crow Road, while Lola called for backup.

They followed the BMW, which was staying close to the speed limit, as it plunged towards the entrance of the Clyde Tunnel under the river.

'I think I know where they're going,' the solicitor said, sitting forward to see through the windscreen.

Lola turned in her seat.

'Cat and Fiona lived in Paisley for some time after their parents died. Cat told me they'd get the bus up to the Braes.'

'The Gleniffer Braes? The country park?'

'Yes. They'd go there and sit and look out over the town and watch as it got dark and the lights came on. Fi used to like watching the planes landing and taking off from the airport. It was just a thing they did to escape their lives.'

'The Braes cover a wide area,' Lola said, eyes on the tail lights of the BMW as it left the tunnel, heading south.

'I know. But if they got the bus there, it must have been to one of the main spots near the road. There's a car park, isn't there?'

Lola was on her phone, updating Command and Control on the BMW's current position, and asking for cars from Paisley to meet them at the Braes. She also asked for a firearms unit to go to the main car park. 'Situation is dynamic,' she told the initial tactical firearms commander, signalling there wasn't time to seek sign-off from a higher-ranked officer.

They passed the hospital and joined the M8 going west. The motorway acquired more lanes to accommodate traffic heading to and from IKEA and the huge out-of-town shopping centre. Cars slowed and began changing lanes. The BMW pushed on, jumping ahead of a truck then nipping out and round an SUV. Kirstie sped up, grabbing spaces that opened up, but the BMW was getting away.

'Keep as close as you can,' Lola said, 'and we'll try to catch them as they go through Paisley.'

The BMW's tail lights shrank into the distance.

CHAPTER SEVENTY-EIGHT

8.30 p.m.

'Nice and tight,' the man said to her, and Cat blinked as consciousness returned.

'Where am I?' She tried to move, but couldn't.

'Out and about,' he said, face close to hers, eyes glittering in torchlight. 'Your and Fiona's special place, remember?'

It was cold. The air felt wet. She could smell mud and pine trees. Undergrowth. Nature.

The Braes? Is that where they were? But which bit? All she could see were trees. Where was the view? The lights of the town?

It was cold and breezy, and fir branches shivered around her. An owl hooted.

He'd tied her to a tree, or a post of some kind.

'My head hurts.'

'Does it?' Mock sympathy as he moved behind her, tightening whatever was holding her wrists. 'Not much longer now. Then it'll all be over.'

'Why are you doing this?'

'Ask your sister, if you get the chance.'

'I don't mean that. I mean, *why*? What made you like this? Who hurt you?'

He didn't answer. He was going into his backpack now, handling a roll of tape. He cut it with a knife.

He lifted the length of tape and fixed it across her mouth and face, pressing it hard onto her skin so that it pulled. 'There. Nice and quiet,' he said, face close again, eyes mocking. 'Shouldn't be long now.'

CHAPTER SEVENTY-NINE

8.47 p.m.

It was pitch black above the town, the car park apparently empty — until Kirstie's headlights fell on a pair of marked police cars at the far end of the car park. The cars were parked close, angled to form an L shape. Lola saw now that they hemmed in a black car. Gerry's BMW, she guessed.

Uniformed officers emerged from the trees with torches as Lola and Kirstie got out of the car.

'We got here just after the Beemer,' one of them, a female sergeant, told Lola. 'The young woman led three men that way.' She pointed into the trees and the blackness between them.

Lola picked a young constable to stay close to Robyn McArthur, telling him, 'She knows both the Balfour sisters. She could be helpful. But try to keep her away from any action.'

More cars arrived. Pierce and Anna Vaughan emerged from the first. Marcus and Jonno were in the second. A third marked car bumped after them across the car park, and the place was soon filled with voices.

Lola pulled everyone into a circle and explained their priorities: first and foremost, to rescue Catriona Balfour from the clutches of a killer, and second, to capture that killer alive.

'We're dealing with gangster vigilantes as well,' she explained. 'They're likely armed and they're no friends of ours. They see us as a barrier to their own prime objective.'

'Which is?' the female sergeant asked.

'To avenge the death of Sean Rennie.'

'Gunfight at the OK Corral,' said one of the uniformed constables, possibly louder than he'd meant to. Lola gave him a look.

'Firearms unit are on their way,' Lola told the circle of attentive faces. 'But time's against us.' She explained that she'd go into the woods and that DC Campbell would come after her. She tasked Anna with bringing their armed colleagues up to speed but instructed her to hold them back until Lola or Kirstie gave the call to engage.

'Now. Here's what might happen,' she said, 'so I need you to be ready. First—'

Raised voices, then an explosion from inside the trees. A gunshot, then a woman's scream, followed by a second gunshot, its echo like thunder off the face of the hill.

More screaming now, from a different woman this time. And the sound of someone — possibly more than one person — crashing through undergrowth. Coming this way.

CHAPTER EIGHTY

9.01 p.m.

Fiona Balfour emerged from the trees, looking stricken with terror but apparently uninjured. She fell into Robyn's arms. Robyn turned a frightened, questioning face on Lola. Lola came to them, pulled them apart and spun Fiona towards her.

'He shot Gerry,' Fiona gasped, tears streaming, snot bubbling. 'He's hiding in the trees and he shot Gerry when Gerry tried to help Cat.'

'Your sister's there?'

'In the clearing. There's a totem pole and benches. It's a picnic place. She's tied to the pole, but he's in the trees.'

'Is Gerry hurt?'

'Gregg shot him and he doubled over. Gerry was trying to crawl. I think . . . I think he shot him again when he was on the ground.'

'Who else is there with you and Gerry?'

'Gerry's friends — I don't know their names. They went into the trees.'

'Are they armed? Fiona — look at me. Do Gerry's friends have guns?'

She nodded, miserably.

'Jeezo . . .' She turned to one of the male uniformed officers. 'Take her away from here. You go with her,' she said to Robyn.

'Boss?' said Kirstie, waiting for instructions.

'Follow me,' Lola told her. 'But at a distance.'

CHAPTER EIGHTY-ONE

9.09 p.m.

'Hello, Johnny,' Lola called into the trees, trying to keep a lid on her horror at the sight her torch had revealed: Catriona Balfour tied to a wooden totem pole, head hanging to one side, her face a mask of blood; and Gerry Rennie, curled on his side, moaning in agony.

'Johnny? Or is it Gregg? I don't know what to call you.'

Rustling from the trees. She turned that way.

'I think I'll call you Johnny,' she continued conversationally. 'I know you as Johnny. Johnny's nice, isn't he? A nice guy. My six-in-the-morning pal.' She forced a smile into her voice, though her heart was racing and she felt sick. 'Put me through my paces a few times, haven't you, Johnny? Putting me through them now as well.'

She listened. Nothing now.

'Damned clever of you, getting a polis to find the crime scene like that. When you told me you were scared of blood I believed you. I thought, poor lad, steering clear of the scene like that! Silly me, eh?'

She walked forward into the clearing, minding a dip where someone had left the remains of a disposable barbecue.

'I'm going to take a wee look at these two people, if that's all right with you, Johnny. They're not looking their best and you know how I like to fuss.'

She approached the totem, saying quietly, 'Hello, Catriona, love. It's Lola Harris. I'm here now.'

She angled the beam of the torch so it wasn't full in Catriona's face, but provided enough light for her to see the injuries. The woman moaned as Lola touched her jaw.

'We'll get you sorted,' she murmured. 'Won't be long now.'

Lola teased the edge of the tape and, finding it came away easily, pulled it free. The woman murmured a word — a name, but one Lola wasn't familiar with — then lost consciousness.

She stepped back and moved carefully to the man curled on the ground, taking her time, knowing she was being observed from the trees by an armed killer.

'Stay still, Gerry,' Lola murmured. She reached for his throat, to find a pulse. It beat strongly. 'We'll get you sorted too,' she said. Then she saw the gun, the handle gleaming in the torchlight, protruding from the back pocket of his jeans. He hadn't even drawn it. So why had Chadwick shot him?

The thought occurred to her: to take the gun, to slip it into her own pocket . . . just in case. But then she looked at the heap of a man on the ground, and at the figure drooping from the totem pole, and thought better of it. Why make herself even more of a target than she already was?

She stood and made a show of dusting herself down.

More rustling. She turned in that direction, arms at her side, torch lighting only the ground before her.

'Come on, Johnny,' she said. 'No good you hiding like this. Come and talk to me. This is over and we've a few things to talk through, you and me. You're the bigger person. You know that. I know that. Come on, now.'

Further noise of undergrowth, then his voice, from inside the trees behind and to the right of the totem pole.

'Where is she?'

'Fiona? Oh, she's away,' Lola said brightly. 'I packed her off for her own good. She was silly to come here, and I think she knows that now. Honestly, I do wish folk would listen to me.'

'Bring her back.'

'It's too late for that. I'm not going to pretend otherwise.'

'Then her sister dies.'

'Come out here where I can see you,' she said. 'Let's have a talk, you and me.'

'I want that bitch here where I can see her.'

'I'm disappointed in you,' Lola said. 'The Johnny I know — he's a decent guy. He doesn't call women names. He's respectful. I used to think how lovely you were to me. I was so nervous getting my trainers on again, and you were so encouraging, and kind . . .'

'You always disgusted me. Fat, ugly cow.'

'Oh, now! Well, look, that may well be the case. But you know, I can live with that.'

'A fat, ugly cow who nobody loves.'

'Johnny, stop it,' she said, calmly. 'It's not nice and it's not *you*. I know it isn't. Not really.'

Another sound from the trees now, but to her left. Who? One of her officers, or one of Gerry's men?

'I'd like to understand,' she tried now. 'Why you did this. Why you killed Darren Flanagan and Amber Wilson. Why you killed Kevin Stainthorpe. Why, Johnny?'

A light appeared in the trees behind the totem pole. A torch, held low, illuminating dead ferns, coming this way.

'All I want to know is, *why?*' she said, keeping her voice light and reasonable.

He appeared, stepping from the trees, passing the totem pole and Catriona's slumped form, coming forward to meet her in the middle of the clearing, among the picnic tables. They were, Lola thought, like tribal enemies coming face to face by firelight in olden times.

'Thank you,' she said.

'What for?'

'For facing me.'

He peered at her curiously. She saw he'd shaved his head — must have done so since the afternoon when he'd kidnapped Catriona. He looked more like Claire Grainger's photofit than before, but there was still something not right.

'They humiliated me,' he said quietly.

'Who did?'

'Amber.' His voice cracked a little. 'Claire. Fiona.'

'They the only ones?'

'There were others.' Maudlin now, a high note of self-pity.

'I meant, are they the only ones you . . . attacked?'

'So far.'

'You waited a good while to act,' she said.

A sly smile tilted his lips. 'I waited till they were going to get married. To have maximum impact.'

'You've had work done, haven't you?' she said now. 'To your chin.'

He reached up involuntarily and touched it, and she knew she was right.

'What else? Your eyes?'

He shrugged.

'Good to make the best of yourself, I suppose,' she said.

He nodded, shyly now.

'Do you really think I'm fat and ugly?' she said, sounding hurt.

He looked awkward, embarrassed. Like the wee boy she'd often thought him. The wee boy who needed a hug.

'I don't mind if you do,' she said, laughing. 'Good to hear the truth sometimes. Might spur me on to hit the gym a bit more.'

'You're not ugly,' he said.

'Thank you, Johnny. That's nice of you. I'm sorry it's come to this,' she said.

'Are you?'

'I am,' she said. 'I think you are too.'

He frowned at her.

'I think,' she pushed gently on, 'you know that it's over, don't you?'

'No.' It was a mewling, miserable moan. 'No. I just . . . I just want her to come here. I want her to be here when I . . .'

'No you don't, Johnny. You don't want that. Not deep down.'

He was looking at her mutinously now. A child who resented his teacher.

'I don't suppose it matters all that much,' he said now. 'If she doesn't see it happen, I mean.'

'No, Johnny. Look. Let's take a walk, shall we?'

He'd taken something from his pocket. It gleamed in the light from Lola's torch.

'Johnny—'

He turned, lifting the gun, pointing at Catriona Balfour hanging from the totem pole, and called, 'Hey, dyke. Wakey, wakey!'

'Gregg!' Fiona's voice cried out from the trees behind Lola.

'And there she is,' he said, a mad grin lighting his face. 'Well, hello there!'

'Let my sister go, you fucking lunatic.'

He moved to the totem pole, lifted the gun and pushed the muzzle hard against Catriona Balfour's left temple.

Fiona screamed, then a man's voice barked from inside the trees. 'Oy! This way, prick!'

Johnny's head snapped round, and Lola turned, in time to see the flash from a muzzle. Johnny yelped, dropping his gun, then rising and seeming to spasm in the air. The gun in the trees spat again, and again, and he danced under fire, before twisting and falling at the foot of the pole.

'*Stop!*' Lola yelled, torch beam raking the trees. She saw eyes, a mouth, teeth — and then the shooter was gone.

CHAPTER EIGHTY-TWO

Thursday 3 November
10.13 a.m.

'I saw Rita Rennie downstairs just now,' Fiona Balfour told Lola, coming back into Catriona's private room at the hospital. She spoke quietly, eyes on her sister asleep in the bed. 'She'd been in to see Gerry. Says he's doing loads better.'

'She spoke to you, then?'

Fiona nodded and took her chair. 'She . . . well, she didn't exactly *apologise*, but I could tell she was sorry about how she'd treated me before. That she felt bad, at least.'

Lola raised a sceptical eyebrow. 'What did she say?'

'She said, "Our Gerry's pals helped you." I said, "What do you mean?" She said, "You'll not be bothered again, so that's us square."'

'Not much of an apology,' Lola said drily.

'I thought I might go in and see him,' Fiona said now. 'Gerry, I mean. Do you think I should?'

'You're a free citizen, but . . . I suggest not. Strongly. One of his associates shot and killed Gregg Chadwick. Vigilante assassinations aren't legal here, no matter how convenient they might be.'

The young woman bridled a little. 'What are you saying?'

'I'm saying,' Lola said steadily, 'you were part of the mob that went armed to the Braes last night. You could be charged with murder, "art and part". In other words you could be liable for actions that led to a death.'

'What? *I'm* the victim in this—'

'I'm not saying you will be, but Gerry Rennie may find himself charged. You could find yourself a witness, so my strong advice is to keep clear of him and the rest of the Rennies too.'

'But that's unfair! What happened to me and Sean had nothing to do with him being a Rennie.'

Lola didn't reply.

'I want a Coke,' Fiona said huffily, rising. 'I'll be back in a bit.'

'I'll wait for you but then I'll need to head off.'

A minute or so after Fiona had gone, Catriona woke up, groaning and blinking her eyes.

'How you doing, Catriona?' Lola said gently when the woman's eyes focused on her. 'It's DCI Harris.'

'Face hurts,' she managed, slurring her words, groaning as she touched a bruised cheekbone.

'It will,' Lola said. 'But hopefully not for long.'

'Where am I?'

Lola told her where she was, that the doctors were confident she'd be okay — maybe even find herself discharged today — and that Fiona was fine and would be back any minute.

'The man . . .'

'He's dead.'

'I thought he was, but . . . Thank God. I know that sounds awful, but . . . he was . . . beyond help. I've met some angry men, but there was something cold driving him. Something evil.'

'He was not a well man,' Lola said mildly. 'Your focus now needs to be on you — and on Fiona. Though I'd say she's going to be perfectly fine. Still a wee bit of growing up to do, but she'll get there, with your help.'

Catriona was tired, and Lola decided to go. There'd be time to talk later. Then she remembered something.

'Can I ask you about something you said? It was just before we helped you down from that pole — you were in and out of consciousness.'

'What?'

'You said a name. You said the name "Lynne".'

Her eyes grew wide and the unbandaged skin of her face paled. 'Did I?'

'You don't have to tell me who she is. I just wondered, that's all.'

'She was a friend,' Catriona said, eyes away to the window. 'Just a friend. That's all.'

As Lola watched, the woman seemed to relax a little. She let out a long sighing breath and appeared to sink into the bed. She closed her eyes.

'You get some rest,' Lola said.

CHAPTER EIGHTY-THREE

12.43 p.m.

'I know what you did,' Lola said when she and DS Anna Vaughan were alone. They were in Elaine's office, waiting for the super to finish a prior meeting in another part of the building.

Anna looked alarmed. 'What do you mean?'

'I wanted to say thank you, that's all. DS Pierce. Elaine says you ripped him a new arsehole.'

Anna's mouth fell open in shock.

'Sorry. One of the "quainter" expressions.'

'He was out of order,' Anna said, recovering her composure. 'I told him so. I think he got the message.'

'Oh, I think he did.'

'Afternoon, ladies,' Elaine said, coming in without knocking. It was her office, after all.

'Afternoon, boss,' Lola said.

'That's the press conference settled with corporate comms for three p.m.,' the superintendent said, once she'd taken a seat. 'Merseyside and West Yorkshire colleagues are content for us to make reference to their cases. They'll be releasing their own statements in the coming days. So, what are we telling the world?'

'That a man called Gregg Chadwick, also known as Johnny Blake and William Cavendish, and possibly by a number of other names, has been killed in the commission of murder,' Lola said. 'That he was shot by an unknown third party, whose whereabouts we are seeking. That Chadwick is suspected of the kidnap and murder of Sean Rennie and of the kidnap of Rennie's fiancée Fiona Balfour. And that we are working with colleagues in two forces in England to identify whether Chadwick was behind multiple murders there in the past few years.'

'Press will ask about the Rennies,' Elaine said. 'There's no way rumours aren't currently flying round newsrooms saying it was a Rennie associate who got to Chadwick.'

'We won't be drawn on that, boss,' Lola said calmly.

'Shouldn't the public be concerned that there's a vigilante assassin at large?' Elaine asked, playing devil's advocate.

Lola shifted in her chair as she reached for the right words. 'We don't believe the public should have any immediate concerns.'

Elaine nodded, satisfied. 'Have you spoken to Gerry Rennie yet?'

'He's still unconscious,' Anna answered. 'Rita Rennie has the lawyers lined up, by the sounds of it. Sounds like she's hiring a PR outfit.'

'God help us,' Elaine said.

They ran through some further possible questions that might arise during the afternoon's presser, then Elaine told Anna she could go.

Lola sat and waited, observing Elaine's expression as she decided how to say what Lola knew was coming.

'You shouldn't have gone in there,' the superintendent said at last. 'You should have waited till the firearms crew arrived.'

'Boss, I—'

'I know why you did it. And, yes, it had a positive outcome, for Catriona Balfour and for Gerry Rennie. But we lost the suspect, Lola.'

'In the grander scheme of things, boss,' Lola said, red edging her vision, 'I think that's acceptable, don't you?'

'Possibly. But now we have another killer, one who got away. Gerry Rennie won't tell us his name, no matter what we charge him with. It sounds like Fiona Balfour won't be speaking either. Won't even give us a description of either of the other two men in the car.'

Lola said nothing.

'There'll be questions.'

'I know,' she muttered, resigned.

'Then there's that other wee matter,' Elaine said now, her tone becoming dry. 'The . . . traffic incident.'

Lola shifted in her seat and tried not to appear mutinous.

'I've recorded the verbal warning on your file,' Elaine said. 'It'll expire in twelve months' time.'

'Boss—'

'Take it, Lola,' Elaine said. 'Then it's done: what you did is acknowledged and dealt with. It leaves Pierce powerless. Understand?'

She breathed then nodded.

'Good. Now, you need some rest — and a chance to decide what to do about that useless bloke . . .'

'Oh, that's decided,' Lola said, miserably, getting up to go. 'Don't worry.'

'Good,' Elaine said, her voice gentle. 'I'm glad for you. Look after yourself, Lola.'

She tried to smile, but her face wouldn't cooperate. Instead she nodded, and reached for the door.

* * *

1.35 p.m.

Halfway across the office she stopped in her tracks and stared in amazement at the flowers covering her desk. A tonne of them, or so it looked, frothing white and yellow and pink. At least four bouquets in plastic pouches of water, and baskets of roses.

Kirstie and Anna had been reading the labels and now stepped away, as if caught in the act. Pierce was watching from over his VDU, eyes narrow and darkly suspicious.

'Came in a oner, boss,' Marcus called across to her.

She approached and read the tag on the nearest bouquet:

FOR A LADY WHO IS TRUE TO HER PROMISES

The label on the second read the same. And on the third, the fourth.

They were all from the same sender.

Not from Joe, *surely* . . . But who? Rita Rennie?

She looked at Kirstie, bewildered.

'No idea, boss.'

'Someone getting married, or is it a funeral?' a voice asked behind her.

Graeme Izatt had swaggered in from somewhere.

'Secret admirer,' Lola told him drily. 'One with deep pockets, by the look of it. You're looking cheerful, Graeme.'

'Life's beautiful,' he said, a big smile cracking his face. He went on his way.

'What was that about?' Lola asked Kirstie.

'Word is DCI Izatt's shortlisted for a new role at the MIT,' Kirstie said, lowering her voice. 'Superintendent in charge of special operations, or something like that. He's been telling folk the job's his.'

'Has he, indeed?' said Lola, hiding her amusement. 'Well, good luck to him . . . and them.'

She wondered if he might like to take an aspiring young DS with him, but doubted it very much.

Her phone was buzzing. A withheld number. She steeled herself and answered.

'Is that Ms Harris?'

A male voice. Familiar.

'Speaking.'

'Did you get the flowers?'

'I did. Who is this, please?'

'It's Kenny Flanagan. You found the man who killed my son. And I . . .' His voice became choked. 'I can . . . I can never thank you enough.'

'Hello, Kenny,' she said, suddenly choked herself, eyes on the massed blooms. 'You didn't have to do this — but I do appreciate it. Thank you.'

'You're a woman of your word, Ms Harris.'

'Please, it's Lola. Call me Lola.'

'Lola, then. Patricia and me — you've given us the best present we could hope for, short of giving us our children back.' Choked again. 'And I don't care that the bastard's dead. I thought I would. I was looking forward to facing him, but this is fine.'

'I'm glad for you.'

'We're going to go for dinner — Pat and me. Tonight. To the eatery Darren owned near the park. It's someone else's now, but they kept the name. Good of them. Anyway, we're going to go to the park first and put some flowers down. Then we'll go eat and remember them.'

'Please give my best to Patricia,' Lola said.

'I will, Lola. And thank you.'

She came off the phone and said, to the waiting faces, 'A grateful parent.' She touched the cool, fragile petals of a yellow rose, not quite open. 'Let's get these out of here, though, eh? There's a care home the other side of Bellahouston Park. The residents will enjoy them.'

Jonno had joined them, arriving from the stairwell.

'Visitor downstairs for you, boss,' he told Lola.

'Really?'

'Not work related, apparently. "Personal" stuff.'

She stared, embarrassed, while at the same time her heart thumped and her fingers began to prickle. Joe. Who else could it be?

'Thanks, Jonno. Where is he?'

'Meeting room two,' Jonna said. 'Oh, and it's not a he. It's a she. A Mrs McIntyre. Boss . . . you okay?'

'Aye. Aye, I'm fine,' she said, swallowing her panic, trying not to think what could be so bad that Joe's wife would pay Joe's mistress a visit at work.

CHAPTER EIGHTY-FOUR

1.50 p.m.

She didn't bother to knock.

'Tell me,' she said, voice catching in her throat. 'Just me tell me what's happened.'

Marie, in a chair facing the door, raised a single eyebrow.

'Joe's fine,' she said.

Lola grabbed the back of the nearest chair, squeezing its cool realness.

Thank God. Thank you, God . . .

'Then why are you here?' She stared, hating the woman more than she ever had.

'To talk,' Marie said flatly. 'I phoned and they said you'd be here. Sit down, why don't you?'

Marie McIntyre was a wee woman, thin and pale in an unhealthy way. Everything about her was sharp: her nose, her chin, the bones of her shoulders and clavicles that made points under her cream blouse. Her manner could be sharp too, not to mention sarcastic and downright nasty. She'd been pretty in her youth. Softer. Warmer too, Lola seemed to remember, though it had been years since the three of them were at school together.

Lola sat, taking her time, determined to appear unruffled.

'Well,' she said, when she was good and ready, 'here I am.'

Marie tilted her head and studied Lola through narrow eyes. 'I know about the car.'

Lola didn't reply. She sat, tiredly, and waited.

'It's the talk of the street. Bit pathetic, really.'

Lola shrugged and made a "see if I care" face, though her cheeks were burning.

'Why are you here, Marie?' Her voice was pleasingly icy.

Something changed. The sharp little woman across the table seemed suddenly to sag. She closed her eyes and sank in her chair, head down.

Lola waited, curious.

Now Marie was crying. Tears streamed silently down her face. She sniffed and shook herself.

Lola sat on her discomfort and waited some more.

'Joe . . .' Marie said at last. 'He . . . his health . . . he . . .'

'What about Joe's health?' Lola swallowed.

'He's struggling. The cancer's one thing. But these past few days . . . it's as if he's giving up.'

'Giving up?'

Marie looked at her. 'His will is breaking. His will to go on.'

'Marie, I'm not going to see Joe anymore,' Lola said. 'I'm not going to contact him either. Not because I don't want to, but because it's terribly destructive for both of us. For me, certainly. I can't live like this. There . . . now you know.'

The woman was looking at her with open-mouthed quizzical horror. 'You don't understand,' she said. 'You don't understand at all! I'm here because . . . well, I want you to see him.'

'What?' Lola kept very still.

Don't let this happen. Don't let her do this to you.

She must be stone. A statue. One zipped up in bubble wrap. Impervious.

'I want you to see him,' Marie said, in a tiny voice. 'He won't get better like this. He won't heal! And I need him to. And so . . . and so I've realised, that the price is worth paying.'

'The price?'

Marie nodded miserably.

'You need him to be alive too, don't you? Surely that's what you want?'

The bubble wrap was frayed. Big holes here and there. And the stone was the wrong kind. The friable kind.

'Please. *Please*. For Joe! We'd plan it, of course. I'd be there. But I could stay in a different room. We could say thirty minutes a time, maybe twice a week.'

'I can't believe this,' Lola said to herself, to the room, to the heavens above. 'Why is this happening?'

'An hour, then!'

'No.'

Marie stared. 'What do you mean, "no"?'

'I won't be controlled by you.'

'Controlled? What do you—?'

'Because that's what this is really about, isn't it? Control. Controlling Joe. Controlling me. *Managing* us.'

'I just want him to be better. I want—'

'Do you know about coercion? The word — what it means?'

'Co . . . ?'

'Coercion. You should know it. Because you're very good at it. You practise it.'

'What are you talking about?' She was getting cross now, her face sharpening more than ever.

'Coercive control. It's a recognised form of domestic abuse. It's against the law. It's been on the statute books in Scotland since 2019. Look it up.'

'How dare you!'

'Oh, I dare. I dare call it out — whether it's you doing it to Joe, or me, or some horrible bloke doing it to his wife.'

'I'm leaving.' She got up and made to leave.

'Fine,' Lola said, rising too. 'Take a good look at yourself, Marie. It won't be pleasant for you, but do it. Try to be better.'

They faced each other by the door. 'He'll never be yours,' Marie said. 'Never, ever. Never in a million years.'

'I know,' Lola said. 'I know that.'

'Good.' Marie smiled.

'I know it, and I'm ready to move on with my life. And I'm happy with that.'

Marie reached for the door handle. Lola got it for her.

'That's the way out,' Lola said cheerily, pointing down the corridor.

Marie scurried off, muttering to herself.

'Goodbye, Marie,' Lola murmured, eyes on the woman's retreating figure, adding, quieter still, 'Goodbye, Joe.'

She turned and climbed the stairs, back to the office and her desk that overflowed with flowers.

THE END

ACKNOWLEDGEMENTS

A huge thank you to Chief Inspector Kirsty Lawie of Police Scotland, whose advice, guidance and suggestions have made this a better book.

Kirsty introduced me to retired Detective Inspector John Shaw of the Scottish Police Recreation Association, who showed me around SPRA's fitness facility in Pollok Park before it was handed on to a new owner, and who kindly explained how SPRA works. John in turn introduced me to retired Detective Superintendent Graham Mayo, now a personal trainer and owner of GBM fitness in Glasgow. I'm grateful to both John and Graham for their generous insights into policing and fitness.

Thank you to Victoria Drew (and to my friend Nicola Hepworth for introducing us) who explained cancer treatment and followed up with further thoughts and helpful notes.

Readers of early drafts are the most trusted of all. Thanks to Katharine Bradbury, Alison Winch and Gordon Munro, who all offered thoughtful comments. My Mum (Lola's biggest fan, and my personal North of England PR machine) helped me get the last scene right — I think Lola is happier with the new ending! Janice Fraser read a later draft (fast!) and gave me reassurance.

Niall Kinsella built me a lovely website and populated it with Campbell David Parker's great snaps. Thanks, both.

Simon and Chris lent me their cottage in Kintyre to write chunks of the book.

Clare O'Donnell helped me with names for various members of the Rennie family.

I spend a lot of time writing at the Perch Café in Garelochhead and at the Park Pavilion Café in Helensburgh. Thanks to Diane and Jamie and their respective teams for letting me gurn and mutter to myself while typing in corners, and for keeping me fat. Thanks too to Zoe and Hugh at Harvest Moon Deli for their support and championing of the first book.

Thank you to the VPDS Book Club for listening to the opening section of an early draft and 'oohing' and 'aahing' in the all the right places. Hope the rest of the book meets your exacting standards!

I've made lovely new writer friends in the past year. Thanks for the advice, support and general gossip/lolz, especially to Sally-Anne Martyn, Linda Mather and Lynda Florence Hughes — colleagues and pals.

Emma Grundy Haigh is a superstar, and her colleagues at Joffe Books are great to work with. It's a pleasure to be published by you!

The biggest thank you of all goes to Margaret Murphy, master crime writer, mentor and friend. Margaret is my guru and I value her wisdom, kindness and generosity beyond measure. Thank you, Margaret, for your continued confidence and support.

THE JOFFE BOOKS STORY

We began in 2014 when Jasper agreed to publish his mum's much-rejected romance novel and it became a bestseller.

Since then we've grown into the largest independent publisher in the UK. We're extremely proud to publish some of the very best writers in the world, including Joy Ellis, Faith Martin, Caro Ramsay, Helen Forrester, Simon Brett and Robert Goddard. Everyone at Joffe Books loves reading and we never forget that it all begins with the magic of an author telling a story.

We are proud to publish talented first-time authors, as well as established writers whose books we love introducing to a new generation of readers.

We have been shortlisted for Independent Publisher of the Year at the British Book Awards three times, in 2020, 2021 and 2022, and for the Diversity and Inclusivity Award at the Independent Publishing Awards in 2022.

We built this company with your help, and we love to hear from you, so please email us about absolutely anything bookish at: feedback@joffebooks.com.

If you want to receive free books every Friday and hear about all our new releases, join our mailing list: www.joffebooks. com/contact

And when you tell your friends about us, just remember: it's pronounced Joffe as in coffee or toffee!

ALSO BY DANIEL SELLERS

DCI LOLA HARRIS SERIES
Book 1: MURDER IN THE GALLOWGATE
Book 2: MURDER IN LOVERS' LANE